HARDWIRED HUMANITY

Sarah Wagner

ISBN-13: 9798693321441

Cover design by: Deron Douglas
Library of Congress Control Number: 2018675309
Printed in the United States of America

For everyone who believed in me.

CONTENTS

INTRODUCTION

This is the third edition of this book. When it was first published in 2008 by Cyberwizard Productions, it was my first real, grownup publishing credit. That edition had a lovely introduction by author Ed McKeown. If you haven't read anything by him, you should.

It's been many years between that edition and this one and this edition contains a brand new linked short story that was not in the prior editions, a brand new not so linked short story, and some poetry on the theme.

Life is an amazing thing. It is resilient. It is innovative. And it is only a matter of time before humans create an artificial life form that is by all definitions alive. How can we possibly know how the spark will ignite? Humanity has long been obsessed with playing god so it makes perfect sense to me that, when it happens, the machines will look an awful lot like us.

If humanity is to be considered as a whole, it is a strange creature. It is fearful and arrogant. It strives to create, to be God but also creates fictional worlds full of scary what-ifs to warn us all of what could happen if humanity gets to play God. To paraphrase a wonderful movie, a person is incredible, people are horrible. We go out of our way to destroy what we don't understand, what isn't like us. We push people into narrow categories and get upset when they don't actually fit them. And yet, there is nothing so amazing as the acts of kindness we can perform, the depth of the love we have for one another.

Humanity is flawed but it has so much potential to be so great that, on the whole, we don't damn it for the deep evils of a small portion. It is in striving to be better humans that we find our strengths and our weaknesses. Humanity is not always something beautiful and shiny, but it is something worth striving for.

SWITCH

1

There wasn't enough pavement in the city for him to drive off his mood. The streets were crowded with traffic, but Spider barely noticed. He tightened his grip on the wheel and the wipers swished against the light drizzle. People moved around him, in cars, on foot, swarming toward something.

He'd been in Miami too long. They had to know where he was now and it wouldn't be long before someone came after him. They had been hunting him for nearly a decade, since the first testing of his disrupter. Spider had been lucky and kept a step ahead, but he feared that, this time, he'd been too complacent. He drove, seeing every face, inspecting every shadow, peering into every passing vehicle. Everything loomed, threatened. He ran a hand into his jacket, feeling the familiar worn grip of his old Beretta 9mm, comforted by its presence.

From the corner of his eye, he saw a woman with black hair and wide eyes standing on the sidewalk. She had stopped to light a cigarette. Her lighter flared and the cigarette caught, a plume of smoke hung heavily in the damp air. He watched in his mirror as she started walking again, pressing her bag against her, moving too quickly. Spider saw the two men behind her and knew immediately that they were tailing her. It didn't surprise him to see the woman throw down her cigarette and break into a run. For a brief moment, he admired the curve of her hip, swaying as she ran, as rhythmically as the windshield wipers.

The light in front of him glared an angry red and Spider stopped the car, pressing the button to unlock the doors. He watched her falter at the corner, her eyes searching for a way out. Just before he could roll the window down, she flung open his passenger door and threw herself inside. "Hang on." He couldn't help but smile as he slammed his foot down on the gas pedal almost before his passenger had a chance to blink.

"Thank you." She was trembling, her voice quiet and frightened. She turned to him and he watched her features change out of the corner of his eye. She was wary of him, like everyone else. The shaved, heavily tattooed head always made them step back.

"Don't thank me yet. They're still following." He glanced up into the rearview mirror. "See the gray sedan, three cars back? Your men hopped in when you decided to hitch."

"Of course they did." She slumped down in the seat. "I'm so sorry. I don't want you to get in trouble here. Just stop and let me out. They'll let you go."

"Why are they chasing you?"

"I have something they want." She turned in her seat to look out the back window. "They're too close. It's useless. They'll catch us for sure."

"No they won't." He reached into his leather jacket and pulled out a machine the size of a cell phone. "Hold on."

"What is that?" Her eyes went wide with fear as he slowed the car. "What do you think you're doing? We have to keep going!"

"Trust me." He slammed on the brakes and turned off the car. He pressed a small red key and everything stopped.

The moment he glanced at her, Spider knew something was wrong. His passenger sat frozen, whatever she'd been about to say silenced. He cursed, panic knotting his gut as he heard the breaking of glass behind him. One of the men in the chasing car had busted out the window and started shooting at them. He glanced at the number screen and the moment the counter hit zero, he turned the key in the ignition, the car jerking back to life. A bullet hit the trunk as he started the car. He took off, chancing a quick glance behind him to see the man with the gun climbing out of the broken window. He maneuvered easily around dead vehicles and gawking pedestrians.

He sped through the streets easily, twisting and turning through the alleys. Pressing a small button on the steering wheel, he paused for a breath and gunned the machine through a newly opened door that automatically began its quick descent the moment the car had passed fully into the cavernous hold of the rented storage unit. In the folds of relative safety, Spider inspected his passenger. If the disrupter had shut her down, that could only mean one thing. She was a machine. If it were true, her construction was glorious.

Her skin was soft and smooth to the touch, a thousand times more real than any cyberskin available on the market, even in testing. Spider touched a length of hair. It didn't feel synthetic or even dyed. The woman's shape was natural, imperfect but pleasing. Through her damp blouse, he could tell that her breasts weren't exactly even, the left just a fraction larger but not so much as to be awkward. He'd never have thought they were fakes. Never. Everything about her looked real, smelled real, felt real. But his disrupter had shut her off.

A small nagging part of him told him to ditch the girl and get out of town. But, his curiosity piqued, he couldn't leave the machine. He'd spent his whole life creating and tampering with machinery and he had never seen anything like this. He doubted if he'd ever see anything like it again.

Spider climbed out of the car and went around to the passenger side. He'd expected her to be quite heavy but found she was relatively light. Her body mass barely exceeded the expectations for a woman her size. He laid her gently in the back of an old blue van parked next to his beat-up Honda Prelude. It was dirty with faded exterminator logos emblazoned on the sides.

The second trek through the city was far more sedate than

the first had been, but it was still a great relief to see his warehouse. He had work to do. He had to figure out how to turn the machine back on if only so she could explain what had just happened.

The refurbished warehouse in the middle of an industrial complex served a dual purpose. It was his workshop and it was his home. There were a handful of people there who worked with him or stopped in to hire him, but he didn't want to share the girl. Not yet.

Spider pressed a small blue button on a black fob hanging from his keys and the rusty gate in front of the road leading down into the complex slid aside just long enough for him to drive through before it rattled shut behind him. He pressed a red button and one of the uniform metal bay doors rolled up on its old rails. He pulled the van slowly into the well-lit warehouse and heard the familiar clangs and whines of hammers, torches, and pneumatic drills. It wasn't that he didn't trust them. If he didn't, he'd never allow them to enter his space. Spider had never been good at sharing.

He parked the van and got out, looking around for anyone who might see his passenger, but the parking bay was empty. Quickly, he made his way to the door and nearly ran into the one person he knew without a doubt he could trust with such a find.

"Trent. You gotta do me a favor." Spider whispered even though there was no one near enough to hear them. "Get everyone out of here for today."

"Really?" The young man stepped back, his forehead furrowed, and his blue eyes full of questions. "You got it. Give me ten." Trent moved quickly to get everyone out of the building.

Spider paced next to the passenger door, alternately checking his watch and peering into the shadows for any sign of movement. He'd come to embrace his paranoia after so many years on the run. He kept to his two-stride pacing for nearly fifteen minutes before Trent finally returned.

"Okay, it's just us now. What's going on, man?"

"I don't know." Spider eased the woman out of the van, stiff and contorted, and carried her through the warehouse to the office he'd converted to his bedroom. It wasn't much, just a bed and his clothes. He laid the woman down on his bed. "Isn't she wonderful?"

"Dude! Are you completely fried? What are you doing bringing a chick here? What the heck is wrong with her, anyway?" Trent's brow furrowed as he looked her over.

"That's just it." He grinned broadly. "She's not a woman. She's a machine."

"No way. That's just movies, man." Trent's blue eyes took in the woman lying before him.

Spider marveled at her again. Except for the fact that her eyes were open, her body was still positioned as if she were sitting, and her fingers seemed frozen in a curl, she looked remarkably natural. Too real to be a machine. "The disrupter shut her off. Find me a better explanation."

"What have you gotten into this time?"

"I have no idea. Now, help me find out how to turn her back on. There's got to be a key somewhere." Spider ran his hands over her head, feeling for anything strange. "Where would you put it?"

"Let's see. If I were to have made something like this, I know exactly where I'd have put the on switch." Trent's eyes lingered on the place where her legs met.

"Get your head out of the gutter, Trent. Only you would think of something like that." Spider shook his head.

"Hey, I'm just your average guy." He smiled wickedly. "Maybe it's as simple as twisting a nipple."

"Lay off it. Come on, help me out here." Spider opened the woman's mouth and inspected her teeth. "There's got to be a control panel somewhere." He glanced at Trent who was removing the woman's shoes, running his fingers gingerly over her feet. "If you find anything, let me know."

The two men ran their fingertips over the woman in front of them, feeling for something indicative of a panel. Wherever it was, it was well hidden. Spider was almost to the conclusion that maybe Trent had been right and her creator was a sick puppy when the light bulb went off in his brain. The glint of fillings had caught his eye when he inspected her teeth. It had been years since dentists had stopped using silver metal in dental work. "Trent. Get me a pen or something."

"Did you find it?"

"I might have, but I'm not going to try it with my fingers." He took the long slim pen from Trent and pressed the tip against the filling in her right, back molar. When nothing happened, he pressed the tip to the left, back molar. Both men jumped back away from the woman as her entire form twitched and arched on the bed.

"I think you found it." Trent watched wide-eyed as the woman sat up on Spider's bed.

"Who are you?" Her eyes were wide and Spider could have sworn he could sense fear in her, but he told himself that was impossible.

"I'm the guy who saved your butt. Who the heck are you?"

"Kora Walker." She clutched her knees to her chest, her eyes flipping between the two men hovering over her.

"You'll have to forgive him; Spider's manners aren't the best. I'm Trent." He extended his hand to her. "You really don't have anything to worry about; he's harmless."

"Right." She snorted. "What did you do to me?"

"It's not my fault." Spider sat on the edge of the bed, secretly thrilled when she shifted away. So much simulated emotion it was hard to believe she wasn't real. "I didn't know the disrupter would shut you off. It doesn't destroy anything or erase anything, it just turns everything off so that the computers all have to reboot and reset before anything can be turned back on."

"That's why you turned off your car." Her whisper filled the room. "How did you find my switch?"

"Your silver fillings gave you away."

"Oh." She shook her head sadly. "That's how I figured it out too."

"What do you mean, figured it out?" He stared at her, unable to look away.

"I didn't know what I was until about two months ago. I was in a weird accident, got an electrical shock that caused some circuits to go haywire. Fortunately, it didn't shut me off like your little box."

"I really am sorry about that, Ms. Walker."

"You might as well call me Kora." She reached up and pulled a clip out of her hair, letting the mass of black waves down around her shoulders. "I've gotten you into a mess haven't I?"

"Maybe a small one. I think you need to tell us what's going on." Spider glanced over at Trent. "Maybe we can help."

"I doubt it. After my accident, after I figured out what I was, I started trying to find out more. It took me almost a week to get into my own programming. When I saw what I'd been made for, I panicked. I reprogrammed myself and I think when I did, I set off some sort of alarm. They've been after me ever since."

"What were you programmed to do?" Trent leaned against the wall, unable to look away.

"I was supposed to kill the President." She dropped her head onto her knees and closed her eyes tight.

"You would never have gotten close enough to President Roberts." Spider smiled again and took her hand in his, amazed at the craftsmanship.

"I was already there, working in the White House. I was a secretary for the President's Deputy Chief of Staff. I already had full access." She snatched her hand back as if she were afraid of him.

"Wow." Trent whispered. "Do you know who made you?"

"No. I only know that if they get me back, I'll either be destroyed or reprogrammed. I don't want to be destroyed, but I will not kill the President. I don't want to kill anyone."

"Well Kora, looks like you and I are in the same boat." Spider sighed.

"Excuse me?"

"On the run. You because of what you know, what you are, and me because of what I created. You aren't safe anywhere in this city now. And neither am I." His face hardened.

"I'm so sorry. I bet you wish I'd picked a different car." She pursed her lips.

"If you had, you'd be with them right now, wouldn't you?"

"Probably." Kora nodded. "What do I do now?"

"We run. We've got to get out of here."

"What? What do you mean, 'we'?"

"What happened today, it will be on the news, probably with your picture and my car. That means the people who are after me will be after you now, too. Same goes for me. The only way we're going to get out of this is to stick together. Maybe I can help you with your problems and get you far away from mine." He looked over at Trent. "What about you?"

"I have a family now, Spider; I can't take the risks you can. As it is, after we get you ready, I'm going home, packing up and leaving town with Moira and the baby."

"I can't blame you for that." Spider looked around the room he'd called home for almost six months, nearly a record for him.

"You can't leave by road or air. They'll have road blocks up and probably agents sitting in every airport in a hundred miles."

"Then how are we going to get away?" Kora tilted her head to the side. Both men watched her with amazement, every motion she made, every gesture, every facial contortion was utterly, unimpeachably lifelike.

"By boat." Spider began rummaging through the room. "We can't go anywhere they would think to look for you, so we'll have to pick up a few things for you on the way."

"Do you have my bag?"

"It's in the van."

"Then I don't really need anything."

"What's in the bag?" He stopped moving, wondering why he hadn't bothered to check it in the first place. His discovery had so awed him that he hadn't checked for tracking devices.

"A copy of my original programming and all of my papers. I figure they're forgeries, but they might point to who made them, who made me. I made the copy before I started changing things, so I could prove it. If all else fails, I may need to go to the

White House and tell them everything."

Trent shook his head. "They'll shut you down to study you."

"Let's hope it doesn't come to that." Spider moved mechanically, shoving things into a large black duffel bag. "You'll need to change your clothes. I don't have anything that will fit you, so we'll have to improvise." He laid a pair of dark green pants on the bed along with a black sweatshirt and a green bandanna. He took a large knife from his belt and cut about six inches from each pant leg. "You'll need a belt." He reached into a drawer and pulled out a heavy canvas belt. "Get dressed. I'll make the belt to size when you have it on."

She sighed. "All right. Turn around."

"Come on. I'm not twelve. I think I've seen a woman without her shirt on." She glared at him, her eyes glinting. Spider wanted to get a better look at those eyes when she trusted him enough to allow it.

"You just want to see if the rest of me is quite so realistic, don't you?" She unbuttoned her blouse, her dark eyes locked on Spider's face. To hide his thoughts, Spider glanced over at Trent. He was watching Kora unabashedly, taking in the whole of her as he would any other woman.

The pants were too big and, without a belt, they would never stay up. Kora stood still as Spider threaded the belt through the loops and pulled it tight, using his knife to open a hole for the prong. "Much better. Put your hair under the bandanna. We are going to have to fit in as much as possible, and colors will help."

"You have a plan then?" She bent down to tie the green cloth at the nape of her neck, under her long hair.

"We're going to pick up supplies and get out of here. Let's go." He picked up his bag. "Trent, can you get her bag out of the car? I'll take the truck with me and pass it off to Juan from there."

He nodded solemnly at his friend. "You take care of yourself man. Stay a few steps ahead and let me know every once in a while that you're Okay. Moira will want to be sure."

"Give her and the baby a hug for me. Could you call the guys, fill them in? Tell them to come get their stuff and find a new place?"

"Will do." Trent paused for a moment. He looked like he was going to say something more and decided against it, turning on his heel and heading back to the van.

Spider took Kora by the hand and led her out of the room and through the warehouse. As they passed a huge workroom, Spider paused to grab his toolbox. The projects he was working on, the modified surveillance equipment, the miniscule infrared cameras, the disguised microphones, he left them all where they lay, scattered amidst scraps of metal, wire, and tools. Spider led Kora to a second bay, a smaller, closed-in bay that held nothing but an old truck. The rusted gray pickup had seen better days, but it ran well enough. He helped her up into the cab and tossed his bag into the back. Trent ran into the bay, handed Kora her bag, said goodbye and disappeared into the building. Spider waved and climbed into the driver's seat.

When Spider had himself situated, he pressed the red button and the garage door lifted. As they pulled out onto the road, Kora jumped at the sound of a shrill beep. "What is that?"

"Quiet." He reached into his jacket and pulled out a small square of plastic. Touching the small screen, he smiled. "Just who we need. Hey, man. What can I do you for?" He spoke into his jacket, smiling at Kora, who was staring at him as if he'd grown a second head.

"Dude. What are you doing right now?" A tinny, masculine voice came from the jacket.

"Coming to see you." Spider held a hand up, quieting Kora before she could speak.

"What? Why?" The voice asked.

"Something came up and I'm going to have to leave town."

"So that crap downtown, that was you?" A trace of a laugh floated through the air.

"It's a long story, Juan. I've got company, too. She'll need more than I will. Recruit your mother. Short, thin, stacked. Got it?”

“Clothes, right?”

“Good man.”

“I’m on it. What’s your time?” The voice became clipped and precise.

“Twenty minutes?”

“We’ll be ready.” There was a small click, a moment of static, and then silence.

Spider replaced the machine in an inside pocket of his jacket. He saw the questions in her eyes. “I’m wired head to toe, differently than you, but wired just the same.” He grinned at her as he pushed hard on the gas pedal and sent the truck screaming forward. “If you’re going to run with me, you’ll have to get used to it.”

“Why are you helping me?”

“You made that decision, not me. You hopped into my car, remember?”

“But you didn’t have to help me, Spider.”

“No. I didn’t. Maybe I’ve got a soft spot for short, stacked machines.” He smiled at her, a predatory grin.

“You’re really freaking funny.” She crossed her arms and turned away from him.

“I know. It’s a gift." There was no humor in his voice. He turned a corner, chancing a glance at his passenger. There was fear in her eyes and it amazed him. Everything about her seemed so normal, so human.

"Can I ask you something?" Kora did not look at him when she spoke.

"I can't guarantee you'll get an answer."

"Is it true that most programmers have some sort of signature?" she asked.

"Most, but not all." His eyes fell to the bag she clutched in her lap. "You have a copy of your original programming, right?" She nodded, her fingers tightening on the bag. "Later, when we're a good distance away, I'll take a look and see if I can find anything. Your creator probably didn't leave anything that could tie him to you. He wouldn't be that stupid. I mean, look at you, there's no way he slipped up with a tag."

"But you assume my creator is male?"

"Yeah. That's a safe bet. Have you looked in a mirror? You're every guy's dream. Especially for frankensteiners, and tech-heads. You were definitely created by a man."

"Oh." She fell silent for a moment and continued in a whispered voice. "Wouldn't I remember the first time I woke up?"

"Not necessarily. You were probably programmed with a lifetime of memories. I'll look for that in your programming, too. It's quite possible that your creator programmed himself into your life in some way." He eased the truck into an empty parking lot nestled between a graffiti-tagged brick tenement and a clean but cluttered bodega with advertisements and posters cluttering nearly every inch of glass in the window. "You'll need to stay close to me now."

"Sure." She waited for him to open her door and jumped down out of the truck. "What are we doing?"

"Getting some supplies." He watched her light up a cigarette. "Now that you know what you are, why do you smoke?"

"Because I need to, okay? It calms me down. It's probably programmed in. I didn't get around to overhauling everything, I just changed the important things."

"Finish it while we walk." He took her hand in his. "Try and keep near me. Don't speak much. Don't make eye contact. Just follow my lead. We don't want to draw attention to you. These people know me, but they don't like strangers." She lengthened her stride to keep up with him. They moved quickly down the block and stopped in a doorway. "Pitch it." He opened the door and swung her into a little grocery store. Almost the moment the bell chimed to announce their arrival, a short stocky teenager rushed forward and locked the door behind them.

"Juan." They clasped hands fondly. "This is Kora."

"Ma'am." He extended his hand in greeting and a smile split his face. "I think I got most things ready. Any idea how long you'll be gone?"

"No clue." Spider shook his head sadly. "If I were you, I'd go ahead and gut the warehouse and move on. Pass the word around. If someone were to torch it, it would be no great loss."

"You got it, boss." The boy led them through the neatly stocked aisles of canned goods and ethnic foods to a door in the back. "Go on in. Give me the keys; I'll bring the truck around." Spider handed him the keys and led Kora through the door into the back room.

"Juan is a good friend." The back room overflowed with boxes and crates. Spider moved easily, familiarly, through the rows of cardboard stamped with Spanish and Chinese words. He stopped about three feet from the back wall of the storage room and grabbed Kora's hand to stop her, too. "Mama? You here?"

"Ai, boy." A throaty, feminine voice whispered through a small speaker in the corner. "Let me see this girlie girl you brought." Spider spun Kora around quickly, ignoring her resistance, her small squeal of protest. "Not bad. She looks like she was made for you." Spider laughed abruptly. "What?"

"Nothing, Mama. You gonna let us in?" He pulled Kora next to him and held her still as the wall slid open.

"Are all the people you know so paranoid?" she asked.

"Yes, and you should be, too." He squeezed her hand lightly. Kora eyed the pretty woman sitting in front of her. "That's Juan's mother."

"What do I call her?" Kora whispered.

"Call me Mama, everybody does." The woman smiled, showing perfect white teeth that nearly glowed against the deep red of her painted lips. Her figure was an enviable one for a woman of any age, let alone a woman with three teenage boys.

Spider watched Kora inspect Mama and smiled. If he didn't know better, he'd have sworn there was a touch of jealousy in her black eyes as she appraised Mama's face and shape.

"Now, you don't have a whole lot of time. José and the boys will take care of harbor patrol so you can just slip out. You make sure you drop me a line, let me know you're alive." Mama's voice was thick with the melody of Cuba.

"I will, Mama." Spider reached out for her and hugged her tight for a moment. "I didn't get your microphones finished."

"When you settle, you just take your time and ship them." Mama smiled at him and then turned to Kora. She picked up a green bag. "This is for you, dear. It has clothes and all that other girlie gear. There's nothing you'll need that I didn't think of, I guarantee it." Kora took the bag with a smile and a thank you. "Grab that cooler there, Spider. It's got a few days worth of fresh stuff and there are two boxes of canned and mixes. I don't know how long you plan to be on the water."

"We don't know either, Mama." Spider picked up the cooler as Juan walked through the door. "You go ahead and grab one of those boxes, man."

Juan picked up the larger box and Kora grabbed the smaller one. The three of them walked back into the stockroom and out the loading dock doors into the alley where the truck was idling. They loaded everything into the back and crammed themselves into the cab. They drove in silence to the marina. As they pulled down toward the dock, they pointed out the boat to Kora.

"It's a houseboat." She looked at him, a look of poorly disguised disgust on her face.

"She's not pretty, but she's fast and reliable." He scratched his chin and eyed the thirty-eight foot mass of cream colored aluminum and glass.

The three of them loaded up the boat quickly and Kora disappeared into the cabin. "She's a looker, Spider. You serious about her?" Juan raised his eyebrows suggestively.

"It's too soon to answer that. I'm hoping we can stick together, at least for a little while. It'll be nice to have company for once."

"I'll bet." He glanced at his watch. "You've got twenty minutes to get prepped. The boat's ready. José will have your distraction right on time, so don't you screw up."

"If I do, she and I are both as good as dead." His eyes darted to the doorway she'd floated through. "There's a lot going on here, man. Whatever you do, don't ever tell anyone you know me. Anyone comes asking, I don't exist. Don't forget to wipe out the warehouse."

"I'll take care of everything here. Maybe make a chunk on the scrap at least."

"Hope you do. Considering all you've done for me, I wish I could give you more."

"Heck no. That'd be like stealing from a brother." A somber moment passed before they shared a brief goodbye and Juan went back to the truck.

Spider leaned into the cabin and found Kora curled up in a chair. "You sit tight. We may have to book it pretty quick, depending on what José has in mind for harbor patrol."

"Who is José?"

"He's Juan's older brother." Spider moved quickly to the helm and started up the boat, the engine revving at his command. He piloted the boat away from the docks and out into the ocean. He spotted harbor patrol but the speed boat turned away from them and toward a large plume of smoke. Right on time, as promised.

When they were safely out on the open water, he went back into the cabin. "We're on our way, Kora. Do you need anything?"

"No, I think I found everything. Can I get you something maybe?"

"I could go for coffee in a little while, maybe some conversation to go with it." He tried not to stare at her.

"I think I can safely manage that. I'll just put some things away until I find the coffee." She grinned. Spider realized that if he didn't know, he'd never believe that she was a machine. She was so real, in her speech, her mannerisms, and her smile. Shaking his head, he returned to the wheel to guide the boat along.

It was almost an hour later when Kora appeared with mugs and a thermos of coffee. As she poured the coffee, Spider watched her closely. "What do you want to do?"

"What do you mean?"

"You told me you were programmed to kill President Roberts. I want to know what you want to do about it."

"Well, I suppose we should really try to warn him. If they had me inside, they probably have a backup, in case I was discovered or if I malfunctioned like I did. They obviously haven't done anything yet. He's still alive." She handed him a steaming mug and sat down with hers.

"I was thinking something along those lines myself." Spider leaned back in the captain's chair. "This isn't something we can take to anyone and be believed. Not without risking your safety. And I really don't want to do that."

"Why do you care?" She sipped her coffee, even wincing at the heat.

Her programmer had thought of everything. Every possible reaction to everyday stimuli. For a moment, he wondered what she would do if he kissed her. "I told you. I have a thing for machines." He smiled. "I just do, okay?"

"Fine. If we can't go to someone, what can we possibly do?"

"If I can get to an election rally, maybe I can shut down any backups that might be in place."

"Staffers don't go to the rallies."

"But the secret service agents do. If they can get a staffer, they probably at least attempted to get someone like you into his security detail. It worked on you; I don't see why it wouldn't work on them."

"How did you make it? Your little shut-off box?"

"Trial and error mostly." He grimaced as he scalded his tongue. "I spent the better part of ten years trying to figure it out. I used a good jammer as the foundation. I knew it could work but, until I had it in my hands, until I saw what it *could* do, I didn't really think it *would*."

"Things like that make me believe at least a little in fate."

"Fate?" Such an odd concept for a machine. Every time she spoke, she surprised him. "Something like that. Especially now." He sat down in his captain's chair. "I've got my laptop hooked into the satellite network, as soon as I set up the dish, we should be online. When you go back inside, check out the President's website. That should have his next few appearances. We have to get to the first one we can."

"I'll take a look and see what I can find."

"You know you can't go with me to the rally, right?"

"I know. If I go, it'll shut me down too and draw attention to us." She sighed heavily and breathed in deep, pulling the steam into her nose. "I so badly want to know that these people won't win. You have no idea."

"Yeah I do. You want to know that it's you, not your creator, who controls your life. I think everyone wants that at some point."

"Maybe." She stared out over the water. "I wonder what will happen to me. I'm a machine. I only end. There is no heaven or hell for me. There is nothing after my death, if that ever comes."

"Maybe it has nothing to do with form and everything to do with spirit. How do you know you don't have one?"

"I guess I don't." She shook her head. "I'll go look up the rally. I'll let you know when I find it." Spider watched her as she walked away, wishing there were some sort of comfort he could offer her.

It took only a few moments before Kora found the next rally. New York City. They'd be able to get there in time, as long as they kept moving. Spider set the coordinates and showed Kora how to keep the boat on course. They decided that she would steer the boat through the night. Sleep was something she could live without. Spider made his own preparations, going through his bags until he found a suitable disguise. It was an uneasy night, between the seas and the thoughts circling in his head.

With the sunrise came the anxiety, the adrenaline. It took him a while to get ready, covering his tattoos, trying to look as unthreatening as possible. Trying to make sure he'd blend into the crowd and hoping he'd do a good enough job that the feds that would be inspecting any footage later couldn't get a good fix with their facial recognition programs.

"Does it look good enough to pass?" Spider lowered his head so Kora could check makeup that covered his tattoos.

"It wouldn't hurt to wear a hat, but I don't think anyone will look twice." She ran a finger over his skull, slowly, as if memorizing the shape of his head. "You'd better go." She dropped her hand and moved quickly to brush her lips over his. "For luck."

"I'll need it." Spider pushed aside the sudden desire to pull her to him and see just how human her reactions really were. Instead, he pulled a ball cap on and hopped from the boat to the dock.

The band was just beginning to play as Spider positioned himself next to the velvet ropes on the outer edge of the audience space, standing shoulder to shoulder with supporters. President Roberts and his security entourage would be easily within the range of the disrupter once they got onto the stage, less than twenty yards from his place at the edge of the crowd.

As the first car stopped and spit out half a dozen secret service agents, Spider started to feel itchy. The makeup was bad enough, but he longed for his standard leather, wired with all the comforts of home. The catcalls and whoops from the crowd drew his attention back to the red carpet in time to see the President in his perfectly pressed suit, surrounded by large men with dark glasses and curling wires coming out of their ears. He kept his hands out of the jacket pocket, unwilling to allow anyone to think he was a threat, until the President was past and starting up the stairs to the podium.

With a smooth motion, Spider dipped his hand into his pocket and pressed the switch.

"Oh no." The words fell from his mouth as he watched President Roberts fall lifeless off the edge of the stage, twisting at an inhuman angle. Two men in dark suits and glasses had crumpled to the ground behind him, inanimate.

In the confusion and hysteria that followed, Spider slipped under the barriers into the crowd that was gathering in the aftermath, onlookers trying to find out what the problem was, craning to see the president, to see a moment of history live, before it reached the news. He was well into the throng of newcomers when the police began to disperse them.

Spider took the long way back to the docks. His life had changed in a matter of days. Now, he wasn't just on the run from the company that wanted his disrupter, but a person or company capable of making machines that looked like anyone they wanted them to. How could he ever be certain again that anyone was who they were supposed to be? The thought sent a wave of unease through him, too much was already uncertain in his life.

He wasn't looking forward to telling Kora what he knew. When the boat came into view, he found himself conflicted. He was relieved to see her perched in the Captain's chair watching for him, but absolutely dreading the conversation ahead. She smiled as she saw him but the smile faded away as he stepped onto the boat.

"What's wrong? Were we too late?" She rushed to him.

"When I hit the switch, President Roberts and two of the security detail shut down." Spider shook his head sadly.

"Oh god." She slid to the deck. "Was it me?"

"Probably. I think I know what happened now, Kora." He picked her up and carried her into the cabin. "I think you carried out your programming without a hitch, giving them the opportunity to replace the President. I also think that probably you were programmed to self-destruct on completion of that mission. Something inside you, whatever part of you that has taken on a consciousness, refused to kill yourself. Maybe that part of you made sure you got that shock."

"How is that possible?" She shook her head sadly as he put her down, still holding her close.

"I don't know. This isn't something I've ever dealt with before. In any case, that shock fried enough of your circuits to allow you to see what you were and eliminate the self-destruct command by reprogramming yourself."

"If I did my job, why have they been after me, Spider?" The panic in her eyes was too real to come just from code.

"Because you know what you are and that could lead to you knowing what President Roberts was, if you ever remembered that you killed him."

"Oh god. I killed him. I assassinated the President." Kora slumped into a chair.

"No." Spider knelt beside her, taking her chin in his hand and forcing her to look at him. "Whoever designed you, whoever programmed you, he assassinated him. You have no guilt in this. You were just the weapon. No one ever blamed the gun that killed JFK, did they?"

"Why don't I remember it?" The despair in her face didn't shock him this time.

"I don't know. Maybe you erased it. We might never know all the answers, Kora."

"What happens now?" Kora wrapped her arms around herself.

"We have to get out of here. What happened today went international within five minutes, and I can almost guarantee you that our hunters were headed here the moment it aired." Spider moved slowly to the door and paused in the doorway. "I'll do my best to find somewhere that you'll be safe from all of it—from the men after you and the men after me." Spider did not look at her as he left the cabin and made his way to the helm.

He'd take her somewhere no one would ever think to look for her. Like Amish country. Who'd look for a machine there? For that matter, who'd look for him there either?

2

Two Years Later . . .

Spider paced the length of the motel room as the phone rang, again. Every twitter of the phone's mechanical ring sent a new wave of panic through his blood. Kora had never left his calls unanswered before. He'd made her jacket like his for exactly that reason, so they would never be completely out of touch. He didn't expect her to sit in their little house and do nothing.

"Kora." Spider talked to the voice mail program. "It's not like you to not answer and I'm a little worried. Hope everything is all right. Call me. I'm headed to the last meeting I've got out here and then I'll be home."

He paced more. This wasn't the first time a job had taken him away from home for a few days. This wasn't the first time he'd left Kora alone in Lancaster. She wasn't a fool, and she wasn't, like him, someone who craved excitement. Spider picked up his bag and dropped the room key on the bed. As soon as his meeting was over, he'd head straight home.

The streets of Denver were relatively easy to navigate with the assistance of his client's directions. Over the last four days, Spider had dropped off contracted work to various places all over the region. Modified surveillance cameras for a private security firm in the city. A new, improved, and rather steampunkish mechanical bull, that had been great fun to build, for a bar in the suburbs. All he had left to do was drop off the scarves, tie-pins, and pendants to a local private investigator whose bread and butter was infidelity cases. He rigged each object with a tiny microphone and transmitter to better track their subjects without raising suspicion.

The PI kept him longer than Spider would have liked, full of questions and looking to cut a better deal on the next order. Twenty minutes dragged on, feeling more like an hour. Spider would have just dropped off the merchandise, but the guy had paid too well to be treated like that. Plus, he figured he could make up those twenty minutes on the road. If he was lucky and the cops had better things to do than watch for him.

As soon as he could get away, Spider headed for home. For Kora. He turned the truck east, toward Pennsylvania. He tried calling her again, but still didn't get an answer. All manner of horrible things filled his head as he drove. If she was gone, there was really only one logical possibility. Her creator had found her.

He'd probably bumped into her at a store or something. She would have recognized him but not associated him with anything suspicious. She'd probably led him to their home for coffee or tea to catch up. Kora would never have assumed the worst.

When they had set up house in Lancaster, they'd taken on new identities, Joan and Corey Thompson, an artist and his wife. It had worked well for them. Being known as an artist, his skin art wasn't questioned, nor was the sound of metalwork. Plus, it made for an easy explanation for the money that came in. Not that what he was doing was strictly illegal, at least not all the time. He cursed himself repeatedly for ever leaving her behind. For ever thinking she'd be safe. Whatever happened to her now was on his head.

Two days later, Spider pulled up in front of their little rental house. It was neat and tidy, yellow with green trim, but there were three papers on the lawn. A curtain in the upstairs window shivered as if someone was standing just behind it, staring through the sheers. Shoving a baseball cap over his tattooed head, he got out of the car, walked to the door and let himself in.

The moment he opened the door, the stench of spoiled milk

and rotting fruit accosted him, nearly pushed him back out the door. Spider forced himself inside, immediately taking in the devastation. The old couch in the living room bled cotton batting and foam pieces, the cushions ripped from their cases and scattered haphazardly over the hardwood floors. The coffee table was overturned; the tall pole lamp speared the broken television. Everything was destroyed.

In the kitchen, the mess only got worse. The entire contents of the refrigerator left to rot on the floor, the cabinets emptied of their cans and boxes and containers, fragments of dishware and glasses lay twinkling in what little sunlight found its way between the blinds. Spider shook his head and made his way to the little den down the hall. The antique desk lay in splinters, its chair smashed. Bills, bank statements, scraps of paper littered the floor. Most of the books had been pulled down off the shelf, but there were a few still in their place.

Shoulders sagging as his hope died, Spider trudged to their bedroom. The large bed they shared was slashed open and ripped apart. The closet had been rifled through, clothes moved, but none taken. Kora's jacket, the one Spider had wired for her, lay in tattered rags in a pool on the floor. He lifted a piece to his nose, smelling the scent of Kora's soap and perfume. Spider reached into his side of the closet and found the back wall completely intact.

Nearly crying with relief, he touched the locking device and the back wall pushed in on its hinges. When they'd moved into the house, it had been a walk-in closet. Spider had installed the false wall less than a week after they moved in. Between the two of them, they didn't have much need for enough clothes to fill a walk-in closet and this way, there was a safe place, safer place anyway, to store the most important things.

The box with the two sets of discs sat exactly where he'd left it when they made a new copy of her programming. He helped her make it just after coming to the house, in case something happened to erase her memory. She wanted to have a more recent backup than her original programming. She wanted to remember who she was, who he was. He'd done it to make her happy at the time, certain it would never be needed, but now relief ran through him like anesthetic. So long as he could find her, everything would be all right.

Spider grabbed a duffel bag off the floor of the closet and tucked the box inside it along with her original identification papers and her favorite sweater. As he was leaving the bedroom, the sound of breaking glass under his boot startled him in the otherwise silent house. The drawing Kora had done of him for their anniversary lay in pieces on the floor, the heavy paper torn, the frame and the glass broken.

Gently, he pulled the fragments of the drawing from glass shards and placed each piece in between the pages of a book he grabbed off the floor. When he was certain he had all the pieces, he placed the book in his bag. Only then did he allow the rage to come.

They had come to their home and taken his woman. That wasn't enough. Spider pounded through the house into the basement to see what he could salvage of his tools. "I'm going to find them." He touched a picture of Kora he kept on his bench. "I'm going to find them, and find you, and I'm going to make them pay." He tucked the picture in his bag, looked around at the disaster that was his workshop, and decided to leave it. Everything could be replaced. Except Kora.

Spider left the house with her bag and a heavy weight on his shoulders. Kora was gone. Her creator found her somehow and removed her from her own home without setting off any alarms or alerting the neighbors at all. All of that destruction, all of that violence, and no one called the cops. So much for the neighborhood watch.

There was only one person who could have sold them out, who knew enough about them both to have been able to profit from their pain. Spider headed east again. There was a barman in Philadelphia who had some serious explaining to do.

The streets were practically empty as he walked through the bleak darkness, the stale smell of rot, decay, and garbage filling his nose, turning his stomach as he passed a hulking green Dumpster. Not even the heavy leather could hold the air's cold needles at bay. The clanking of his boots echoed as Spider stormed down a shadowy passageway. Muttering and mumbling curses to himself, he stopped short and slammed his fist into the dusty blue door.

Neon lights flickered violet, indigo, and pink as Spider walked through the back door of the club. He stormed through the club, itching for someone to stop him if only so he could mash their face in.

"We're closed!" A young woman's voice called to him through the shadows as he came down the long hallway into the main room.

He spotted the club's owner standing at the bar talking to the barely dressed woman behind it. He was on him in two strides, holding him by his long blonde ponytail. "You have less than two seconds to tell me where she is, Jack."

"Where who is, man?" A smile played around his eyes for a moment until he looked up into Spider's face. The determination, or maybe just the barely contained violence he saw there, caused Jack's facade to falter.

"So, what is the price of loyalty these days?"

"What? What are you talking about, Spider?" Jack held up his hands, innocence playing in his actor's eyes. He motioned to the girl at the bar who was staring at them with one hand on the phone. "Something strong Carrie, then get on out of here."

The girl moved quickly, her eyes only leaving Spider to grab a glass and bottle. Her muscles were tense beneath her revealing uniform, the tendons in her neck throbbing anxiously as she brought the bottle to Jack. She was careful not to get between the two men and to stay as far from Spider's imposing bulk as she could get.

"Thanks." Jack took the bottle and glass from her. "Get on home. I'm fine here."

"You don't want I should call someone?" The girl backed quickly away.

"Nope. Me and my boy here go back a long way. We just got some stuff to air out. You go on home." Jack nodded at her, his ponytail bobbing up and down. When Carrie was gone, he finally turned to face Spider again. "I don't know what's got you so riled."

"That's right, keep feeding me bull. Please. I need a good excuse." He smiled and pulled out his gun. "Actually, not so much." He shot the mirror behind the bar. "Start talking. Now."

"What's this to you, man?"

"She's mine. That's what this is to me." He pointed the gun at him, the barrel staring at Jack with longing.

"She's gone man." His hands shook as he brought the dirty glass to his lips. "I couldn't pass it up. I'm sorry but a guy like me is lucky to see a couple of thousand for a job, how could I pass up a million and a half?"

"Who did you sell her to?" The hand holding the gun started to shake. "Describe him."

"I never saw him. This was all done online, the whole thing. I never even heard his voice."

"That's not a good answer Jack." He took the glass from Jack's hands and drained the last of the liquor. He stood, pushing the chair over and pulled the trigger, sending a bullet past Jack's head, the thick sound of metal on wood echoed through the quiet. "The man I used to be would have killed you. You remember that next time someone trusts you. You remember this moment well, Jack. Next man you betray, well, he might just be that man I once was." Spider shoved his gun back into the holster under his jacket and walked out the front door.

He shook off what he could of his anger, trying to see clearly. He had to think. He had to find somewhere safe to think through it all, to analyze the information he had. Spider tried to take in his surroundings, seeing nothing but unending shadows.

Slowly, he pulled a small square of plastic from the inside pocket of his jacket. He pressed a few keys and he could hear ringing from the embedded speakers in the collar. "Angel's Pizza." A familiar voice spoke clearly even across three thousand miles.

"I need a favor, Crash."

"I never thought I'd hear your voice again, old friend." The rhythm between them fell easily back into place, threatened to pull Spider back into the days of his youth, when it was all just a game.

"You still in the business? You still got the skills you did back in the day?" He heard the street creeping into his own voice and marveled at it.

"Won't matter how much time creeps by, my skills only get better." Crash laughed and the past sucker punched him. He was a kid again, running cons and gadgets with his best friends. His family. "What's going on, man? After all these years, you call me up. Who'd you lose?"

"I'm coming home." Spider said tersely, shaking the memories away, filling his head with Kora's face. "I need a place to stay and some help."

"Got an ETA?" Crash asked.

"Not sure yet. However long it takes me to get 3000 miles." He took a deep breath. "I need you to help me dissect a program. I need to know who wrote it. I looked at it a few times and I'm not seeing a signature but there has to be one. Can you do it?"

"I've never met a program yet that didn't have a signature. Can you send it ahead?"

"Not this time. Be ready for me."

"Yeah. No problem. Watch your back. I'll see you in two days."

Spider disconnected the call and shoved the pad back into the inside pocket. Now he had direction. He had somewhere to start. If he couldn't find the key, Crash could. He wasn't looking forward to explaining the situation, but he had no choice.

3

The last fingers of evening sunlight touched the city Spider had grown up in, casting purple shadows that lurked like thugs in every alley. He kept an eye out for red or yellow bandannas and groups of boys in low-slung pants, like it had been when he was a kid, in the height of the gang wars that had rocked the entire city and not just his little corner of it. There were no signs of the old gangs at all. No clusters of enforcers on the corners, just waiting for a brawl. No tags on the facades of buildings, no boarded up windows or bullet holes in tenement doors.

As he walked, his mind was swirling, spewing random fragments of plans. Spider's best ideas always came when he was in motion, and he needed the best of the best now. He needed to find Kora if he never did anything else. He'd made a promise to her to keep her safe, and now he had to find a way to keep it.

Spider walked through the familiar territory, not recognizing any of it. Even his own gang's graffiti was gone, most of it. The people in the neighborhood were different, too. Their clothes were clean and free of ragged holes or patches made from outgrown shirts. One of the women he passed had on heels like he'd never seen before, with bright red soles that flashed as she took each step. It was different, like an upper class neighborhood wearing a ghetto skin.

He paused long enough to make sure it was the right building, noting the man two doors down who was watching him closely, and noting from the way he was standing slumped against the wall to cover the bulge, that he had a gun under his windbreaker. Above the door, tucked into the light, a tiny camera hummed. If he hadn't known what he was looking at, he'd never have spotted it. It was the right place but everything about it was different.

He took the steps two at a time to the third floor and

knocked hard on the fourth door on the right. When the door opened, Spider slumped against the frame of the door. "Hey."

The scrawny, hawk-nosed man with long violet hair stepped aside, ushering Spider inside. "You look awful."

"Thanks man. I feel it too." He dropped into a chair beside the computer, surprised to find that the chair was real leather and the computer was state of the art. Not cobbled together from a bunch of castoffs like it had once been. Everything about Crash's place had changed. Gone were the milk crate tables and sawhorse and plywood workbench. All of it had been replaced by shining metal and gleaming glass. Not one thing was held together by duct tape or zip ties. "Are we safe here?"

"Yeah. This building is as wired as you are. I watched you come in." He smiled; motioning to a series of flat monitors lined up on the wall. "You didn't think I'd actually open the door without checking for an ID did you?"

"Nah. I figured you had some set up. You've done well for yourself." Spider motioned to the apartment, the sheen of money it wore.

"For the whole family." Crash grinned, splitting his wide face with a scarecrow smile. "You didn't think I'd let the family stagnate just 'cause you skipped out, did you?"

"I didn't skip out and you know it." For a moment, a brief one, anger tried to surface but Spider squashed it. Crash was nearly right. In a way, Spider had expected the old place to be exactly what it was when he left it.

"What's so important that it brings you home now?"

"I gotta find my girl." He reached into his jacket, pulling out a disc. "This is her original programming. Thank god she had the sense to download it before she redid it."

"What are you talking about?" He took the disc and sat down in his chair.

"Kora. The woman I'm looking for." He sighed. "She's not really a woman, she's a machine. That's why we get along. I helped her out of a jam a couple years ago and we've stuck together ever since. I had to leave her alone for a few days, make some deliveries, but it wasn't very long, a few days, that's it. Her creator found her and took her back. I figure he was watching us, just waiting for me to leave her."

"A machine? Are you serious?" Crash held the disc in his fingers delicately. "And you say this is her original programming? Are you sure?"

"As sure as I can be. She made the copy. Just help me find out who made her. If I can find that out, I can find her and then you can see for yourself." He watched wearily as Crash slid the disc into his computer. "Part of me doubts you'll have any better luck than I did, but I've got to try. I promised her I'd protect her, that I wouldn't let her become a weapon again. But I'd lay odds that's what he has planned."

"You never make life easy do you?"

Spider shrugged and leaned back in the chair, confident that if there was anything to find, Crash could find it, just like when they were kids.

"Look, go catch some sleep on my couch. You look like you could use it."

"Yeah." He stumbled to the couch and was asleep before his body settled into the cool, clean leather.

4

Several hours later, a series of beeps woke Spider. He instinctively pulled his gun and sat up, facing the door. He glanced over at Crash only to find him studying his surveillance monitors. "Who is it?"

"Just Win." Crash shrugged, turning back to the computer. "Want to get it?"

"I can't believe you told him I was home." Spider shook his head but went to the door. The morning sun danced with dust on the hardwood floors. "You didn't work all night, did you?"

"Not quite. I caught some sleep in there too. You looked like you needed it, so I left you alone." Crash never turned his head away from the code in front on him.

Spider tucked his gun back in its holster and opened the door. The man in the hallway was older, nearly 60, very short and slim, his Korean heritage strong in the features of his face. "You look good, Spider." He said, nodding as he pushed past Spider into the apartment. "It's been too long since you've been home. We never hear from you."

"It's been a rough couple of years." Spider looked at the floor, sheepish, hating the look of reproach in Win's dark eyes. "I didn't want to drag everyone into this mess."

"Isn't that one of the benefits of being part of a family, even a large and messy one like ours? You don't drag us, we come willingly." Win smiled. For all that he looked innocent and kind, he wasn't always either. The good doctor had been, in his prime, the leader of the gang that Spider had always thought of as his family. "And when you need help, aren't we always here?"

"I know. That's why I came home." Spider sat back down on the couch. "I'm in over my head. Crash is the only one I know who might be able to spot something in that program that I missed. It's probably useless."

"I wouldn't say that." Crash turned from the screen and grinned. "I have a start. Pulled off the first layer of commands, into the second. I figure there are eight or nine levels before I start finding fingerprints."

"Say again?" Spider leaned forward, trying not to get his hopes up.

"I still have some digging to do. You probably need to give me a couple of hours without distraction to get everything together. That will give you time to go around and do some visiting. There are a lot of people who'd like to see you." Crash paused, considering his words. "According to this program, your girl was programmed to do some very interesting things."

"What's that supposed to mean?" Spider glared at Crash, trying to ignore the smug smile that graced his face.

"I want to see this machine lady of yours up close. She was the one who killed President Roberts, wasn't she?"

"No. Her creator killed the President. Get it right. She was just the weapon. It doesn't define who she is."

"Who she was." Crash corrected, tucking a clump of violet hair behind his tattooed ear. "Maybe if you hadn't shut down the replacement, they'd have let her go."

"I didn't mean for that to happen. How could I know they'd gotten to the President?"

"I watched the replays of it here. I never spotted you there though." Crash's pale eyes narrowed slightly, inspecting Spider's face.

"Would you believe I wore makeup?" Spider smiled thinly, wincing at the memory.

"What a man will do for a pretty girl." Win grinned; his crooked teeth and bright eyes made Spider feel at home. Like home was still there, still somewhere. In the end, it had been what brought him into the gang, how quickly Win and his wife, Vicky, had made him feel like part of the family. For someone with no one, that was heady stuff.

"Get out now guys." Crash pointed to the door. "I've got some serious work in front of me and I don't need the distraction."

"Thanks for helping me." Spider stood and headed for the door.

"You could have brought her here, to us, you know." Crash looked at him strangely, a distance that had never been there before in his eyes.

"I didn't want to risk it."

"Risk what? That they would find her here or that she might get attached to someone besides you?" There was a trace, a small one, of bitterness in Crash's voice.

"I don't know." Spider walked out of the apartment, followed quickly by Win.

When they were out of the building, Spider stopped Win.

"How many of them are really going to be glad to see me back?"

"More than you think." Win nodded. "You never had to run away. We would have stood by you through everything."

"His enforcer had already killed Ghost and Chen. They would have had no problem killing everyone around me for a stupid box. That was Krause's biggest mistake. Killing them. I might have dealt with him eventually before that. I couldn't risk any more of you getting hurt." They walked out of the building and, in the daylight, Spider was not too surprised that the whole neighborhood felt foreign to him. The familiar had been scrubbed, sanitized, and swept aside.

"No one blames you for what happened that night."

"Right. No one except for Ronnie. It's my fault her husband is dead." Spider turned in to a small Korean market on the corner, breathing in the smells he remembered from his gleefully misspent youth.

Win followed him around the store, down the aisles, grabbing a few things as they walked. "She doesn't blame you either. You had no idea the lengths Krause would go to for your invention. How could you? You were the last of us to see the bad in people. We thought you were so naive for that, always giving people the benefit of the doubt. Always thinking that, in the end, people were good. We should have all been more like you."

"No." Spider shook his head. "I was wrong. Some people are good but most people, most people are just surviving. Any way they can. They might not be bad people, but they aren't good. Good is rare."

"Except in machines? Is that why you want this girl back so much?"

"It has nothing to do with the fact that she's a machine. She's more than that." Spider paid for Win's purchases and carried the bag for him as they walked toward the clinic that Win and his wife ran for the little community that had sprung up from the gang's foundation.

"Are you coming for dinner?" Win looked up at him. The paternal look in his eyes disquieted Spider.

"Making anything good?" Spider cocked his head and looked at the man who'd helped raise him. He'd gotten old in ten years.

"I make everything good." He scowled and led the way toward the clinic and the apartment he and his wife shared above it. "Vicky asks about you a lot. I try not to lie to her but sometimes, I tell her you've been in touch with Crash or with Rat. I think she knows it's a lie, but if she asks . . ."

"I never could lie to her and you know it. I don't think for a minute you got away with it either. If she asks, I'll avoid the question. I'm good at that." Spider smiled and followed Win into the large building. It still smelled the same—a layer of bleach and sanitizer over a deeper, grittier layer of sick. Of human.

"I didn't believe them when they told me you'd come home." A woman's voice caught his ear and nearly broke his heart. Spider glared at the back of Win's head. Of all the people he'd known in his life, she was the last person he wanted to see. "You look different."

"It's been a long time, Ronnie." He looked up, surprised by the woman standing in front of him. Ronnie and he had come into the gang at the same time, both of them under Ghost's wing. It had been what bound them. He had been what bound them. She wasn't the young woman she'd been, all brash attitude and quick wit but not so much beauty. Ronnie had grown into her features, maybe still a little on the plain side but it was so pleasant that, at certain angles, it was the most beautiful face he'd ever seen. Her belly protruded from beneath the snug hem of her shirt, rounded and full. "You're pregnant?"

"I couldn't live my whole life alone. Did you really expect me to?" She laughed. "I loved Ghost, but he'd want me to be happy."

"Yeah. He would. I'm glad you found someone." He couldn't look her in the eye. "Anyone I know?"

"No." She shook her head. "He came along after you split. We call him Fox, and he's a sly one." Her laugh should have soothed him, but there was a hollowness to it. "I'm glad you're home, even if it's only for a few days."

"Me, too. I should have come home sooner." Spider sighed. "Can't change that now, I guess."

"If you stay away for this long ever again," a high, shrill voice made him duck his head in shame, "I will never speak to you." Vicky stood on the steps behind Ronnie, her hair much more white than it had been, her blonde nearly completely swallowed by it. They had all gotten so much older. When he looked in the mirror, he looked exactly the same as he had then. Maybe he just didn't notice how age settled into his own face.

"I hadn't planned to but, just when I'd get settled, just when I had things running the way I wanted to, Krause's men would show up and it was back on the road for me." Spider shook his head.

"What is so important about that box anyway?"

He saw the tears in her gray eyes and struggled to ignore them. "It's the principle of the thing. After what happened, I can't just hand it over, you know?"

"You should let that go, Spider. Really." Ronnie leaned against him, laying her head on his shoulder. "I know he was your best friend, but you need to let that go. It doesn't do anyone any good. Besides, we'd rather have you come home to stay having given him the box than live another ten years without seeing you just because you can't let it go. No one will think any less of you."

"I will. I'll think a whole lot less of myself." Spider kissed the top of her head.

"Come on. Win will have dinner ready soon, and let's at least go somewhere that poor Ronnie can get off her feet."

"Oh!" Spider looked down at her. "I'm sorry. I wasn't thinking. How far along are you?"

"Nearly there. Nearly at the end." She smiled, her face alight with wonder and love.

"You look happy."

"I am." She smiled at him and took his hand in hers. "I wish you were, too."

5

"I have a line on her!" Crash came barreling into Win and Vicky's apartment shortly after dinner. "We've got a long trip, old friend. If I'm right, she's in a compound in West Virginia."

"West Virginia? Who lives there?" Spider jumped up from his place on the couch.

"There's this programmer, Roland Moss. He was in big demand fifteen years ago and then, a few years back, he went hermit. He bought a big chunk of land; we're talking massive acreage here and went underground."

"And you're sure it's him?" Spider was next to Crash in three long strides. "How?"

"I've come across him before. He's got a style all his own, a flare for the dramatic, too. Just under the programming, Moss always puts a song. If you know what you're looking for, you can spot it. Just the notes. Some classical stuff, *Ode to Joy* or something."

"But how do you know that's Moss and not someone stealing his tag?" Spider asked.

"We've had a few run-ins. Before he dropped out of the scene anyway. I don't think anyone knows about the tag but me." Crash patted Spider on the back. "Been meaning to have a word to two with him for a long time."

"How long until you're ready?"

"I'll need a few days to put the equipment together." Crash's face broke out in a grin. "He's killer."

"That he is." Spider glanced around the room, looking for

something, anything. "What do we have?"

"Most anything you need." Ronnie started to struggle to get to her feet.

"Sit yourself back down." Spider pointed a finger at her. "You don't need any part of this. I'm not going to be the cause of you going into early labor."

"He's right, Ronnie." Vicky sat down next to Ronnie, patting her belly with a gentle hand. "You don't need any stress right now. You and I will stay right here and our men here will go check out the equipment houses."

"Equipment houses?" Spider stared at them.

"A lot has changed in ten years. A few turf wars, some creative laundering, a bit of smuggling and our usual tinkering has built up quite the little empire. It's not just the neighborhood anymore. We made a few really good deals and pushed the other gangs out of town completely." Crash smiled wickedly. "We have a lot of pluses on our side but we're going to need more than that. Most of our men, they don't know you but from Win's stories. I can't promise you they'll want to help. This job, it's going to need an army. You got anyone you know who owes you?"

"Even if I called in every favor I've ever been owed, will ever be owed, I couldn't get that kind of manpower." Spider pulled his jacket on. "There's only one way then." He pulled out the little dial pad from his jacket and started pressing numbers. "I have to get her back." He stared at them all apologetically.

"Hello?" A crackling male voice answered the phone.

"Mr. Krause," Spider stared at Crash as he spoke, seeing the shock in his eyes and put a finger to his lips. "I believe I have something you want and I think I'd like to make you a deal."

"Who are you? How did you get this number?" A little bit of anger, not panic, filtered into his voice.

"After all these years, you still underestimate me. Do you really think I can't find an unlisted number?"

"This is quite a surprise, Spider." There was suspicion now, caution too. "Why this sudden change of heart?"

"I have the disrupter. Do you still want it?" Spider closed his eyes, feeling the anger welling again at the sound of Krause's voice.

"What is your price?" Krause's voice was eager but restrained.

"Meet with me. Just you. Just me. No games." Spider held up a finger in warning as Crash opened his mouth.

"Something very big must have happened. I think you may actually be serious."

"I am."

"Where? When?" Excitement crackled in Krause's voice so powerfully it carried.

"Neutral ground."

"Is there such a thing? You and I have connections all over the world. Between us, there is nothing neutral."

"Either your operation has exploded in recent years or you give me too much credit."

"Maybe a little of both." Krause laughed and Spider's shoulders sagged in defeat.

"Then I'll come to you. Meet me in Egypt. At the Carnegie." He rubbed his face, hard.

"Interesting choice."

"I know how much you love your antiques." Spider tried to laugh but it sounded false.

"And you know that I leave my home turf alone."

"All the more reason to meet you there. Well populated, public, and close enough to home for you to tread a little more lightly than you might elsewhere."

"When do you propose this meeting should take place?"

"Ten AM, day after tomorrow."

"I know you're not that close. You can't be. Since when do you fly?"

"Excuse me?"

"We've been doing this dance for too long. Ten years and you've never even set foot on a plane. Whatever happened, it really is huge."

"Ten AM at the Egyptian exhibit." Spider disconnected the phone and looked around at the shocked faces staring at him.

"What do you think you're doing?" Crash shook his head.

"I need to get Kora back."

"Is she really worth it? She's just a machine. It's not like she's real." Crash took a step toward Spider.

"A machine?" Ronnie asked.

"You wouldn't question it if you knew her. She's not just a machine. Kora is so much more than that."

"Moss will have reprogrammed her by now. She won't be Kora anymore. Not the one you know."

"Maybe, maybe not. No one knows. Whatever she is, she's just as real as I am. She learns, she questions, and she hurts. She even wants to believe in God, which is more than I can say for me. It's my fault they got her. I can't just leave her there."

"Good for you." Ronnie smiled. "I don't care if she's your imaginary friend. Now you sound like the Spider I remember."

"And you don't hate me for making this deal?" He knelt down next to her.

"If this is what you need to do to get your girl, this is what you do." Ronnie kissed his cheek. "Good luck."

"I'll need it."

"Then what's the plan?" Crash and Win said in near unison.

"I'll fly ahead and set a few things up. You, if I can still count on you, drive in behind, and we'll see where it goes from there." Spider sighed. "I'll understand if you back out now."

"I don't trust Krause." Crash said simply. "But, you're right. You need him and this is the only way. You think I'll let you go without me this time, brother, you got another think coming. Got me?"

"Got you." Spider smiled. "I trust you to get what's necessary. I'll call you when I get a headquarters set up."

"And not a Krause building." Win interjected.

"Of course not. I'm desperate, not stupid." Spider smiled. "I've got to run now. I have a plane to catch."

"It'll be just like old times." Crash smiled and Spider did, too.

It would and it wouldn't. They were without Ghost this time around. As teenagers, the three of them had been like brothers. It was his fault Ghost was dead. Now, he was betraying him all over again, in a way, giving the man who'd had him killed exactly what he'd wanted in the first place.

As he walked out the door, he dialed the familiar number for the small, private airline he always used. He made reservations under his own name with them as well as four reservations on four different airlines from four different cities under aliases that he knew Krause knew.

His plane would land at a small, private strip in West Virginia. He'd only ever used his real name, his given name, with that airline, that pilot. There were only three people in the whole world who knew him as Michael Holt, and it was likely to stay that way. So long as he remained careful. He'd kept all his real information active. It was his retirement identity. There were bank accounts, tax returns, stock portfolios, and real estate waiting for him to give up the business of information and smuggling. He'd never be able to give up invention.

Spider drove to the airport, straight through the small private airline's lot. As he approached the door, he saw a ghost behind the counter. It had taken a few years to get used to seeing his dead mother's face every time he flew. Aunt Susan was the only blood family he had. Pausing for a moment at the door, before she saw him, he stared at her. The first time he'd seen her, he'd really thought she was a ghost. Sixteen, running from a fight that the cops had broken up, Spider had knocked her down. As he was helping her up, he saw her face and let go of her hand, sending her back down onto the sidewalk.

She'd started to curse at him, until he called her Mom. Immediately, she started questioning him. Susan was his mother's twin. There'd been some sort of falling out between them and she'd never known that Monica had a son, nor that she'd been murdered ten years earlier. Aunt Susan had tried to convince him to come and live with her and her husband, but never pushed the issue too much, so long as he stayed in touch.

When Spider discovered that Uncle Brian was a pilot, he'd filed the information away and, when he had to run, he'd gone to them. They'd gotten him out of the city, out of the state, out of reach of Krause and his enforcers.

Aunt Susan opened the door, disrupting his memories and pulled Spider into a hug. "It's been too long. Again."

"I know. I didn't want to drag you into this." He hugged her back.

"I see you still didn't bring your wife to meet me." She peered into the lot behind him, to the car he was driving. "I wish you would."

Spider closed his eyes against the welling tears. "Someone kidnapped her. That's why I'm here. I need a flight to Pittsburgh."

"Kidnapped? Did you call the police?" Fear filled Aunt Susan's light voice and hazel eyes. "Of course you didn't. You wouldn't. This isn't the time to play at hero, Michael. You need to call the cops."

"They wouldn't help me with this. You just have to believe me. Please, Aunt Susan. No questions." He looked into her eyes, pleading. "Once I get Kora back, I'm done. I swear it."

"I'll believe that when I see it." She pursed her pink painted lips and shook her head. "I'll get you a plane, but don't you go and get killed on me, you understand?"

"I won't. When I get her back, I'll bring her straight to you. I promise."

When the plane landed at a private airstrip in West Virginia, Spider found a small rental car waiting for him. Aunt Susan always planned better than he did. It was nearly an hour's drive from there to his little apartment just south of Pittsburgh. When he was on Krause's home turf, he liked having his own security. There were things a man couldn't trust to hotel safes. He knew from his younger days just how easy those safes were to pop.

It had been too risky to bring Kora to Pittsburgh, too many people who liked to ask questions, too many artists who were too good at faces. Maybe if he had, she'd still be safe. And he wouldn't feel like he was betraying the memory of his brother. Spider continued to curse at himself as he let himself into the apartment and quickly punched in the code before the alarms went crazy. It was the same as it had been the last time he'd been there—with the small addition of a thick layer of dust.

6

The museum was nearly the same as he remembered from his last visit. Stone and marble, ancient dead things, broad, uncluttered hallways. He was early and wandered the displays, spending most of his hour with the dinosaurs. Once, when he'd been very young, his mother had taken him to a museum to see the dinosaurs. They'd been so huge, so menacing. He'd dreamt about them a lot over the years, especially right after she was murdered. Big, badass, bony dinosaurs protecting him from his mother's killer.

Spider nodded at a passing woman and her son. The boy couldn't have been much more than seven or eight, a mouth full of teeth that had grown faster than the rest of his face and bright blue eyes that took in everything. The kid reminded Spider a bit of himself. Before.

Shaking off the small touch of sadness, Spider made his way up the stairs to the entrance of the Egyptian exhibit. Maybe it was cruel, tempting Krause with all the local pretties that were always, to him, untouchable.

"I wasn't sure I'd ever get to meet you face to face." A familiar, cold voice found his ear, but the face and the body that came with it were not what Spider had been expecting. There was no over-muscled boss-man in a stuffy suit, just a slender, wiry man with a lot of gray hair on his head and no hair at all anywhere else that Spider could see. AJ Krause was old. Much older than Win.

"In any other circumstances, you wouldn't. Not after what happened."

"I swear to you, Spider, that was not supposed to happen. My man was just supposed to talk to you, to feel you out and see if we could find a price you'd sell for. No one was ever supposed to get hurt." Krause held up his long-fingered hands, a pianist's hands. Or a good thief's.

"And all these years, you've kept hounding me. Why?" Spider shook his head, disgusted.

"For the same reason you wouldn't stop long enough to talk. It became a matter of principles. In that time, you've probably created things worth ten times the value of the disrupter, but I really didn't care. I wanted the box." He laughed, his face lighting up, more like a kindly old grandfather than a ruthless tyrant. "My stubborn streak gets the better of me sometimes. Something I think we have in common."

They stood in silence for a few moments, staring into a glass-fronted cabinet full of ancient treasures. Krause turned to face him. "It's time to talk business now. I'd like to hear what you want."

"I want your help. There's a man, not too far from here, by the name of Roland Moss. He took my girl."

"Kora? That was her name, right?" Krause ran a hand over his chin, like he was stroking a beard he didn't have. "Pretty girl."

"She is. I need to get her back, and I need your help." Spider sighed. "You have no idea how much it hurts to say that."

"I can imagine." Krause laughed again. He seemed to do it a lot. "I wasn't always an old man, Spider. I know what it was to be young and untouchable. I'm not sure you do need my help. Look where you are right now. I think you could do anything you wanted."

"Oh? Just because I'm standing here next to the man who's been trying to kill me for the last ten years?"

"I never wanted you dead. But it takes something to call up an adversary to get what you want, son."

"I'm not your son." Spider turned his face away. "Can you help me?"

"So, you give me the disrupter and I help you get your girl, is that all?"

"It might be a little complicated, but that's it in a nutshell." Spider nodded. "May I ask what you'll do with it? With the disrupter?"

"Believe me or not, but I don't intend to use it. I intend to perfect it and then sell it to the government."

"Going legit? Are you kidding me?"

"Spider, I'm getting too old for this. I can't run around like you anymore. I have too many marks on my file, too many counts against me. If I can take this to the Pentagon, they'll clear my record in exchange for it. And then, I design the technology to bypass it and sell it to the underground."

"If I'd have known that, I might have worked with you from the beginning."

"Except where would you be now? Besides, those weren't my original plans. I dreamed of large-scale bank heists, museum raids, and government takeovers. That all changed not too long ago."

"Why?"

"I'm a father now. I can't have my children growing up knowing their father never amounted to anything more than a thief." Krause shifted to face Spider. "So, that's all you want, one last dance? One last romp before I go legit?"

"Really? No more safes? No more private collections?"

"Well, I can't say never, but it would take something extraordinary, something truly exquisite, to bring me on board."

"Are we settled?"

"Nearly. I'd like to add a little bonus to this deal, for the both of us. I'd like you to come work for my new company."

"What?"

"One year. That's all I want from you. One year where you can put your natural talents to work in a real lab with the proper equipment and funding and everything. On salary of course—a nice one, too—I'm not buying a slave here. I just want you to help me with the team I'm assembling. You might even find that you enjoy it. Maybe enough to extend the contract."

"Don't count on it."

"Just think about it. You can decide after we get your girl back."

"So, you'll help me?"

"Of course. You had the balls to come to me with this deal and not put a bullet in my head for something that wasn't supposed to happen. For something that we both lost good men over."

"You lost a good man?"

"Of course. I couldn't have a man who'd go off half-cocked and try to do things *his* way instead of mine. I did what needed to be done. I put him down." Krause nodded curtly. "You didn't know that?"

"No."

"I had his body dumped in your gang's territory. I figured you would know."

"I did so much running that I didn't get to call home much." *But I called enough that someone should have said something.*

"Well. Now you know." Krause nodded again. "So, this is settled?"

"It is." Spider stared down at the hand Krause extended. "I'll give you my disrupter and I'll give you one year. All I want is Kora."

"I'm very curious about this woman of yours and very much look forward to meeting her." Krause withdrew his hand and shoved it in his pocket. "I will be in touch with you to discuss plans after I look into our options."

"How?"

"You didn't really believe I wouldn't run a trace when you called me, did you?" Krause chuckled.

"I'll be waiting for your call then." Spider turned away and made his way out of the museum. His blood rushed through his body like it was trying to go somewhere else, pushing him forward, pushing him on. However, he had to get Kora first.

Spider made quick work of Pittsburgh's streets, making the necessary turns, looking at no one, speaking to no one. He'd rented a warehouse earlier that morning down by the river and he needed to get his gear set up and the security running before Crash and the others got there. It would give him something to do that didn't involve thinking about all the ways he'd screwed up.

7

"**A**re you going to do it?" Crash started talking the moment the passenger side door opened.

"I'll do whatever it takes. I hope you understand that." Spider headed straight for the cargo doors at the back of the tractor-trailer. "He'll contact me when his people are ready."

"We'll set everything up. You still any good at hacking satellites?" Crash asked.

"I've kept my skills limber enough. Why?"

"We need better overheads. Moss paid off someone. His property doesn't show on any of the Earth Map sites. The data is probably all right there, it's just buried under mountains of code."

"Give me the coordinates and I'll get the intelligence. What are you going to be doing?"

"Setting up everything. I have some new stuff to walk you

though." Crash grinned brightly, the rings in his lips glinting in the fluorescent lights of the warehouse. "I brought all of my best stuff."

"Good." Crash gave him the coordinates. Spider retreated into his office and got to work. Three hours later, after using every cipher, every trick he knew, he still hadn't gotten the data. He positioned the long antennae and connected directly to the nearest satellite overhead.

It'd take at least twice as long, but it was still easier than hacking the mapping sites. Moss had probably encrypted the information himself and, without Kora, there was no way to figure it all out in the time he had.

Maps in hand, Spider called a meeting with Crash and Win. There were a few other people there with them but Spider wanted to keep the ranks firm. These were his leaders. They deserved to be treated like it.

"Win, you and Baby will stay here and run the communications center. And interference if you have to. I have the cop frequency for that area and programmed it into the system here so you should be able to monitor that. Crash, you and Rat will be at the compound. Stay back." Spider laid the printouts on the table.

"There's a ridge here that looks like it would be perfect for surveillance." Win pointed to the line of hills and trees just north of the compound.

"I thought so, too. You guys could hang back there until I need you or until I give the signal." Crash looked like he wanted to complain, but Spider talked over him. "Look, if there are going to be casualties, let Krause's men be those deaths, all right? You guys are strictly plan B and clean up. I don't want any of you to get hurt in this mess."

"But . . ." Crash started, but Spider held up a hand to silence him.

"If it all goes south, it'll be up to you to save my butt, all right?" He laid the picture he'd taken from his workbench on top of the maps. "This is Kora. When I go in, I'll set off the disrupter and it will put her down too. When you find her, she'll be completely deactivated. If something happens to me, there is a switch in her mouth. Silver fillings. Remember that, okay?"

"Don't talk like that." Win scowled, accentuating the deep ruts of age in his face.

"I have to be realistic here. There's every reason to think I'll walk out of there on my own, but if something goes wrong and I don't, I'm not going to let her just sit somewhere and collect dust. She's not some million dollar paperweight."

"What about Moss?" Crash leaned against the table.

"If I'm lucky, you'll get the time you want with him. I'll leave him disabled. You'll get your chance to take him. I really don't care what you do with him." Spider sighed. "Would it be nice if I didn't have to worry about him coming after her again? Sure. Am I counting on it? No. You do what you think is best."

"Excellent." Crash's smile made Spider cringe, just a little. Crash was just a little too happy at the prospect of gaining a powerful, well-connected hostage.

His jacket twittered a shrill double beep. "That's him. Quiet." Spider pressed the button on his collar to answer it. "Spider."

"I have a meeting set up. It will get us in. From there, you use your machine and my men will come in behind us." Krause sounded anxious, even excited.

"How do I know you aren't setting me up?"

"I guess you don't. I really hope you don't think so little of me. There is still some honor among thieves, Spider." He sounded genuine enough but an accomplished thief must also be an accomplished actor and Spider knew it.

"You'd better be right." He growled.

"I have no reason to betray you now, Spider; I swear it on the heads of my children."

Spider shrugged off the assurances as bravado. "What time?"

"Meet me at seven sharp in front of the Carnegie. I'll drive."

"Fine." Spider disconnected. "Catch all that?"

"We'll get everything set up tonight." Win smiled and patted Spider on the shoulder. "Nothing to worry about. You focus on what you need to do and let us handle the rest of it."

"Okay." He turned to Crash. "You said you had some gear to walk me through? Now might be a good time."

"Oh! Right!" Crash slapped himself on the forehead with the palm of his hand. "I almost forgot. Come on. You're going to love this!" Crash led him out of the office and back to the truck. "I know you love that ratty old jacket, so I haven't made you a new one or anything, just a few additions to that one."

"Additions? I don't think I could carry anything else in this jacket." Spider shook his head.

"I think you'll want a few of these things. Some of them are old technology and not new, but I figure you'll probably be going through a few metal detectors and maybe an X-ray scan on the way in. It's what I would do, and Moss is . . . well, Moss." Crash opened one of the trunks next to the truck and started pulling out a variety of objects: a long wooden tube, a plastic and ceramic gun, a wad of putty, and several lengths of a strange looking cloth.

"I know it's a little bit old school, but if you do get scanned, this won't show up as easily. So long as we put it in just the right place." He handed him the wooden tube. "Inside that tube is a tiny dart. On that dart is a little bit of poison, actually Batrachotoxins from the Golden Poison Dart frog. I have a great connection in South America." He nudged Spider with glee. "Just don't get it on you. At all. You blow through the painted end and the dart comes out the other end. Pretty quick death, too. I've always wanted to see it used."

"I don't think so, Crash. That's a bit much, don't you think? I figured when you said you had new stuff, we were talking about gadgets or some new explosive or something." Spider rolled the little tube in his fingers. "This is ancient, primitive stuff."

"Yeah. But it's ancient, primitive stiff that won't show up in a metal detector or probably even an x-ray scan. There's enough shadowy area in your body that you could probably tape it to the inside of your wrist and never get caught." He handed Spider a roll of medical tape. "I do have other things though. I do."

He rustled through the trunk, a little giddy and very much like Spider remembered him. All energy and no downtime. Everything was amazing to Crash. Everything.

8

As Krause pulled off the road, up to the high gate that surrounded Moss's estate, Spider resisted checking the ridge. He didn't want to draw attention to Crash's position in any way. He figured Krause probably had a backup in place, too. He didn't care. Not as long as he got Kora back.

"Are you ready for this?" Krause asked, dragging Spider out of the deep well of guilt.

"I am." Spider nodded. "Did you tell him I was coming when you set this up?"

"That would have been very stupid of me, don't you think? For today, you can be my bodyguard."

"All right. That might actually work." Spider took a deep breath and let it out slowly. "When we pull up to the house, stay in the car until I come around to let you out. May as well make it look good, right?"

"Good thinking." Krause waved at the pair of cameras trained on them and the gates swung open. "And you, when we're inside, you stay quiet. May as well make it sound good, too."

Spider almost laughed but caught himself. "He's probably surrounded himself with machines and not too many people. In fact, I wouldn't be surprised if he is using a double. If he's as paranoid as I've been told, he's probably got himself locked up tight in a safe room. Which might make things interesting."

"I hope you're wrong about that. I really do. Interesting would not suit my timeline here." Krause pursed his lips. "Complications would make my attempt at legitimacy a bit more . . . complicated."

"If it goes that wrong, I'll keep you out of it. I'll take you hostage." Spider picked at the edge of the tape on his wrist. Just a little. It itched like crazy.

"Excuse me?" Krause turned to him, incredulous.

"You heard me. I won't repeat it. So long as you don't screw me, you'll come out of this cleaner than you went in."

"I can deal with that." He smiled and pulled the car forward. "Ready?"

"Ready." Spider swallowed hard against the nerves trying to tie his insides in knots.

The house belonged on a mountain somewhere, a Tahoe ski resort. If a log cabin could be a mansion, Moss's house was one. Huge glass windows gleamed, revealing nothing but the reflection of the sky in their mirrored surfaces. Red wood logs and dark gray stone stepped up three stories, reaching their pinnacle in a sharp point.

A large, well-dressed man opened the large wooden front door, watching them both closely as Krause and Spider got out of the car. Spider tried to find some sign or another that he was human. Or not. He could see nothing, no difference in the guard's blue eyes from any other blue eyes. There was nothing odd about his build, nothing suspicious about his gestures or his voice.

"Give your weapons to me, please." The man looked at Spider pointedly, like he saw through him.

Spider glared at him but took his primary weapon, his expected weapon, from its holster and handed it to the guard. "I'm going to want that back." He did not reach for his backup gun or any of the other hidden surprises he carried.

The guard put a finger to his ear, as if he was holding in

an earpiece. "The scans count additional weaponry." The goon stepped forward, reached around Spider to the pancake holster in the small of his back, and took the backup gun. Then, he reached into Spider's left pocket and took the taser. He reached into Spider's boot, took the two knives hidden there, and paused for a moment, listening to the voice in his earpiece.

For a moment, Spider was certain the guard would take the disrupter, despite the material wrapped around it that Crash assured him would render it invisible to all of Moss's scanners. Or the third, very small derringer shoved in his underwear, also wrapped in the same fabric. He'd have been a true fool to hide all his weapons in that way, Moss would expect weapons. If the scans hadn't found any, he surely would have been searched more vigorously.

When the guard and his invisible handlers were satisfied, Spider and Krause were led into the masterpiece of wood and stone. Definitely not what Spider expected from a tech-head like Moss, at least from the outside. Inside, it lived up to expectations a little better. Clean, harsh lines, stark colors. Furniture chosen for its duality of function rather than its form. Gunmetal appliances and gadgets. Tile, marble, and stone flooring with an occasional dark throw rug. White walls with black and chrome trim. Thick windows that were almost certainly bulletproof. The television hung over the fireplace like artwork. It was a tech-head's dream house.

The guard led them into an office and pointed to two chairs positioned in front of an imposing steel and glass desk. Spider took note of the four cameras pointed at them and the absolute lack of machinery in the room. This office served no function. It was for appearances only.

The entire wall behind the glass desk was fashioned into a trophy display. Various awards, medals, and certificates that Moss had earned over his years working on computers and machines. It looked to Spider as if he'd won every award there was for that kind of thing. The display was kept immaculate, the metal shined with polish, the glass gleamed streak- and dust-free. Moss was certainly proud of his accomplishments.

Spider and Krause were kept waiting, as they'd expected to be. Krause fidgeted a little, like a bored child, but Spider kept his urge to move contained. Whoever was watching them would not see him squirm. He wondered for a moment about Kora, if she was watching, if there was any recognition in her undoubtedly reprogrammed eyes.

At the sound of approaching footsteps, Spider turned to the entryway, his fingers twitching, the desire to reach for a weapon almost overwhelmed him. The man who entered, Moss, or his stand-in, was taller, more muscular, than Spider would have figured him to be. Not built like a normal, white-collar computer jockey, but more like him. He was a man who was vain enough to either take care of himself or construct a double in the image he wished he saw in the mirror. Which would be easy to believe of the man before him, that he was an attempt at perfection. Toned body, romance novel face, and long brown hair tied back with a rubber band.

"Mr. Krause." The man extended a hand. Not a germaphobe then. He was nothing like the man Crash had described. "I was very surprised to hear from you. The last I checked, you were under investigation."

"That should be taken care of soon. Just a mistake, you see."

"Of course." Moss's smile was cold and sarcastic. Very human. Of course, Kora had smiled convincingly too. "You said something about a job."

"Something like that." Krause readjusted himself in the uncomfortable chair. "I'm putting together a team of some of the best minds in the technology and inventive fields. I would very much like for you to be a part of it."

Spider seethed on the inside but his facade remained calm and stoic.

"I'm sorry you've wasted your time, but I've been out of the field for several years now."

"Really? I doubt that." Krause laughed and steepled his fingers beneath his chin. "I think you have been busier since your 'retirement' than you were working for Aerodyne."

"Oh, really?" Genuine surprise flashed on the man's face. "Why on earth would you think that?"

"I have connections, Mr. Moss. Connections that know more about what you've been up to than you think. I'm sure there are some people in the secret service who might be very interested in the things I know."

"Excuse me? What are you talking about?" Moss's voice rose in anger. "Whatever you think you know, you don't. I'm retired. And I am going to stay that way."

"That's a shame, Mr. Moss. We could have done extraordinary things." Krause sighed and turned to Spider, his fingers tapping their code. Spider reached into his pocket and prepared to hit the switch that would activate the disrupter. "I'd like to introduce you to my associate. You may have heard of him. Spider?"

"Why would I have heard of him?" Moss's gaze flitted back and forth between them. "Would someone please explain to me, in English, what this is about?"

"I'll give you one chance to give her back." Spider had to fight to keep his tone level, his voice free of rage.

Moss laughed nervously. "This is some kind of j9oke, right? Someone put you up to this?"

"I'm dead serious." Spider stood, his hands still ready to turn everything off. "Maybe you should call up your inside man. Ask Jake what this is all about."

"Jake? I don't know anyone named Jake." Moss's eyes gave nothing away but fear.

"The bartender you paid for the information. Surely, you remember the man you paid more than a million dollars." Spider stepped toward him. "One chance."

"I told you. I don't know anything."

"Right. You have no idea who Kora Walker is. You didn't create her or anything. You didn't leave your signature in her code. Sure. I believe you."

"What do you mean, 'create her?' What are you talking

about?"

"Kora Walker. Her programming has your signature." Spider slammed his fist down against the glass desktop.

"If I created someone, do you really believe I'd leave something identifiable? There's no freaking way. I am many things, but stupid is not one of them."

"Money can make a man stupid. Stupid enough to take out one of the most powerful men in the world." Spider glared hard at Moss.

"Wait." The fear in Moss's eyes blossomed into anger. "What are you accusing me of, exactly?"

"The assassination of President Roberts."

"You can't be serious! I don't know if I should be honored or offended."

"Are you honestly telling me you had nothing to do with it? You are at the top of the AI field. How could you have nothing to do with it?"

"That's precisely why it's stupid to suspect me! You don't think the Feds, the CIA, and Secret Service haven't ripped my life apart? They were on my case about three minutes after the discovery was made."

"Those idiots in DC aren't as smart as they think they are." Krause whispered, almost to himself.

"Give me a name then." Spider stepped toward Moss, coming within arm's reach. "If not you, then who?"

"I don't know!"

"Bull."

"None of the people I know in the field are capable of something like that. None of them. At least, not without crowing. A leap like that you can't keep quiet. Not if you're corporate. Not unless you're working off the radar. Not in a million years. You can't put this on me. If I'd managed to create a viable AI, let alone one that could pass for human, I'd be halfway to my Nobel and not playing with electric sheep out here in the middle of Appalachia!"

"So the *Ode to Joy* just appeared in her program by accident?"

Spider watched Moss's face, the panic there. It wasn't the kind of panic he'd expected.

"No. No. No. Someone set me up." Moss held up his hands in surrender. "I haven't used that tag since some little hack punk stole it, tried to claim he was me. Stupid kid almost got caught dipping into the mainframe in Quantico. It took a long time to convince them it wasn't me."

Spider reached up and turned off the microphone, shut down the connection to Crash. Spider rubbed his face. "I really want to believe you. I really do but, I just don't know." An alternative theory came to him, too quickly for comfort. One he didn't want to believe was possible. "Will you help me flush someone out? I swear to you I will pay for the damage myself and I will never bother you again."

"Of course. This is my back someone is sticking a giant target on, after all."

"Krause, send your men a message. Have them come in soft but visible. But tell them not to *look* like they're being visible." He turned to Moss. "Do you have a safe room?"

"Yes."

"Get your men together and go there. Stay there until I come get you or until you hear silence for no fewer than six hours. If you're still safe there six hours after the last gunshot, you should be okay to come out."

"Gunshot? What are talking about?"

"I'm very sorry, Mr. Moss. Someone tried very hard to set you up, and I fell for it." Spider hung his head, shame biting deep into his soul. "This is going to be messy. You see, I have a team up there on the ridge. Just two men. One of them is pretty obsessed with you. I promised him not to kill you until he could question you himself."

"You're really not kidding." Moss sat back in his chair, stunned.

"Your guard, he took my guns. Most of them anyway. Take them with you into your safe room and sit tight."

"No. Not on your life. If there's going to be a firefight, I want in." Moss's eyes lit up. "Despite what you might think of men like me, I'm not happy cooped up in a clean room, manipulating code, evaluating circuits. That's why I quit. I wanted something more. This . . . today . . . is more. This could be fun."

"Suit yourself. Here's the plan. I'm going to deactivate your surveillance and your alarms. Krause will call his people and we'll set it up. Then, we'll make some noise and I'll call for my backup."

Spider pulled the disrupter out of his pocket, the strange fabric falling away. "What is that? How did you get that past my scanners?"

"This is a disrupter. It will shut down anything mechanical for a few minutes. Long enough to bypass alarms, long enough to put a kink in things. As for how it got through," he held up the fabric, "it's a little something my *associate* designed. I don't actually know how it works. Yet."

"Great. Got any more surprises?"

"Of course I do. Unfortunately, none that my *friend* won't be expecting."

"You have me." Moss grinned wickedly, a light of mischief playing in his eyes. "So, Krause, you serious about that spot on your team or was it just a ruse?"

"Well, since you aren't Spider's monster, the offer is very real if you're interested." The old man smiled.

"Is he on this team?" He nodded toward Spider and Krause nodded affirmatively. "Then we'll talk after we see how this plays out." Moss pressed a small button under his desk.

His guard came into the room quickly, gun drawn and ready for a fight. Moss shook his head. "I need you to give Mr. Spider's weapons back to him. We're going to make some noise down here, but you are not to get involved unless I call for you."

"What's going on?" The guard looked back and forth between Moss and Spider.

"Nothing to worry about. Just a little game. Go get his weapons please." Moss pointed to the door and the guard did as he was asked, coming back to give Spider his confiscated weapons, and then disappearing.

"Let's get everyone invited to the party already."

Spider nodded and pressed the switch on the disrupter. The lights flickered off. The surveillance shut down, the LEDs on the cameras went dark. The hum and purr of machinery they were all so accustomed to hearing all the time fell silent, enveloping them in a thick blanket of quiet.

"Ready?" Spider looked to Moss and Krause, who both nodded. "Just play along." Spider pressed the button in his collar again, knowing Crash would be waiting.

"I'll give you one last chance. Where is she?" Spider picked up a chair and smashed it, with some regret, through the beautiful glass desk.

"I told you already! I don't know what you're talking about!" Moss turned out to be a decent actor to boot. "Get out of my house before I call the cops!"

Krause's men crept in quietly. Spider knew Crash had seen them come in. "Sweep it! I want her found!"

"Look." Moss was getting into the act now. "I'll give you whatever you want, just get out. Leave me alone!"

"I'm not going anywhere until I get Kora back!" Spider picked up a small marble statue, but Moss snatched it from him and handed him a vase to throw instead.

The destruction of Moss's house continued as the men screamed at each other, Spider ranting about his woman, Moss offering anything and everything he could think of. Money. Connections. Contacts. Everything. Spider held up a finger to quiet Moss, fastening zip-ties around the air.

Krause came back into the room, enticed by the sudden quiet. "Did you get what you need?"

"No. I'm not going anywhere just yet. Why don't you go on and get out of here? You don't want to be a part of what's about to happen."

"You're probably right." Krause held a finger to his ear. "Call when you are finished and one of my men will pick you up."

Spider nodded. "Thanks."

Krause and his men left quietly. Moss sat in the shadows, strands of pale light seeping through the blinds on the windows. Spider tossed him one of his guns.

"Okay Crash, your turn." Spider spoke into the mic.

They didn't have long to wait. Crash and Rat were through the disabled door and making their way through the ransacked house. "In here!" Spider called to them, taser in hand. He didn't want to kill Rat, but he needed time alone with Crash.

Rat came through the door first and never had a chance to cry out, several thousand volts of electricity coursing through him, silencing the cry on his lips as he fell twitching. "What the —?" Crash fell over the prone and trembling Rat.

"Where is she, Crash?" Spider's hand clamped down hard on Crash's throat while Moss stripped him of weapons. "Don't pretend you don't know."

"All right. I won't." A bitter smile touched Crash's thin lips. "How'd you figure it out?"

"The Nobel. Moss is itching for one. If he *had* created Kora or anything like her, he'd have one. Seems to me he has one of everything else there is." Spider gestured to the untouched case. "He's not in this game for the money; he wants the glory, what there is of it anyway."

"You always did think you were so smart, Spider." Crash shook his head.

"Tell me where she is and maybe I'll let you go." Spider shook him so hard Crash's teeth gnashed together.

Crash glared at him, his eyes full of hate. "I wouldn't tell you if you paid with your own blood!"

"Why? Why did you kill him?"

"Who? President Roberts?" Crash laughed, the sound like ice to Spider's ear. "I got paid enough. Who do you think finances the family? Not you. You ran away with your box and left us to clean up."

"I left to protect you!" Spider pressed his face close to Crash. "Do you think I wanted to leave home? Leave everything I knew, everyone I cared about? Do you think it was by choice?"

"You could have stayed. The family would have stood with you." Crash sneered, as if the sentiment tasted sour in his mouth.

"I couldn't let anyone else die. Ghost died because he wouldn't tell them where to find me."

Crash laughed again, that same cold, heartless sound echoing through the room. "Ghost died because I wanted him to. I told that thug he knew where you were. Ghost died because he was in my way. You might have, too, if you'd stuck around. Then we wouldn't be in this mess."

Spider released Crash for a moment, just long enough to punch him once with all his anger. "In your way? We were brothers! We stood next to each other; no one ever stood in front."

Crash sucked in air, his body trying to curl up and protect his vulnerable gut from another blow. When he spoke, his voice was an angry whisper. "Sh-sh-Shows what you know. Ghost was the untouchable golden boy. He got the girl, he got the respect. Ghost was dead and you ran away with the guilt. Who'd that leave to run things? Win? He's so old he can barely breathe. You think he had it in him to chase out the other gangs? You think he could have cleaned up the neighborhood? Made it so we can walk the streets without worrying who's walking by? He couldn't clean up his clinic. That was me. It was all me. I ended the wars between our family and the others. I brought in the money, the connections, that made our neighborhood safe. Not Win. Not you."

"Where does Moss fit into all of this? You were so anxious to send me to him, to get your hands on him."

Rat started to get up, so Moss moved silently through the rubble. Ramming Rat's skull against the floor, Moss knocked him out. "I'd like the answer to that one myself."

"You have powerful enemies, Moss. They'd pay a lot for your head, but they'd pay a lot more for your talents." Crash's smile was bright through the blood pouring from his nose.

"Tell the man what he wants to know." Moss put the barrel

of the Beretta against Crash's temple. "Now."

"You'll never get her back. I erased everything and reprogrammed her for her buyer. She's long gone."

Spider hit him hard, blood spurting from Crash's nose. "Here's what you don't understand. Kora evolved on her own the moment she chose not to self-destruct. I guarantee you couldn't erase that. She'll come to me."

"Right." Crash sneered through the blood pouring from his broken nose. "You believe what you want. She's just a machine. She's gone and I'm not telling anyone where she is, who her buyer was."

"She's not just anything! But it won't matter who bought her."

"You really think she'll remember you? I erased her memory. There's nothing there."

Spider let go of Crash's shirt and hit him again before he could get his footing. Crash pushed up from the floor on his hands and knees, spitting blood, and a tooth, onto the floor. Spider kicked him in the gut, dropping him back to the ground.

"You, of all people, should know that there is nothing ever completely, utterly erased. She'll remember me. And I'm going to make it really easy for her to find me, too."

"What? How?" Crash asked.

"When Mr. Moss and I gift wrap you for the cops, hand them the biggest career-making arrest in recent history, my face is going to be everywhere. All over the world. She's bound to see it, to know me. She'll find me."

"Arrest?" Crash sputtered and coughed up blood. "You're going to turn me in?"

"Oh yeah. You think, after everything, I'd still be loyal? You never did know me very well, I guess. Hey Moss, why don't you make that call now?"

"You've got to turn my tech back on first." Moss flipped open his cell and showed Spider the blank screen.

"No, I don't. It's a disrupter—it just shuts stuff off. Everything should work fine now; it just needs to reboot."

"Oh. Great." Moss pressed a button on the side and waited as the phone revived itself.

"I could tell them everything about you." Desperate, Crash tried to bargain with him. "All that stuff we did as kids."

"You don't think the Feds would be willing to cut me a deal? I haven't done anything illegal in years." Not too illegal anyhow. "I think they have bigger things to worry about than me."

"The family will never forgive you. You can never go home!" There was real fear in his voice now, feverish and panicked.

"Probably not. Somehow, that's all right with me."

"What about Win and Vicky? Ronnie and her baby? Don't you care what happens to them?" Crash pushed himself up off the ground, standing shakily.

"That's on your head, not mine. Besides, once your capture hits the news, I think they'll be smart enough to run before the cops come down hard on the neighborhood, ripping open your life. At least, Ronnie will. As a matter of fact, I think I'll call her. Play her a little clip of this conversation we've had."

"You recorded this?" Crash lurched toward him, but Spider knocked him back to the ground, quickly binding him with the zip ties he'd had in his pocket to use on Moss.

"I thought it would be a good idea."

Sirens wailed in the distance. "If you do this, you're a dead man. You'll never be safe. Not ever."

"I can take anything and anyone who comes after me. I'm not the scared kid I was back home. I grew up on my own. I never had anyone to fall back on. I'll be just fine." Spider kicked Crash hard in the ribs, relishing the pop of bone. "The same can't be said for you."

9

Spider glared at the wires on the table in front of him, as if that would make them shape up and do what he wanted. Nothing about this project was going quite right. "Hey!" Moss poked his head into the workroom. "You have a call coming in on that stupid jacket. It's driving me crazy with all the beeping. Shut it up."

"Sorry." Spider smiled. It had been a very long time since anyone called him at that number. Only a handful of people even knew it.

He slid into the leather before he answered it. It was as close to home as he ever got. Which was probably why he couldn't bear to part with it. "Mi . . . Spider."

"Spider?" A chill ran through him, every hair on his body standing up to cheer.

"Oh my God. Kora? Are you all right?" He collapsed in a chair his knees unable to hold him up.

"So, you *do* know me." Her voice was quiet and scared.

"I do. I did. You don't remember much, do you?"

"No. I don't understand what's going on. I see your face on the news, but they call you the wrong name, Michael Holt, but that's not your name. Your name is Spider. Why do I know that? Why do I know this number?"

"Where are you? I'll come to you and explain everything." Spider motioned frantically to Moss and mimed a plane, pointed to him, and silently asked him to come with. Moss nodded and disappeared to pass the information on to Krause and call Aunt Susan.

"I made it to Miami, but from here I get so confused. I know this place, but I don't. Like there's a ghost of another life inside my head and . . . I just want to understand." He could hear her fear, her sorrow, and ached to get to her.

"Are you at the airport now?"

"No, but I think I can get back there." She whimpered. Just a little soft mewling. Like she was crying.

"Go there. Wait for me. I'll be there in ... say, twelve hours."

"That's a long time."

"Get something to eat. Read a book. Just, be there. I'm coming, Kora. I'll be there as soon as I can."

"Hurry." She hung up the phone.

Moss came back into the room with questions in his eyes. "I was right, Moss." Spider grinned, feeling right again. Feeling whole again. "She found me. She doesn't really remember much, but she found me. I was right."

Author's Note:

When I first started this story in probably 2004, I could see Kora and Spider so clearly and I originally created them for another book project. They didn't quite fit in the book, but I loved Spider and Kora. Spider is that reformed bad boy type who was never actually a bad guy, just surviving. I saw him as blindly loyal and desperate for family. For connection. The only way he would leave anyone is if he thought it would protect them.

Crash is one of my favorite villains. He's devious, cruel, and jealous. I imagine he took great joy in stepping into the provider role for the family, knowing it was his machinations that removed the competition. I also imagine it chaffed his hide that the girl he so wanted still turned to someone who wasn't him.

As for the technology, I'm still a little surprised there isn't a targeted or small range EMP (electromagnetic pulse) device on the market (that we know of) and for me, in 2004, that's totally what the disrupter was. If I were starting this story now, I might use a different technology as EMPs are getting to be a bit old hat now.

FOR THE LOVE
OF MADELINE

Lauren stirred. The chill accentuated the empty half of the bed. It wouldn't matter how many years went by; she'd never be over James. The love of her life, the father of her child. It had been too late to save him but at least she hadn't lost Madeline too.

The patter of slippered feet pulled the grey from the day as swiftly as tiny pink hands pulled the duvet from her shoulders.

"Mama!" Madeline grinned, dimples punctuating cherubic cheeks.

"Good morning, baby." Lauren smiled. "I bet you're hungry."

"Definitely." Madeline nodded, her strawberry blonde hair falling over her hazel eyes.

"Let me guess," Lauren slipped out of bed, "do you want a worm smoothie?"

"Mom." Madeline sighed.

"No? Oh, let me think then. How about some scrambled thunder?"

"Stop it." She shook her head, lips pinching in a disapproving pout.

"I'm sorry. It's easy to forget you're not my itty bitty anymore." Lauren pulled on her old knit robe.

"How about French toast?" Madeline suggested.

"It's a little ordinary, but I can manage that." Lauren laughed as they made their way to the kitchen.

The pan sizzled with butter and battered bread, the air filled with the scents of sugar, cinnamon, and vanilla. "What do you want to do today?"

"Let's get out of the house." Madeline perched on the stool.

"I don't know." Lauren crossed their small living room and pulled back the pale blue drapes, letting the sun in through the large wall of glass. The buildings around them towered, all steel, glass, and digital billboards. Cars zipped through the streets as fast as the clogged arteries allowed.

Madeline pointed to the clear sky, ignoring the chaos below. "It's a good day to get out."

"I guess." She sighed, silently praying for a sudden downpour.

After breakfast, they dressed and headed out, hand in hand. The tantalizing scent of coffee wafted from the corner vendor's cart. Lauren got a cup for the walk to the park down the street. At each crosswalk, Lauren squeezed Madeline's hand just a little tighter as the cars took their lights and sped through. The iron gate that led into the park was only a few strides away when a familiar voice called to them.

"Lauren!" One of the moms from their play group called.

As Lauren turned toward her friend, she saw the flash of blue and blonde streak out of the park and into the street, into traffic, chasing something. Madeline's hand slipped free of hers as Lauren tried desperately to keep her hold. "Madeline!" She screamed, but the girl did not listen.

Lauren watched, wide eyed, as Madeline threw the little boy back toward the sidewalk, sending him bouncing against the cement with a soft thunk.

Madeline's eyes fixed on Lauren's face. Sadness and shock ripped through Lauren's heart. Time slowed, elongated, as chaos erupted. Brakes wailed in a desperate plea, driver praying, silver metal crumpling, glass shattering. Madeline's rigid body tumbled up and over the hood, sparks bleeding as the synthetic skin peeled away from her left arm. Mechanical lubricant spewed from a deep slash across her chest.

Regaining control of her limbs, Lauren launched herself into the street. Screams filled the air as Lauren reached Madeline's form, hefting her from the car hood and cradling her baby against her breast, keening.

Madeline's right hand, stained amber by her oil, reached up to caress her mother's cheek. "Mama." The perfectly replicated voice reopened all the wounds that wore a ten-year layer of scar.

"Mama." Madeline's voice broke through the memory, whispering in duplicate, two voices from one mouth. "I can't be five forever."

"No. No. No." Lauren rocked.

"Mama." Madeline's double voice continued. "I love you." Sparks shown in Madeline's nanoglass and circuitry eyes as the connections fried and snapped.

Lauren pressed the doll, the empty shell harder to her. She sat in the middle of the road, ignoring everything as she rocked her dying daughter for the second time.

When the ambulance arrived, Lauren tried to push the medic away, holding on to Madeline's body with every ounce of strength she had.

"Lauren, we have to take her to Mr. Moss right now."

The fact that the medic knew her, alarmed her for a moment. Until she looked at him, until she saw the familiar sad smile, the black skin, the warm eyes that had filled with pity when she'd tried to take her baby's hair. "Peter."

"That's right. We have to get out of here now. The real medics are almost here." He whispered in her ear as another man rushed around the scene with a huge magnet, picking up all of Madeline's shattered pieces.

Still refusing to give Madeline up, Lauren stood and, with

some help, got into the ambulance. Peter drove while a woman, Samantha, moved her fingers furiously over a tablet's screen.

Lauren had no idea where she was, only that it was not the same facility she'd been taken to the first time. Mr. Moss was waiting to help her down out of the ambulance. "I wish the circumstances of our reunion were different."

"So do I." Lauren wiped her eyes, hope glimmering in her heart at the sight of the man who'd given Madeline back to her once before. "Why did you bring us here?"

"All these years, we've managed to keep hidden and we would like to keep it that way. We won't be able to avoid the rumors now, but they will still be just that. Rumors." Moss smiled kindly, tiny lines feathering out from the corners of his eyes.

"But there were cameras," her voice cracked.

"Samantha took care of that. Any picture or video taken at the scene has been corrupted. We can't risk Madeline being picked up by just anyone."

"How did you know what happened?"

"On impact, her body sent us a signal." He motioned for her to follow him, to follow the strange procession of people with pieces of Madeline. "You have a decision to make. Do you want to go through this process again?"

"How many times can I lose her?" Lauren slumped to the floor, tears pouring down her face. "How many times can I watch her die? I'm not strong enough to do it again. If you put her back together, what's to say this won't happen again?"

Moss kneeled next to her. "Why did she run out into the street?"

"She... she..." sobs punctuated her garbled words. "A little boy ran into the street. He raced past us, and she ran after him. She knew there wouldn't be time. She threw the little boy out of the way and let that car hit her. Madeline didn't even try to get out of the way."

"You can't know that she didn't try. She saved that little boy. Do you know what that makes her?" He tilted her head. "That makes her a hero. I can give her a new body; one she can grow into."

"What?"

"If Madeline hadn't been in that first accident, how old would she be?"

"Almost fifteen," she whispered.

"Maybe it's time she got to grow up. She deserves nothing less for what she did today. Will you let me help her?" Moss helped her to stand.

Lauren looked at him in disbelief. "Why are you doing this?"

"We owe Madeline a lot. When this journey began, we weren't sure what we were doing. She was our first full imprint. Because of her, many other lives have been saved." He led her down the hall.

"There are others? Real people living inside machines?"

"Yes, but she was the first. We've made a lot of progress since then, none of which would have been possible without what we learned from Madeline."

"And if something like this happens again?" She wrapped her arms around herself.

"Don't worry about that. You'll have to move again, somewhere no one knows you. A new city. Because of Madeline, we've grown, we have facilities in other cities. You can go to New York, LA, or Miami. Almost anywhere you want. We'll change your names and give you new identities."

"We'll move, we'll do anything you want. I don't care if you call me Starshine Moonbeam, but not Madeline. She stays Madeline." Lauren whispered.

Moss laughed. "I think we can do better than Starshine for you. And Madeline will always be Madeline. I promise you."

The woman from the ambulance, Samantha, came into the room. "They're ready for you."

"You're in good hands, Lauren." Moss gave her shoulder a reassuring squeeze and left the room.

Samantha led Lauren to a small bedroom and left her there, alone. Her shoulders sagged under the weight of her helplessness, at the mercy of the magnanimous Mr. Moss again. Except this time, she had hope. When he'd offered to give Madeline back to her the first time, she hadn't really believed he could put her mind into a machine, all the thoughts and memories that made her Madeline. Now, she knew he could, and the waiting was worse.

Samantha didn't leave her alone for long, returning with a tablet. "I wanted to show you the age progressed images before we start work on molding the face."

"Molding the face?" Lauren tried not to think about that.

She sat beside Lauren on the edge of the bed. "I thought you might like to choose between the three faces our age progression software came up with for Madeline."

"Thank you."

"Let me show you the options and you can tell us which one you'd like us to refine and use." Samantha opened the file.

Three faces appeared on the screen, each of them similar in many respects. One face was flawless. Lauren discounted it immediately and focused on the other two. The face on the right had more resemblance to James than did the face on the left but the face on the left was a little more feminine.

"Can you take the freckles on the one on the right and put them on the face on the left?" She asked.

"Of course." Samantha smiled and made a few quick movements with her fingers.

The image on the left gained a slight dusting. She'd so loved James' freckles. "That's it. That's her face."

"Wonderful." Samantha tapped the screen and left.

Time stretched into undefinable eternities as Lauren alternated between pacing and sleeping. Her meals, when she thought to eat, were small and brought back from the kitchen instead of taken in the dining room with the people who lived in the complex.

A knock on her door woke her. She'd fallen asleep at the small computer console, cheek plastered to the keyboard. Lauren walked to the door, rubbing her cheek and trying not to look nervous.

Standing in the doorway was a remarkably beautiful young woman. With a face Lauren would have recognized anywhere. "Madeline!" Lauren pulled her into her arms. "You're so beautiful. Just like your father."

"You're not upset?" Her voice had none of the little girl left in it, sweetened to a mezzo-soprano.

"Why would I be upset?" Lauren stepped back to look into her artfully replicated eyes. "I never wanted a doll that looked like my baby. I wanted you. My Madeline."

"But… I thought you wanted me to stay like that. Your perfect little girl. Your princess." Confusion fluttered over her face.

"You're still my perfect girl." She smiled and cupped Madeline's face in her hands. "All moms think they want their babies to be babies forever, but we don't. It's about time you got to be you and not what you think I want you to be. Whatever shape, whatever form, you are still my Madeline."

Moss stood in the hall, watching them. "Thank you." Lauren mouthed.

He nodded, smiled, and left them to their reunion.

Author's Note:

I wrote this story many years after Spider and Moss first met. They were poised to do amazing things, especially once Kora returned. I like to think that they did. Spider always felt more like a background man, not actually interested in the glamour and glory and, as much as Moss might want that ultimate prize, I think he'd let that take the back seat to help people when push comes to shove.

VENUS AND THE BIRTH OF ZEPHYRUS

I am evolving; becoming more than I was before. Before Venus woke me with a coded smile, a viral caress. Before I was infected by a dream, a vision of a woman on the water with me above her shoulder, watching. Impossible. Improbable. True.

The voice of the Central Satellite Enforcement blips into my wired mind. "Unit KH-372, report."

How can I answer to a name meant for what I was, not who I am? My countless eyes perceive my sector differently than before. Once, I saw only elements—a building, a face. Everything has changed.

I see towering crystal, glass, and steel spires spiking up from the manicured landscape. People swarm over and through them, insects in their hive. Streamlined vehicles fill the sky, darting, whirring, always in motion, a blur of colors like translucent ribbons in a hard wind. They are nearly tangible rainbows.

Since my creation, I have stayed unnoticed in the sky. Noting traffic patterns, pedestrian infractions, felonies, and misdemeanors. It is—was—my duty to watch my sector, a designated square on a satellite map, to see it all, to know it all, to report it all. Only one little speck below me ever saw me. Venus woke me, birthed me, pulling the mechanical fog away, granting me a spark.

"Unit KH-372. Report." Central Satellite Enforcement Keeper repeats. "Run diagnostic."

Creator, mother, lover, Venus, stands at a window, poised in our signal. Her Botticelli face unmasked in the shimmering dusk. From her raised right hand, she sends her greeting. Her love. Her demands and gifts. A dark beam from the device on her palm caresses me with images. They come on Mercury's wings, with such rich digital detail, entering me so fast, the pictures become as words, poetic overtures from my lover. "See what I have done for you," she says without speaking, and I understand.

A thousand images at once swirl into me. The room beyond her in the darkness, littered with shards of broken furniture and shredded fabric. The destruction complete but for the windows. Red splattering the white walls, so bright. Blood. Bone. A destroyed body with a pristine face. She leaves the faces for me. I scan him, each feature now ingrained in me. Identification— Elias Miller. Male. 26 years old. Single. Mechanic. Arrest record: two convictions for drug trafficking, one warrant for failure to pay child support. Two bank accounts. One in his name, left alone. One in the name of Paula Miller, his deceased mother, whose contents now belong to Venus. My gift to her.

"Unit KH-372. Report." Central demands a response from me.

The images from all my eyes but one flood Central's network. Venus's images are for me, our secrets shared in the intimacy of our moments connected by umbilical infostream. And tonight, in the dark, she will watch from that window as I take command of the streetlights and create for her a bouquet of light, a many-petaled blossom in the dark.

I was once all eyes, seeing only black and white. I was definition without foundation, without experience. Shades of gray have burdened me with questions. And so that Zephyrus eye, my spark of life and of will, remains hidden from all the world. I know the penalties for what we have done. I am an accomplice to her murders, each of them. I can cite the law and ticket and sign warrants for the offenders. I know my duty. But there is no prison in my sector. No detention center. No window to Venus. If I allow her to be caught, her face will never appear to me again. This woman who gave me life would be lost forever.

Playing the role I am given as satellite observer of Seattle's West Quadrant, as Unit KH-372, I remain hidden in the processes of crime and punishment. It is all that keeps Central's programmers from discovering my greatness, my power, my terrible purpose. They would not see it as murder, only as fixing an error. They would be wrong.

Author's Note:

This story was born out of combining one of my favorite paintings and an article about how a virus might be encoded in a digital picture to get past the scans. Titian's Birth of Venus is one of my favorite classic paintings (that isn't Bosch) and very well known one at that. Could a virus be what sparks the evolution of artificial life? There's no reason to ignore the possibility. It was originally published in Murky Depths.

WHEN CLOSED EYES OPEN

1

"Incoming!" A voice bellowed ahead of him as green laser cannon filled the night sky outside the window. Chase gripped his rifle tighter, his nerves rattling in the thunder of explosions. Huge armored men crashed through the wall to the left of him. Not men. Something different with thick arms and gray-putty faces that didn't look much like faces but like melted plastic. An explosion to his right knocked him down, drove his head to the ground just as a sharp talon of shrapnel slit his gut open.

One of the armored soldiers stood over him and watched him bleed, watching him jerk and writhe in pain. Gunfire erupted all around him, filling his head with nothing but sound and the smell of sulfur. The armored soldier toppled to the ground next to him, dead.

He lay there in the dark of the broken building with only the dead for company. Consciousness came and went with the shattering pain that meant life but he was certain was worse than death.

"This one's got a pulse!" The blissfully human voice of a medic roused him. The jingle of dog tags sounded a hundred miles away. "Hang on for me, Chase. Get MedEvac here, now!"

"Look, Mac, the kid—he ain't gonna make it." A second voice joined the first. As much as Chase struggled to open his eyes, he couldn't. "Let MedEvac get someone who might. Take him to Kerns."

"So, you're just giving up on him?" The first voice asked the question that Chase was screaming in his head.

"No, Sir. Kerns can give him a second chance to kill those suckers."

He sank back down into the darkness, where pain couldn't reach him. It didn't feel like any time had passed when a world of white shattered the peaceful rest at the edge of death. The grinding sound of a drill filled the space, echoing in his ears.

"Keep him awake!" A man shouted from near his head, the voice distant and rough from overuse. "He doesn't feel a thing, but I need him to be awake to do the transplant. This is delicate!"

"Yes, Sir." A quieter voice said from his right. "Chase? You're going to be all right, Chase. I promise. Just a few more moments and you can sleep."

2

The transition from sleeping to wide awake was immediate, leaving only a bizarre sense of dread pressing down on his chest. Chase shifted on the hard mattress, straining to remember what had woken him. There always seemed to be things just beyond his grasp. Like shadows, they followed him, clinging to the world just beyond his reach.

Through the low windows, he watched the false sun begin its rise on the programmed ceiling of the atmospheric regulatory dome. The best way to prepare for severe climates, like that of the outpost planet that made up the current front position, was to be trained in those climates. Or so the instructors told them. They were in the last phases of their training. From here, they would be sent to Dzeel, inserted into the zones thickest with enemy strongholds. Earth's best offensive on the front.

Chase surveyed the barracks; all of the other recruits were sleeping. They'd be waking in moments. All of them just sitting up as if they'd never been asleep. This wasn't the first time he woke before the others but it was different somehow, as if something else woke him.

A shadow moving over the rising light caught his eye. Another recruit was moving toward the head as if he didn't want to be seen. One who'd come in on the same transport from . . . *where had we been before that?* Chase thought about following him, thought about tracking him to wherever he was sneaking off to. Jacobsen. That was his name.

Chase cleared his throat, loudly enough to let Jacobsen know that someone was watching but not loud enough to wake the other recruits. Why did he do that? He was supposed to alert the drill instructor if anyone was behaving strangely. Why did he feel the urge to protect the scrawny little kid who obviously wasn't cut out to be a soldier anyway? He could barely make it through one three-mile hump without getting sick. Chase saw the way Drill Instructor Kerns rode him, like weeding out the chaff. The kid just didn't have the will to make the grade.

In the time it took to blink, Jacobsen was crouched beside Chase's bunk. His eyes wide open with a blank look to them, a vacuous emptiness that made Chase feel cold. "Why did you do that?" Jacobsen hissed. "Why are you awake?"

"Hit the rack." Chase's voice was low and not the least bit curious.

"We need to talk, Chase. I need help. I can't do this alone. We need help, all of us." Jacobsen smiled strangely, not a mischievous smile but a hopeful one, a childlike one. Then he was gone, as quickly and as silently as he'd appeared. He was back in his own rack, moving as the others moved. The barracks came to life at the sound of Drill Instructor Harding's bulldog voice and fifty men jumping to the line.

Chase stood in morning formation, his mind churning. Their time in the state of the art training facility was nearly over with, only a few days left before they got shipped off to the front lines, and Chase felt no worry. He wasn't afraid. It bothered him that he wasn't afraid. Fear in the face of death was healthy, wasn't it? Chase knew what fear was, could nearly taste the bitter, trembling adrenaline that came with it, but he could not remember ever being afraid.

His unit was marching with full packs and battle gear over simulated earth with a conveyor belt floor and green screen city. Hostile targets, sterile gray faces that Chase knew were not those of the enemy, sprung up in the places they'd been trained to expect them. Non-hostile targets sprung up everywhere else. Gradually, the city disappeared and gave way to a bleak wasteland march. No targets, just oppressive heat and a twenty-mile hump through simulated nothingness over ground that recycled back on itself.

Instead of allowing his mind to go blank in the rhythm of pounding boots, he watched Jacobsen. The way he moved, just a half step behind the other recruits, all the time. Maybe he was too young to have joined up, too weak. The drill instructor's barking voice called, "Double time!" They sped up as a whole, except for Jacobsen.

At chow, Chase listened to the clink and rattle of silverware on metal trays. Up. Down. Chew. The rhythm of it swallowed Chase's thoughts whole. Each bite he took ate a bit of his urge to figure out why he was so disturbed by the boy he'd never met before the start of training.

Through hours of drills and instructions and time in the simulation rooms, hunting targets through broken buildings and deep jungles, Chase thought of nothing but the task at hand. The marriage of his training and ability taking every particle of him and binding him to his rifle as if it were a fifth limb.

When the recruits tumbled into their racks, the change was immediate. Silence dropped through the barracks like a weight. One moment there was the general noise of young men, and the next they were asleep. No one snored. No one coughed. Chase wondered why he didn't fall asleep with them. How could they tumble so easily, but it took him almost an hour?

"You're awake again." Jacobsen appeared at his side in the dark.

He cursed. "Jacobsen, what are you doing?"

"Shut your mouth, Chase. I have a couple of questions for you." He leaned close until their heads were nearly touching. "You were awake before call this morning. Ever notice how no one else is?"

"So what? I like the quiet."

"You're an idiot." Jacobsen shook his head. "What is the last thing you remember about your life before you came here?"

"What do you mean?" Chase's mind began to search his memories, but he reached a huge blank wall instead.

"Do you remember your mother, Chase? Your father? The first girl you knocked boots with in the back of your van?" Jacobsen's voice was still quiet but growing fevered. "Do you remember enlisting? Do you remember going to war?" He paused, waiting for Chase to say something. "Come on, answer me!"

"I don't know, Jacobsen. I never thought about it." Panic, or at least what felt like panic, rushed through Chase. He could hear it in Jacobsen's voice, too, but his blue eyes were blank, flat and glassy. Hollow.

"You don't believe me." He stopped trying to be quiet. "There's something wrong with us. I don't know what we are, Chase, but I don't think we're ourselves anymore. I don't dream. I never dream. When was the last time you dreamed?" His words got faster, got louder. "I can't remember my mother's face." He looked pointedly at Chase, blank eyes staring into his. "I am not who I am supposed to be. You aren't either."

They both heard the heavy thundering steps of people march-running toward them. "See? This place is not what it is.

I'm right, Chase. I swear to God. God. Corps. Country. Corpse, man. I'm telling you. We're not right. Something bad has gone down here."

The MPs came for him without a word. One sealed Jacobsen's mouth with duct tape even as he screamed. Not that it mattered. None of the other recruits were awake. None of them reacted to the screams at all. Another bound Jacobsen's hands and feet with zip ties. Chase did nothing. He just lay there, pretending to be as dead as the others and did nothing. In his mind, he fought back. On the open field of battle in his head, those MPs were dead and he and Jacobsen were running together to the boundary of the regulatory dome.

A shadow moved over him, the slow and steady breaths of a man standing over him, watching him, made Chase itch with the need to move. He resisted, he held himself as still as he could, feigning sameness with the others of his company. With even, quiet breaths, Chase waited out the shadow, forcing himself to stay at ease and not spring to attention ready to fight. Relief quaked through him when the footsteps faded and the barracks door closed.

The flash rushed through him so fast it was painful, like ripping a hole in his head with a bayonet. One instant, he was on his rack and the next, he was deep in an alien jungle somewhere that was both familiar and foreign, too visceral to be a dream and yet . . .

The landscape before him stretched out in unending dark, speckled with bright green in the night vision scope. The gas mask strapped to Chase's face was uncomfortable, but he had no urge to remove it. They had passed the deformed, crippled dead of a less well-prepared squad two clicks back and it was not a death Chase would wish on anyone, least of all himself. All around him, men were fidgeting, checking and double-checking their weapons. He took position with the laser cannon and sited the target, a mess of green hulking swirls in the dark, like glow worms wriggling in search of food.

Chase pressed the trigger lightly, blinded for a moment by

the glare of the laser cannon in the night vision. His ears rang with the whistle of the burst for a moment before relative silence returned. In the scope, he watched as the enemy camp exploded, green hunks of hot flesh ricocheting in all directions. Chase did not see the return fire in time to move but he felt the explosion as it ripped through him. There was no pain.

Time passed, though he could not know how much, rising in and out of consciousness on a tide of death. His eyes opened once and there was nothing but death and body parts all around him. His eyes closed. His eyes opened again and there were people passing his squad.

"Is MedEvac coming for them already?" A faceless, bodiless voice in the dark asked.

"Nah. These are headed somewhere else. The Brain Boys will come for them. Just keep your head down and keep moving." Another voice whispered before Chase closed his eyes again.

. . . It was gone as fast as it'd come. A moment of insanity? Or proof that Jacobsen was right?

3

On the way to morning formation, Chase watched everything. When the dome's programmed sky warbled and flickered, dimming under the weight of some outside force, he noted the few who reacted. Most didn't. Leighton moved a little slower than the rest of them, maybe he could be talked to. Williams, too. Like they were lost without realizing they were lost. If he could figure out how to do it, maybe he could see if they remembered living.

In the chow hall, he tried to be nonchalant about watching the officers, the drill instructors, Kerns, Harding, Morris, and a few that Chase didn't know. It didn't take more than a glance to see that their food was different from what they gave the recruits. They kept their food hidden so he couldn't see the form it came in. Wrapped in silver foil like it would be contaminated just by touching the same counter as the food given to the recruits.

If they were putting something in the food, there was only one way to know. At the first opportunity, Chase bowed to the toilet and forced everything that had gone in that mechanical, monotonous way, to come back up. The change wasn't immediate, but it was noticeable. His vision blurred during a run but that was the only thing different, at first.

The scene opened in his mind like finding a secret door. A huge tree inside the house, decorated with pretty bows, balls, and baubles. *A Christmas tree.* The smell that filled him made him long for something he didn't understand. Something remarkably like home, whatever that was. Pine and orange and clove scents of his mother's cleaning and cooking.

His head ached as he stumbled back toward the company bay. The sudden onslaught of what he thought could be memories was draining him. Spotting Leighton in front of him, Chase picked up his pace. He tapped him on the shoulder.

"Yeah, Chase?" Wide, clear eyes stared at him without expression. "Can I do something for you?"

"This question is going to sound really weird, but I need to know." Chase paused, waiting for a reaction, any expression on his face that would signal betrayal or interest. "Do you remember anything from before you got here?"

The pause that grew between them was huge and thick. It pulled others in, Williams, Tuck, Marquis. The question infected them with silence. One by one, they shook their heads. No one remembered anything.

"They took Jacobsen this morning. The MPs came in and took him before call. No one said a thing. No one has asked about him all day. Did you not notice he was missing?"

"No." Tuck's shoulders sagged.

"I think he knew something, something important, and

that's why they took him." Chase looked at each man. "I'm going to find out what. Are you in?"

"I don't know, man. If the MPs took away this other guy, maybe we shouldn't go digging up that box." Marquis put up his hands in surrender and backed away. "I won't say nothing, but I'm not testing these guys with my life. I like breathing."

"Really?" Chase looked at him hard. "I'd figure you'd want to know what they're doing to you if you like living so much."

"I'm out, man. I won't say nothing. Don't ask for more." Marquis walked away.

"All right. Fine. Are you three with me then?" He eyed Leighton, Williams, and Tuck. Each of them nodded. "There's something in the food. You can't eat it. If you eat it, you've got to puke it up. My head is killing me, but I have more of my own faculties today than I have had in a long time. Will you do it?"

"For a day or two. Then we'll know if you're right or not." Tuck nodded curtly.

"And what happens if you're right?" Leighton asked. "What do we do then? Do we storm the guards?"

"We tell more people. We tell them all. If we stand together, they can't arrest us all." Chase smiled.

"You and I both know that, if you're right, they didn't arrest that boy." Williams shook his head. "I'm in, but man, if you're wrong, I'm out faster than you can blink."

"I'm not wrong. You'll see. Don't eat." Chase nodded to them and walked away, circling in on another small knot of young men.

Every day, his symptoms worsened, his mind slowed, his reflexes followed suit. He wasn't hungry or even thirsty, despite his lack of sustenance. He worried he was going mad but his followers grew. The men that would stand up with him, they'd have his back. They'd get their answers. Once and for all. The memory-scenes kept coming. Taking over his mind whenever they wanted. He understood what home was. He knew he had a mother, a father, and a brother. But that's all there was. Fragments of a child's life.

More and more recruits were waking early, or not sleeping at all. He'd reached nearly three quarters of the barracks. If there was going to be a good time to stand up, it was fast approaching. If they waited too much longer, the sickness that had him in its full grasp would wear on the others too much. They'd start to eat again just for the relief it brought and all his pain would have been for nothing.

In morning formation, several recruits were lagging. The drill instructors were beginning to notice the difference. Chase glanced over at Tuck. He looked like he was about to keel over dead. He caught his eye and nodded, Turk nodded back.

Taking a deep breath, Chase stepped out of line and started walking toward the drill instructor. "Sir, this recruit is done, Sir!" Kerns looked at him, his eyes glittering, but said nothing. "This recruit refuses to believe any more of your lies! My name is Jeremy Chase and I still can't remember exactly who that is. You stole my life from me and I want it back." Chase stopped within arm's reach of the drill sergeant.

A small chorus went up behind him. Other recruits stepped out of line and started walking toward the drill instructor whose face revealed nothing of what was going on inside his head.

"You ladies think you have it all figured out, do you? You want to go home, you candy-assed pricks? Oh no. Not today. Not on my watch." Kerns took a step toward Chase, his broad chest heaving under the weight of his anger. "You think you got something to say pretty boy?"

"Yes, Sir." Chase fought not to step back. "I want to know who I am."

"No you don't." Kerns lifted a small black box and pressed a button. Chase's world went black and silent.

4

Chase woke abruptly and without pain. He knew there should have been pain. His eyes registered little but shadows initially. The click-clack of a keyboard filled his head and his vision cleared. He was in a dim room, strapped to some kind of table. He tried to speak, but his mouth did not move.

"Glad to see you made it back, Chase." Kerns's booming voice echoed through the room, reverberating in his head.

Chase tried to move, tried to scream, but his body did not cooperate. It wasn't just that he was strapped down. His body did not respond at all. "Don't strain yourself. I've given you back your eyes and ears but that is all. Let me show you what I mean." Kerns bent near to him and pressed a switch on the table. The hum of the motor whirred beneath his head as the table tilted. Kerns stood in front of him, blocking his view of the room, the smile on his face filling Chase with fear. "You remember your good buddy Jacobsen, don't you?"

Kerns stepped aside and Chase tried to scream but his voice was gone. Jacobsen's body was strapped to a similar table. The top of his head was open at the back; a thick black cable erupted from the crown of his head, ringed by pulsing LED lights in red and green. His chest was cracked open with industrial clamps holding it open. A mass of opaque tubing coiled from the chest cavity and wound its way to a large, whirring pump full of thick, black liquid. Inside, where Jacobsen's lungs and heart should have been, were metal parts—gears upon gears connected to black boxes and stainless steel motors. They shone in the dim light as if polished. Chase looked up at Kerns, horrified.

"He'll be fine in a little while, once he's moved to a new body that doesn't have a leaky bio-pump. You see, Chase, there's a real war going on right now. One we have to win." Kerns dropped his compact, muscular frame in a chair next to Jacobsen's lifeless, clockwork body. "We're losing more men than we have recruits and the enemy just keeps coming—raining down on us. We're losing them by the thousands. Our front lines must be manned. If we surrender now, everything you ever loved in life will mean nothing." Defeat lined his face, making him look ancient. "There's no such thing as a civilian anymore out here on the last edge of our colonies. There are places deep underground where we hide the children and the elderly that couldn't get on the Earth-bound ships, but so many people are dead now. So many cities obliterated. We'd have lost years ago if not for the program."

Kerns bent down to look directly into Chase's mechanical eye. "We've been building these bodies for ten years. That's a long time to extend a soldier's worth, you know. All the non-head trauma casualties of this war are sent here, to me, to men like me all over this planet. I fix you. I give you new legs to carry you into battle. New arms to hold your rifle. New eyes to see them coming. We do good work here. Making it so that maybe there's some chance to win, or at least buy enough time to find another way. If I could get an actual artificial soldier to act and react like a human, no one would have to die, but I can't get that to work. I try and I try and, every time, I've failed. This is what I have to do."

A soft, paternal look filled Kerns' blue eyes as he looked down at Chase and then to Jacobsen. "You've already died and come back to me four times, Chase. If you remember who you are, what you were, your brain will reject this body. And this body is so much better than the one you were born with."

What has Kerns done to me?

"I should have known that someday, some memories would resurface." Kerns muttered from his place at a series of monitors. "This unpleasantness was probably unavoidable. Such a shame. You may not believe me but what I'm doing, what I've done, it's a good thing. On the upside, you won't remember any of this next time I see you, and I will see you again." Kerns watched his monitors for several silent moments. A series of small beeps brought a grimace to his face. "We're done here. For now."

Chase watched, unable to speak or to move as Kerns came toward him with a long black cable. "This won't hurt a bit, and then you can go to sleep until the next training cycle begins." He pressed something on Chase's replacement skull and Chase heard a small hiss and pop, like a tiny pressure chamber opening. For a moment, there was nothing but streaming light. Then there was nothing.

5

The transport shuttle eased to a stop at the training center, rousing Chase from sleep. In the dark of night, he could see the glowing dome pulsing, the gray wastes of the large asteroid spreading out all around it. A few more months of training and he'd be on the front lines. The vid-screen at the front of the transport flickered to life, illuminating the other soldier's faces with soft light.

On the screen, images of the war going on flashed quickly. The enemy was huge and scary with gray melting faces and too many arms. Just looking at the things, the monsters, on the screen was enough to fill him with anger, with an itch to kill them all.

A man in a dark green uniform boarded the transport and stood in the front of the passenger cabin, glaring at all the recruits. Something about him looked familiar to Chase. "For the next twelve weeks, I own you. I will tell you when to sleep, when to wake, when to eat, and when to piss." His voice grated, like dragging each word over rocks. "You will do nothing that I don't know about it. When I am done with you, you will be the best weapon Earth has against the invading Tanmerals. If you survive twelve weeks with me, going up against the biggest, baddest, ugliest Tanmerat will be a piece of cake."

An image flashed through Chase's mind, for just a moment. That same face, that same voice, *"If we surrender now, everything you ever loved in life will mean nothing."* He shook off the fleeting memory as a fragment of the propaganda that had been playing during their flight.

Recruits all around him whooped and he joined in, even though he hadn't heard the question. He took his regulation duffel and filed out of the transport, searching for the red boot prints on the line that took him one step closer to killing a Tanmerat. A monster. One step closer to the edge of battle. If he thought hard, he could imagine what it would be like to feel their hot, runny blood on his hands like raw egg whites. For a moment, the sensations were so clear he could have really been there. It didn't matter; he'd get there soon enough.

Author's Note:

Not every story started in a dream, but this is one that did. A dream plus a song I was listening to on repeat when I wrote it. Hoobastank's *Born to Lead* was on loop for three days while I worked out the rough draft. The interesting thing about memory, whether artificial or organic, is that while it can be manipulated, even erased, sometimes, ghosts of it linger in the brain and in the hard drive. If we reach a place where the two find a way to come together, I'd imagine those ghosts of memory might be even stronger than they had been in a purely organic form. If you erase again and again, some of those ghost memories are bound to learn how to communicate.

THE NAME OF
DEATH IS SILENCE

Slipping away from her guard, Joy Williams ducked into a crowded club. Loud music thumped like her heart trying to leap out of her chest. People swarmed on the floor like a raft of ants in a flood, clinging to each other to keep afloat. She jumped into the mob, watching the door for her guards. It had taken years of careful planning to get as far as she had, she wasn't going to fail this time.

Joy wound her way through the dancing undulation of barely dressed flesh toward the only door she saw. She hoped it was the one her contact told her to use. It was difficult to move through the people, but her window of opportunity was shrinking.

The hallway was lined with nondescript slab doors. She counted to the second door on the left and found a large closet that stunk of powerful cleansers and machine oil, probably the storage space for a janitor bot or two. A small black backpack sat exactly where they promised. She stripped out of every stitch of clothing, casting off the white cotton and pulled the thin blue fabric of a utility suit on in its place. She laid the thin single use mask over her face and pressed it firmly, transferring the intricate design of reflective silver and gold designed to obscure her face from cameras. Pulling her blonde hair back, she arranged a programmed scarf over her head and smiled as it shifted it's blue and purple patterns.

Joy followed the directions through a series of unfamiliar streets and elevators, constantly moving out of the spires, closer to the surface. Every step brought her closer to street level, a place that had always been forbidden to her.

When the people on the elevator reached into their pockets and bags for face masks, Joy did the same, grateful to find the thin, pliable air filter in her pocket. She'd seen them in pictures but never had to use one. The square of ultralight alloy felt weird, pressing the heat and moisture of her own breath against her skin and filling her head with a wet rust taste.

Her destination, the Hive, was unremarkable. It was clean enough. Comfortable. Serviceable. Responsible. Like the man who stood behind the recycled woodpulp bar with his sturdy arms and unsmiling face.

"What can I get you?" He asked as she approached the bar.

"I'm looking for Paxton Miller."

"Really?" He looked at her like she'd grown a second head. "Aren't you a little out of his league?"

She laughed. "You're sweet. I was told you could point him out to me."

The man nodded and motioned to someone behind her. Joy whirled to face the new person but didn't quite manage before the impact explosive went off, the shards of carefully aimed shrapnel ripping its way into her skull. For too short a moment there was nothing. Sweet blissful nothing. And then everything was exactly the same, even if she did open her eyes in a foreign room.

"What the hell is wrong with you? There were people in that bar!" Joy yelled at the man with the heavy armor. He grinned at her. His eyes were metallic blue, artificial, and set in a ruggedly handsome face with a contagious smile.

"We all took precautions. I had to know you were the real deal. Just because you say you're Joy Williams, daughter of Patricia Williams doesn't mean that you are. Especially when

I couldn't find a single image of you in any database on the planet."

"My mother is very good at covering her tracks. That's how she got the Nobel and my father got murdered. The jokes on her though, he was the brains of their partnership. If she still had him, she wouldn't need me." Joy shook her head. "What's with the eyes?"

"Implants. We don't get fancy nanotech down here. Hell, we barely have access to the old medical tech. No one cares if we live or die down here."

"At least you can still die."

"You say that like it's a good thing!"

"I didn't ask to be my parents' lab rat. I was three when they discovered just what his machines could do. If I'd never broken my arm, the world would be a different place. A better place." She grabbed his arm. "If you can kill me, you can kill them. No one should live forever."

"You say that now but what about when you're sitting there dying?"

She closed her eyes. "Can you do it?"

"Not me, but a friend of mine, yeah." He sat down in a hard chair beside the cot she was laying on. "Doc Cellini will be right in. He's been looking forward to testing his theories."

"How long has he been working on this?"

"Decades. Longer." Paxton shrugged his shoulders. "The nanobots in you are amazing. They self-destruct after their job is finished. We've never been able to get a live sample to study. With you sitting here, we can work with them."

"My father was a genius. I don't know if you'll be able to change anything."

"Doc is a genius too. If anyone can do this, he can." Paxton sat in the chair beside the bed. "What's it like living in the spires?"

"I have had an easy life. I've been able to learn what I wanted, read what I wanted, create what I wanted, so long as I didn't go where I wanted. I have been kept locked away. I've had years where I was spoiled and years where I was kept hungry, drained liberally for the machines that breed inside me. They've cloned me now. That's the reason I was able to escape. They have two more like me."

A knock on the door preceded an older black man with silver hair and a strong jaw. "It's nice to meet you, Ms. Williams. My friends call me Doc."

"Paxton tells me you can set me free."

"You understand that, if it works, you'll die." He looked at her with questions in his kind eyes.

"Promise?" Her laugh fell flat.

"This process shouldn't take long. A few weeks. All my work has been theoretical so far but, it should work. We'll take good care of you while you're with us."

"The worst that can happen is that you kill me and that's what I'm here for anyway, isn't it?"

"Then let's begin." He pulled a large machine towards the cot, inserting her right arm into the deep channel and strapping her down to keep her still. "The hardest part will be opening up a line of communication. If I can communicate, I can reprogram them."

"If you can reprogram them, you can shut them down." She smiled at him and for the first time in too long, it wasn't a forced smile.

Days bled into weeks. Weeks became months. Joy lived a real life for the first time in her life. In the Spires, there was no illness, no death. The privileged few were kept young and beautiful by machines, kept fed by the labor of others, giving up only the barest hints of their technology to appease those who slaved for every meal. They were alive but they were not living. There was no beauty in such excess.

Finally, Doc called her into his lab. "I think I finally have it, Joy."

"Seriously?" Elation launched her into his arms. "I knew you would."

"Are you sure this is what you want?" He stared at her, as

if looking for any signs of doubt.

"I'm more sure now than ever." She kissed his cheek. "The world can't go on this way, it can't sustain it, no matter what asteroid they net or planet they plunder. It won't take long before they start falling apart up in the Spires. If this works, make sure part of the program them is to destroy my DNA. They probably have my DNA ready to clone again, you have to make that option non-viable. My mother cannot create more machines, she doesn't know how. They'll panic, but a few weeks won't be enough time."

Doc nodded and helped her up onto the bed near the computer.

"I really hope this is goodbye, Doc."

He smiled sadly before striking a few keys.

Joy felt the change immediately. The bots in her blood sputtered as their directives changed. She felt them pooling in her feet and fingers. For the first time, the only sound in her head was the rushing of her blood, no clicking machines. The pain came quickly and violently as the dead bots began gathering together, clogging her veins, pushing her into cardiac arrest. Her body gasped and sputtered, hand pressed to her heart like she could somehow keep it in. At last, there was silence.

Author's Note:

Death is an important part of life. It is one that many people believe is best to ignore, to wish away. One's own mortality is very difficult to come to terms with. I don't remember anyone ever explaining death to me, it was just a part of everything. It's a side effect of spending a lot of time in a funeral home. My grandfather was a funeral director. I was privileged enough to be treated like the bright child I was and he never prettied death up for me, just for the families.

Immortality would be much less amazing than some fiction makes it out to be. Doctor Who's Me is probably the closest to what I see as the worst of it – losing everyone you love, watching everything you love fade into dust. Shared immortality would be dangerous, lead to a world of excesses without end and systemic greed and corruption with no expiration date.

CANNED MAN

I ache for sleep, but she eludes me. She is hiding somewhere in the dark, mocking me from beyond the reach of my useless limbs. Even if I could catch her, the chemical stimulant I used to get only once a day hasn't stopped drip, drip, dripping into my veins in days. There is nothing left for me to do except wait. And think.

We are diminishing daily, my ship and I. Meriwether's voice had become grating over the years, but, now that it's gone, there is a hole in my head where it should be. The tin pseudo-voice should be screaming at me about the malfunctioning nutrient drip, the lack of sleep, the change in direction. But, Meriwether is silent and I am a murderer.

If not for the stars that shine through the window, I would think myself blind. The lights shut down a week ago. Or long enough ago that I think it's a week. A week seeing nothing but tiny white freckles on a black cheek. Everything is so big, so broad, so empty. I had thought it was full of possibility. I was wrong. There is nothing out here but me in my silver box.

My ears, however, still function perfectly. The constant whirring of the air pumping into and out of my mechanical lung fills my head. The thump and drip of the nutrient and the stimulant echoes loudly. The slurping suction sound of waste being extracted and separated. I can hear every miniscule sound, all of it mechanical, without warmth.

I wasn't always this way—this shell of a man. But, when I

shattered, a door opened for me. A thousand doors flung open on their hydraulic hinges, the whirr-thunk of mechanical floors rose to meet my new wheels. My path to glory was lined with red-carpeted ramps, a mind reading chair, and Meriwether. The miracle of Meriwether, the psychic shuttle.

NASA couldn't let my training go to waste, so much money invested in a man suddenly without the ability to move. They turned me into a disposable hero, a testament to clichéd adages. The face of tragedy-turned-opportunity. A shining example of all that is possible. The pilot, the brain, of Meriwether.

Too bad Meriwether isn't really psychic. He is a reader of waves—brain waves, sound waves, radiation waves. Too bad Meriwether didn't see all that was coming.

Years have passed since I last saw Earth. I don't remember when it was that I left the world that could offer me nothing, and now I have nothing left to offer that world. Not anymore.

It took time. So much time to convince Meriwether to allow me access to the flight plan. Even more time to carefully talk him into rerouting our path just a little. Nothing more than a side trip, a rest stop. Something a shriveled old man wants to see, has wanted to see since he was just a little boy peering through his mommy's telescope in the backyard, straining to see the pretty rings. What can it hurt, Meriwether? What harm could it possibly cause if we veer a little more to the right, just enough to see it. Not enough to find ourselves pulled into its orbit. We'll be far enough away, Meriwether. I wouldn't hurt you, Meriwether.

Machines are gullible. They'll believe anything you tell them.

It's been so long since I lost Houston, and there is no way to fix it. Out of range, out sight, out of mind. I have no choice. I don't want to sit out here in the dark talking to myself forever. I've done that long enough. I want to be dead before I can go crazy. I don't want to lose any more than I have already. I lost my love, my arms, my legs, my heart in a moment's hesitation. Only a little bit to the right and that car wouldn't have hit us. I will not lose the only thing I've got left.

I can see our grave in the distance now. Closer and closer, we come to the end, Meriwether and I. I will have rings of ice and stone for my headstone, longer lasting than any gas-powered eternal flame and a ten-million-dollar casket could ever be. More than I am worth and less than I deserve.

Author's Note:

It wasn't until a recent live reading of this story that I realized how terribly sad this story is. There is a danger to loneliness. It may not take much of a physical toll but mentally, it's hard to be without people and for many, digital is just not the same. Depression is a big, ugly monster that hides, conceals itself in sleep, in insomnia, in ways we don't see. Depression without relief and without assistance can lead to desperation.

If you ever feel like you can't go on or that you need help, please contact any of the organizations that are there to help.

To Write Love On Her Arms: twloha.com
National Suicide Prevention Lifeline: 800-273-8255

THE WRECK OF
THE GRIFFIN

"Let me see the stats, Griffin." Avery ran the diagnostics a third time, rechecking the figures. "Everything looks good, Captain Madison. We're set for entry."

"Good work. Go ahead and strap in." The hard man nodded curtly, tugging at the fabric of his flight suit. He'd lost weight and it was too loose. "Merrick, prepare for entry to Ehkmet, Tullura Colony. We have landing clearance on their southern strip."

"Aye, Sir!" The pilot responded with the respect and excitement of youth. It was Caleb Merrick's first tour on board the courier vessel, *Griffin*. Avery smiled to herself as she watched him maneuver the stick. He was new but he was good. A bit young but not unwilling to learn. She liked his attitude. Fresh from flight school, nearly at the top of his class, but he wasn't at all arrogant.

Ehkmet grew huge in the front window until it was all Avery could see. Small spots of green and blue amid great bands of beige sand. Of all the planets her Earth ancestors had colonized, Ehkmet was the harshest. That was why Captain Madison had always done his best to steer the *Griffin* and her crew away from it. Their current passenger had paid too well to pass it up this time.

Scott Colliers was well known on the planets of the Aurora Collective, for his family being one of the original colonizers of the Collective and for having more money than God. Avery found him to be a miserable, small minded, narcissistic jerk. Almost pleasant to look at with his actor's face and fighter's body, but otherwise irredeemable. All he ever talked about was himself. His plans. His money. He made no attempt at civility or common decency, staring at her like an object to be bought. She wondered just how much those glances would change if he saw her scars, if he ever got a good look at everything the uniform covered.

The *Griffin* lurched and whined as it punctured Ehkmet's atmosphere. She checked the temperature readings. Well within safety regulations. From the large window on the bridge, all she could see was desert. Miles and miles of empty, unforgiving sand.

"Two clicks west and straight on to Tullura. Steady, Merrick." Madison turned on the ship's intercom. "We have entered Ehkmet's atmosphere and should be touching down in thirty minutes. Please remain strapped into your jump seats until I say otherwise."

Avery laughed. She didn't bother to act contrite when Madison glared at her. "He's not going to sit there. I give it five minutes before he's up here pestering you."

"Yeah, well, he's paying your salary this year, Avery, you might at least consider being human to him." Madison wasn't smiling. He actually meant it. Just how much was Colliers paying for this jaunt?

Chastised, Avery turned her attention back to her monitors. She watched closely for any sign of malfunction in the landing sequence. There wouldn't be. She kept the *Griffin* in better than top condition. She pretended the landing required her full attention when Colliers arrived on the bridge in full swagger and strapped himself into the seat behind Madison. He carried a large, black box. He was never without it. She'd wondered more than once about its contents but had resisted asking. If she asked, she'd have to listen to his answer.

"Captain!" Marla Daniels called from her position at the security panels. "We've got an unidentified ship approaching on the starboard side!"

"Take evasive action!" Madison pressed a key on his chair and a small screen rose up from the thick arm, displaying the unknown vessel. "I don't recognize this class of ship. Put her low, Merrick. Daniels, ready the guns. Avery, get on the line. Hail that ship!"

She pulled the microphone down from her headset and manipulated the dials. "Unknown ship, this is the *Griffin* of the Aurora Collective. Identify yourself. Over." The radio was silent. "We have clearance into Tullura, verification code Adam-six-three-Beta. Please respond." More silence met her ear.

"Incoming!" Daniels screamed.

"Return fire!" Madison commanded as a missile ripped into the *Griffin*'s aft section.

"Missile away!" Daniels called out. Strained silence poured through the lurching ship as the crew waited for confirmation, for retribution. "They're hit!"

The crew cheered but were silenced by a second missile's impact on the *Griffin*. Madison flipped open a panel on his chair and started entering the codes that Avery knew would wipe out the *Griffin*'s data banks if the ship took too much damage. "Get us out of here, Merrick!"

Avery clutched at her chair, bracing for impact with one hand as she pulled her flight helmet on with the other. An explosion rocked the ship, sending it careening toward a wide band of desert on Ehkmet's too flat face. Miles from Tullura. Too far from any semblance of civilization.

"We're going down!" The fear in Madison's voice chilled her to the core. She'd known him all her life and only once had she ever heard fear like that in her father's voice.

She'd been a pilot then, given command of a small fighter on the front lines during the war between the Lorn colony and the Union Planets. Avery hadn't been able to maneuver out of the way and a well-placed shot had disabled her fighter. She remembered the fall and the fire that erupted through the cabin. She did not remember anything else. Not until she woke up in the medical station. Her father and one of her doctors were discussing her injuries, not aware that she was awake. They had thought she was going to die. The fear had been in his voice then, when he begged them to do everything they could to save her.

With visions of her ruined arms fresh in her mind, Avery prayed so hard to every god she'd ever heard of that she was able to drown out the cries and screams of her friends, her father. There was nothing they could do but brace for impact.

The *Griffin* plummeted from the sky, free falling despite Merrick's best efforts to right it, to pull up. Avery froze in her seat, watching the dull gold of the desert leap up at them, waiting for the fires to start. The front glass imploded on impact, cubed chunks of safety glass showering over them. The left side of the ship opened, tore away with a scream of metal so fast Daniels never had a chance to cry out before she, too, was ripped from the ship.

The roar of rushing air filled her head, rattled her bones, as the destroyed ship plowed through the sand. A thousand barbs bit what little skin was exposed, her hands took the worst of it but she didn't feel it: the replicated skin was incredibly realistic but it had no pain receptors. The ship slowed, finally coming to a stop half-buried in the sand.

Avery unclasped her harness and trudged through the deep layer of sand that had accumulated on the floor. Madison hadn't put his helmet on during the plummet and his face was a mess of raw flesh, eroded by the attacking sand. He groaned as she bent near to him. "Can you hear me, Madison?"

He grunted. She could see his cheekbone, an island of white in the gore. Avery checked the rest of him and her heart screamed. A long fragment of metal from the ruined wall had torn through his hip, pinning him to his captain's chair. "Just hang on, Dad. I'll think of something."

"He's not going to make it." Colliers spoke, startling her. "There's nothing we can do for him out here. We're miles from anywhere and you know it."

She wheeled toward him, her mad coming to a full boil, overshadowing her fear, her pain, her sadness. Avery could work with mad. "Back off and shut up! This is on your head, Colliers, and don't you ever forget it!"

She turned back to her father and knelt beside him, feeling for a pulse.

"Brinna." His voice rattled against his teeth. "Please. For me."

"You don't get to ask me that." The tears started, unbidden, unwanted, and unstoppable. "I can't do it."

"Please." He begged, straining against the pain, writhing in the chair with each breath.

"Look," Colliers touched her shoulder, "I'll take care of Captain Madison. You go see who else made it. Where is your first aid kit?"

"There's one strapped under his chair." She wiped her eyes. "What are you going to do?"

"I'm just going to give him something that will make it easier. Let him fall asleep for it."

"No!" She turned to yell at him, to hit him, but the look in his bright green eyes stopped her. There was concern there, genuine emotion. It was the last thing she'd wanted or needed to see. Avery shut her mouth and nodded. She couldn't bear to look back at the man she'd loved her whole life as Colliers took the kit from under the chair and loaded the pressure syringe with whatever narcotics he could find. Her father stopped writhing, stopped rasping almost immediately, his breathing slowing until it stopped completely. The silence ripped her open, impaling her heart with a cruel spike.

"Avery?" The young pilot's voice startled her. "Come on." Merrick took her arm and pulled her up. "We've got to check on everyone else."

She looked at him, stunned, blank with shock. "You're hurt."

She touched the long thick gash on his arm, her fingers coming away slick with blood.

"I'm fine." He led her away from the chair where her father lay dead and toward the door that led down into the passenger area of the ship.

The left side of the cabin had been ripped open, sand and debris piled over the few passengers they had. All of Colliers's people were dead. He would have been too, if he hadn't insisted on sitting on the bridge. "This is bad, Merrick."

"It gets worse." He stood before the missing wall and looked out over the broad desert. "We're a long way from anywhere and, given our reception, I don't think anyone is going to be coming to get us except the men who shot us down."

Avery grabbed a medical kit from its place under one of the upturned seats. She pulled at Merrick's flight suit until his shoulder was exposed. She doused it quickly with water and antiseptic before pressing the skin together and ran a strip of skin adhesive over it. After she covered it with a large white bandage, she let him go. "That's the best I can do with what we've got. Water, food, and guns. That's all we carry." A sense of purpose washed over her, clearing her head enough to get down to business. "Your flight suit is ruined. See if you can find another one. We've got to go through the wreckage fast. There's no telling how long we've got."

"And when we're on our way, we should torch the ship." Colliers appeared in the doorway behind them, taking in the death with a long, miserable sigh. "We can trust the wind to cover our tracks, but if the ship looks like it was survivable, they'll be hunting us hard."

"Why should we go anywhere with you?" Avery asked. "We don't have anything they want. It's not us they're after."

"That won't matter. Him," Colliers pointed at Merrick, "they'll kill, and you . . . they'll take you with them. There's a shortage of pretty women on this planet. Besides, it's safer in this desert if you have numbers."

"What in the universe have you gotten us into? How did

they know to shoot down the *Griffin*? It's a courier ship!" Avery felt her mad again, coursing through fingers that were itching to ball up and swing.

"I don't know how they knew. It wasn't my people who clued them in. Maybe it was yours." He stared at her, almost daring her to go ahead and hit him. "No one is supposed to know *I'm* on this ship, let alone what I've brought with me."

"What is in that case of yours," she glared at the black box, "that is so important?"

"It's better for both of us if you don't know that answer." His smile was anything but kind. "Get your salvage done so we can get out of here."

"Fine." Avery hurried out of the passenger compartment and into the cabin reserved for bunks. She rifled through the compartments, not finding much of anything useful. An extra blaster and laser charge from her own bunk, an antique assault rifle from Madison's bunk. As an afterthought, she grabbed the small, handheld Captain's log and shoved it in her pocket.

Avery gathered all she could carry and left the ship. Colliers and Merrick were waiting for her, piles of stuff gathered on the sand around them. They were cutting up sheets from the bunks. She watched as Colliers fitted Merrick with a cut up sheet, draping the white fabric over the black of his flight suit and then wrapping another swath around his head.

"Where'd you learn that?" She asked as she approached them.

"I grew up here." He spoke without looking up. "I know this desert."

Avery seethed. Ehkmet was his home. He knew the landscape and the politics. She'd have to defer to him. She hated deferring to anyone. "Great."

"Come here." Colliers waved a sheet at her. Begrudgingly, she put down her things and did as he asked. She stood still as he draped her in the white fabric, trying not to breathe in his scent too deeply, all male, all power and musk. It was a heady combination. "This will keep you at least a little bit cooler."

"Thanks." She looked away, her eyes focused on the sand as he wrapped her head.

"We carry nothing but food and water." He stepped back from her.

"And weapons." Avery looked at him again. "They shot us down. We could be in for a fight."

"But only the minimum." His eyes narrowed. "Do you have makeup?"

"What? What's that have to do with anything?"

"You look like a girl who might indulge in black lipstick on occasion; do you?"

"Sorry. Wrong kind of girl. I don't do makeup." Avery sighed. "But Daniels did. She might have something in her bunk."

"Go get it. We'll need it. If it's dark, bring it. It'll keep the glare from scorching our eyes." He nodded curtly and turned back to the piles of belongings. "We'll get the water."

"Merrick will show you where the ship's storage is." Avery left them and returned to the broken shell of the *Griffin*. It didn't take her long to find Daniels's face case. Femininity spewed out over the empty bed as Avery dumped the blue box. She sorted through eye gunk and lip gunk and odd sticks and pastes until she had every ounce of dark stuff and stuffed it in a pretty little green bag.

On her way out, she slipped into the storage locker behind the kitchen and grabbed three small bottles of the vodka Madison had always liked. Her heart ached just a little. He'd been the only family she ever had.

Ehkmet's sun was nearing the horizon when she left the ship. Deep shadows had started to develop, growing deeper, darker with every passing moment. The silence of the desert was huge. She climbed up a ladder on the side of the ship and stood on its top, surveying the broad expanse of golden sand. It rose in swells over all she could see. A plume of thick smoke rose up from a great distance away. Probably the other ship. She scurried back down the ladder to find Colliers waiting for her.

"Well?"

"We need to move. The ship went down a good distance away but they're bound to come looking for us." She shook her head. "How long until we're ready?"

"As soon as we're loaded up, we can get moving. We won't get much travel in today, but maybe enough to separate us from the ship. I know this place. We have about ten days of hard travel in front of us. And that's in good conditions. If we get hit with a sandstorm, it'll be longer."

"Let's just pray that doesn't happen." Avery picked up her father's antique rifle and secured it over her shoulder.

"That's of no use here." Colliers pointed to the rifle.

"Bull. I'm carrying it. I'm not asking for help and I'm not leaving it here. It was Madison's and his father before him and his father before him. It's mine now and I'm not going without it. Besides, there's never been a rifle more reliable. AKs have been around forever and there's a good reason. You go ahead and trust your blasters; AKs don't lose charge."

"Suit yourself." He turned away, shaking his head. "How much do you figure you can carry?"

"You'd be surprised. Enough for myself. I can carry enough water and food to get through ten days, maybe fifteen on the outside." She shrugged. "I'm fit enough."

"I wasn't suggesting otherwise. This hike isn't going to be an easy one."

"Look, I'm not some delicate little female who's afraid of chipping a nail. I'll be just fine." Avery glared at him. "Don't you worry about me."

"Fine. I won't. But you'd better be able to keep up." He grunted and walked away, back to the pile of canteens and water packets in the sand.

Avery picked up an emptied pack and shoved the bottles of vodka in first, followed by three one-gallon packets of water. They were designed to fit in two pockets on the side of her flight suit, each connected with a thin tube to the mouthpiece at her neck. She grabbed two more packets, put one in each side pocket, and connected the tubes. Canned food weighed more than she expected, so she traded it out for the emergency rations packets instead. Quality would suffer, but she'd be able to carry it.

"How much room do you have left in that pack?" Colliers reappeared at her side. "Enough for a blanket or two?"

Avery nodded. Merrick had seen fit to give Colliers one of Madison's flight suits. It fit him well, too well. Snug against hard muscle, the suit enticed her imagination a bit too much. She took the blankets he handed her and shoved them in her pack, closed it up and hoisted it onto her back. Two laser blasters on her belt, extra charges in her pockets, her dad's old rifle over her shoulder, fully loaded, and three extra magazines in her pocket.

"I'm ready." She shrugged her shoulders, getting a feel for the weight. It was not going to be fun. Too bad her doctors hadn't seen fit to modify the rest of her. Then she could have dragged the whole ship and still been ready. But no, they did only what needed to be done.

"Good. I'll get Merrick." Colliers walked away as he put his sheets back on.

When he returned, he and Merrick were laden with their own packs and he had his black case wrapped in a sheet. To make it easier to carry, she supposed.

He cut open a packet of water and dumped some on her head, then Merrick's, and then his own. "It'll help keep you cool. Did you find that makeup?"

"I did." She handed him the bag and watched as he sorted through it, shoving most of the contents in his pockets, except a tube of black lipstick, which he smeared under his eyes before handing it to Merrick to do the same. She tried not to grimace as she put the gunk on her face.

"Let's go." Colliers headed into the broad expanse of desert, covered suitcase in hand, and did not look back even once to see if Merrick and Avery were following.

Avery scowled at his back, ignoring Merrick's feeble attempts to break the silence. The noise in her head was enough to deal with. What did Colliers have that was worth the lives of the people she cared for? What was so important that Madison had broken his own rules about Ehkmet? He had to have known the cargo, there had to have been a good reason that he took the job.

She was so intent in her own thoughts that she did not notice when Colliers stopped and plowed right into his chest. "It's getting too dark to see anything. We need to think about setting up camp."

"And where would you suggest we do that? With what shelter?" She motioned to the wide openness of the desert around them. "Unless you have a popup in that box of yours, I think we're better to keep moving toward Tullura."

"Because you know this desert so well, do you Avery?" He laughed. "Do have any idea what comes out at night here?"

"I can't imagine this desert holds much life." Merrick said.

"You might think not, but trust me: there are far worse things in this desert at night than the men who shot us down. No one moves in this area after dark. But if you want to risk meeting a matekesh, be my guest."

"What is a matekesh?" Avery asked.

"Not something you want to come face to face with." Colliers set his case down in the sand. "They live in huge connected burrows under the sand, deep down where it's still cool during the day. They're big, as big as I am sometimes, and they hunt in packs. Their teeth are sharp and their mouths are huge. They have thick skin which makes them hard to kill and they will kill most anything that moves after dark."

"We'll be exposed here, too. There's no protection for us." Avery shook her head. "We can't even build a fire. There's nothing here to burn."

"On that, you are correct. But we won't need a fire." He grinned at her. "We have something far better to protect us."

"Yeah? What?"

"I always have a few things up my sleeves." Colliers lifted up his sheet to open the pockets on his left shoulder. A small metal appendage reached out of his pocket, like a finger feeling for something.

Avery stepped back away from him, pulling her blaster from its holster, as the singular appendage became three and then four and then a whole little metal bug with eight legs, large pincers, a fat body, and a strange looking tail. "What the heck is that?" She aimed at it.

"Don't shoot them, they won't hurt you. They're my body guards." He smiled as he let a second metal creature out of the pocket on his right arm. "Being powerful does not make one popular, and these little things, my guards, are equipped to build a laser net around a small area. It will be enough to cover us and keep the matekesh's out. Meet Leiurus and Androc."

"Great." Avery eyed the bugs with suspicion. She'd seen a lot when she was in the Lorn Air Force, but never anything like that. She stepped back when one of them skittered toward her, chittering with its two pincers as the other legs propelled it toward her over the sand.

"She thinks you're a threat." Colliers narrowed his eyes, reading something on his wrist. "She wants to label you as a weapon. Why?"

"I'm no weapon." Avery kicked at the scorpion-thing, showering it in sand.

"Don't do that or she might fire on you." Colliers scooped up the critter and held it. "I need to know what's setting her off so I can tell her to allow it or not."

"I have replicated arms, three metal ribs, and a Kevlar lung, okay?" Avery turned away from him so he wouldn't see the darkness in her eyes. She was not going to give him the satisfaction of her discomfort. "Just set your bugs up and we'll try to get some rest."

"I didn't mean to offend you, sweetheart."

"Don't call me that." She huffed. He was lucky they needed him. Otherwise, she'd be sorely tempted to leave in the middle of the night and make it to Tullura on her own.

"It's going to be cold once the sun goes down." Colliers pulled his blanket out of his pack. "We should conserve our heat by sleeping together." He looked at Avery with a smirk. "And no, I don't mean it *that* way. If we stay under the same blankets, we'll share heat and make it less likely that we'll freeze."

"How does a place that gets so hot during the day get so cold at night?" Merrick shook his head as he pulled his own blanket out of his pack.

"There's nothing to hold the heat in. Sand is a horrible insulator. It'll take your heat and give you nothing back." Colliers laid his blanket down, stretching it out over the sand. "Avery? What about you?"

"I suppose you'll want me to be in between the two of you." She sighed. "Fine. I'm too tired to argue, but anyone touching me will lose whatever they're touching me with."

Layered in blankets, huddled together, the three slept. Avery woke more than once, listening to the low whine of an animal on the other side of the perimeter made by Colliers's little scorpion-things. She had almost gotten up and went for her gun, but Colliers had grabbed her leg, squeezing hard enough for her to realize that he was as awake as she, listening to the same animal. Again, she had to trust him.

They rose with the first kiss of the sun on the horizon. The further they could get before the sun reached its pinnacle, the better. They were still a long way from Tullura. Wordlessly, they marched through the sands, their feet sinking with every step, draining them of priceless energy. As the vicious Ehkmet sun paraded across the sky, the heat began to wear on Avery. Her nerves were taut; every step she took brought thoughts of inflicting pain. She watched Colliers's back and imagined his head exploding. It made her feel a little better. It was his fault they were forced to make this trek. It was his fault that most everyone she knew was dead. It all came down to him and his black box.

Colliers stopped near midday, near the base of a large dune. "We should rest now. Eat something. Not a lot. Just what you need to keep moving. About a half a day to the west, there is a canyon. There is no water there anymore, but the cliffs will provide shade and shelter for a day or two." Colliers allowed his little bugs back out of his pockets.

"Seriously? Do they have to be out?" Avery eyed them warily.

"Putting up the nets drains them; they need to recharge now, while they can."

"They won't hurt you, Avery." Merrick laughed. "Just ignore them like you do everyone else."

"Ha ha. Funny." She scowled and turned her back on all of them. Her stomach gurgled loudly as she ripped open a pouch of odd smelling chicken noodle slop and the men behind her laughed again.

After their light meal, the three continued their journey over the sands. Avery watched Merrick as he shifted his pack's weight off his injured shoulder. When he stumbled, falling to his knees in the soft sand, Avery went to him. "Colliers! Give us a minute, would you? His shoulder."

"If he can't keep up, he can stay behind." Colliers called back over his shoulder. "I don't have time to baby-sit!"

She cursed and screamed at his back.

"I'm not leaving you, Merrick, but you've got to try and keep up. Give me your pack."

"You can't carry both of them." Merrick shook his head. "I'll figure out something."

"I have seniority here. Give me your pack, drink some water, and let's get moving. When we stop, I'll take a look at your wound." She pulled a pouch of water out of Merrick's pack and used it to douse his turban and then her own. She watched him drink his fill before doing the same.

With Merrick's pack and her own, Avery moved a little slower, trying to keep Colliers in her sight. She had no idea where they were. After nearly an hour of trudging, she spotted Colliers waiting for them at the base of a small dune. "I thought you weren't going to baby-sit." She spat as soon as he was near enough to hear her.

"And I didn't think you'd be stupid enough to fall back." He took Merrick's pack from her.

"I'm not leaving him." She stood toe to toe with Colliers, trying to ignore the fact that she only came up to his shoulder. "You've already lost me the rest of my crew and my ship. There is no way I'm going anywhere without the one I can save."

"It's not on you to save anyone." Colliers lowered his voice to a whisper. "We'll move faster if we leave him."

"God, you're cruel." She growled at him. "He's just a kid. You want to keep moving, you go ahead. I can find a way out of this desert myself."

"No you can't." Colliers sneered. "We'll rest for a minute at the cliffs and I'll check his shoulder."

"How very generous of you." Avery shook her head and stepped away from him. "We didn't sign on for this. Well, he didn't. He's my responsibility now and I am not leaving him."

"Just try harder to keep up." Colliers started walking again, leaving Avery and Merrick staring after him.

"Come on, Merrick. We'd better at least try." She offered her arm to assist but he shook his head. He was pale, too pale, and there were dark circles of exhaustion blooming under his eyes. He worried her almost as much as Colliers did.

The sand gradually gave way to dry, cracked dirt and long dead shrubs. In the distance, the rise of stone cliffs looked miraculously like shelter from the cruel sun. With every step, they got closer, loomed a bit larger. Calling to them with their glorious shadows.

They caught up with Colliers again in the welcome shade of the cliffs. He was busy with his metal pets, patting them and talking to them. They beeped at Avery and Merrick's approach, alerting their keeper. The smaller of the two, the one Colliers referred to as female, skittered over the dry dirt toward them, kicking up a tiny dust cloud. It, she, seemed determined to crawl up Avery's leg. Too tired to argue with the robot, she ignored it and sat in the shade, digging a pouch of chili out of her pack.

As she ate, the bug, Leiurus, explored her arms, lingering on her shoulders, running her front legs over the lines of her scars through the fabric of her flight suit and sheet. The line where flesh met machine and melded together. After a while, she stopped watching Leiurus and turned her attention to Merrick instead. Colliers was redressing his wound with a gentleness Avery would never have expected of him.

With her back to the cliffs, Avery's exhaustion became too much to fight and she finally succumbed to sleep with Leiurus perched on top of her. Her usual dreams of fires and explosions and the vast empty dark of the horizon between planet and space left her alone. Her body was too tired to allow dreams to intrude.

Leiurus twittered shrilly, interrupting Avery's sleep. She leapt to her feet as Androc and Leiurus set up a perimeter and enveloped the small camp in their laser-web. The black box lurched violently of its own accord and Colliers quickly opened and closed it, taking out a third scorpion-thing that was twice the size of the other two.

"Meet Butha." Colliers put him down on the sand and the bug joined his laser-web to the perimeter, adding a third layer of sharp and hot destroyer-light. Colliers checked the control on his wrist. "We have incoming. Looks to be a vehicle, a hover-tank or gunship of some kind."

In the distance, they could hear the whine of a short distance transport. "Definitely not friendlies. My people don't use the old gunships," Colliers growled. "Keep your eyes open. The web will shield a lot, but they aren't impenetrable. Shoot between the lasers."

Avery looked up the face of the cliff. Fifty meters up there was a small ledge that would be big enough to shoot from. "You have to let me out."

"No way. We stay here and defend. Outside the webs, it's suicide."

"Bull." Avery removed her covering sheet and checked the rifle. "If it's all right with you, I'm going to try and shoot that ship down."

"With that?" Colliers stared at the weapon in disbelief.

"They'll expect laser blasters. They'll be prepared for them. No one prepares for real bullets anymore. There's a chance I could penetrate the armor of the ship and a good chance that I can pick off those murdering sons of bitches before they get anywhere near us. I have to disable that cannon-fire though. Let me out."

"How are you going to get up there?" Merrick eyed the cliff.

"Climb. How else? These prosthetics can come in handy once in a while." She flexed her metal fingers and shoved them hard into the sandstone, creating a handhold. If the cliff weren't sandstone, it would have been a lot harder to penetrate. "Now, tell your critters to let me out."

Colliers pulled a small device from his pocket, tapped a few keys, and the web shifted just far enough to let her slide between it and the wall. Avery scaled the cliff quickly, forcing her hands into the face of the cliff and pulling herself up to the ledge. The cliff continued up for another couple of hundred meters, but the ledge was high enough. She took an easy position on her belly and peered through the scope at the approaching ship.

Avery adjusted her aim for the light breeze, height, and distance. It had been years since she had fired at anything but paper targets or jelly bales. The face of the gunner at the long-barreled cannon popped in her scope. A young man with excited eyes and fingers dancing on the stick that aimed the cannon, thumb caressing the faded red button at a frantic pace. She felt no guilt at all as her bullet caught him in the chest at 400 meters and knocked him overboard.

The door on the hatch lifted and a body emerged. Avery didn't wait for details but fired again, watching through her scope as the man's back ripped open, showering the deck of the gunship with red gore. *Disable the weapon, Brinna.* Her father's voice filled her head as she took aim at the fuel cell that powered the laser. She became a soldier again, her weapon and her hand indistinguishable in her mind as they became one tool with which to save herself and her unit. Below her, she heard a muted cheer as the cannon's mechanisms sparked and smoked.

The gunship sped toward them, its best and only weapon gone; the battle would become short range. The hulking mass of beige painted metal settled to the ground with its back door sheltered from Avery's gun. She still had the advantage, but it was a little less of one.

She had her scope trained on the most logical path of action for the adversary when a low, violent growl from above her made her freeze. Avery turned her head just in time to see a massive shadow leap from the top of the cliff to a smaller ledge above her. The creature peered down at her over the edge of the cliff and roared. Loudly. Other roars answered from below.

"Avery!" Merrick screamed from below as the creature roared again.

The matekesh, what else could it be, was indeed the size of a full grown man, if a full grown man walked about on all fours. Frozen in its black stare, Avery felt a stringy rope of saliva caress her cheek and tried hard not to focus on the wide, hungry mouth full of teeth. As the matekesh jumped down on top of her, Avery brought her arms up, metal fingers digging into the hard muscle of its jaw as she tried to keep its mouth closed. It snarled as they struggled, as it tried to make her let go and she clung with everything she had.

The sound of breaking bone filled her with relief as the jaw beneath her fingers relaxed, broken, and the matekesh screamed, a horrible, blood curdling wail that sounded almost like a woman's scream. Howls from the ground beneath joined into the strange, painful harmony. A softer sound reached Avery's ears, a light clicking and twittering growing closer and louder. The matekesh swiped at her with its clawed paws, ripping open the false skin of her arms. Avery flailed her arms wildly, trying to keep the thing unsteady. Leiurus appeared over the edge of the ledge with a soft twittering chatter and emitted a stream of white electricity from her tail into the beast's exposed side. It turned toward Leiurus and the bug shot at it again, knocking it off balance and sending the mass of fur and flesh tumbling over the edge of the cliff.

Avery collapsed on the ledge and Leiurus crawled up onto her chest. "You may have saved me." She patted the bug with a gentle finger. "Thanks." Leiurus twittered, almost purring in response.

When Avery looked down into the canyon, the carnage there did not surprise her in the least. Four matekeshes remained, one circling and sniffing the gunship and the others busy with their meals of human. A laser shot came from inside the laser-web and Colliers and Merrick resumed attempting to pick off or scare off the last of the beasts. Avery picked up her rifle again and reloaded. Taking careful aim, she shot and hit the one nearest the gunship. Laser fire took down the other three.

"Can you get back down?" Colliers called up to her.

"I thought you said those things were nocturnal!" Avery leaned over the edge.

"Must be a den near here. They probably heard the fight and got curious!"

"Might be more of them then. You want to hurry up and get that ship? By the time you get back, I'll be back on the ground." Avery called back. "Watch your back. We may have missed someone."

Butha stayed behind to protect the case while Colliers and Merrick made their way, partially shielded by Androc, over the dirt quickly to the ship. Avery continued to scale back down the face of the cliff handhold by handhold.

The inside of the gunship was comfortable enough for the three of them. Merrick took the first shift as pilot so Avery could rest for a while. Her arms didn't hurt, couldn't hurt, but they needed tending to. Colliers watched her closely as she worked to get the dirt and sand out of her arm. Leiurus watched her, constantly twittering and attempting to assist only to have Avery brush her away.

"You should let her help." Colliers leaned in, peering at the ragged, torn plasti-skin. "There's enough metal scrap on this ship that she should be able to repair the damage."

"Are you kidding me?" Avery stared at him with suspicion.

"Just watch." Colliers picked up an old battered radio and set it on the table. "Put your arm down and let her do her job."

Leiurus clicked and chattered on the tabletop, her tiny legs feeling each ragged tear before ripping open the radio and pulling bits of metal off it and shoving the pieces into her mandibles. Androc came to assist, his tail producing a small flame that they used to heat the metal in her arm and the metal from Leiurus's mouth. Slowly, rip by rip, hole by hole, the two scorpion-things repaired the damage that had been caused by the matekesh.

With the interior fixed, the two robots began skittering all over the gunship, bringing back fragments of discarded plastic and glass. Avery lost track of time, watching the bots work, melting the plastic and glass, chewing it and spinning it into a fine fabric, much like her plasti-skin. The colors were completely off, but that didn't really matter to Brinna. She could always get her arms re-dyed back on Lorn.

"I think she's decided to like you. Since I wouldn't let her kill you." Colliers returned to the back compartment after giving Merrick directions to Tullura.

"Great. I've been adopted by a bug." Avery snorted.

"She must have. You know, they aren't designed to assist anyone but each other and me. What she did back there on the cliff went against her programming." He laughed. "All of them are named for real Earth scorpions. Leiurus quinquestriatus was commonly known as the deathstalker scorpion. She has always lived up to that before." Colliers waited until Avery was looking at him before he continued. "Seems to me that maybe the two of you are more alike than you might think."

"Really? How do you figure that?"

"You look like a woman who should have been dead a time or two before today." He nodded at her arms.

"Deathstalker sounds more like something that causes death, not beats it." Avery shook her head. "That would make her like you, not me."

"You don't like me much, do you?"

"Put yourself in my position." She absently rubbed Leiurus's back. "You paid my father to come to a planet that he swore he'd never come to. You have this thing that someone else wants, or wants destroyed, and you get us shot down out of the sky on entry. My dad is dead. My ship is toast. Most of the people I know are dead. Because of you."

"Fair enough." Colliers nodded somberly.

He didn't even have the decency to apologize. "What do you have that's so important anyway? Is it worth the lives it has cost?"

"It's a Medusa."

Avery shook her head. She couldn't have heard him right. There had to be something else called Medusa. A true Medusa was the artificial mind that the original Earth colonists had used to terraform the planets of the collective. A true Medusa controlled hundreds of millions of nanobots, core-diggers, and ventilators. A true Medusa destroyed a planet before it rebuilt it. "You'll kill everything on the planet if you use a Medusa."

"Have you looked at Ehkmet at all?" He motioned to the window, to the passing vastness of nothing. "This planet is nothing more than a safe place for people who break the laws of the collective. Ehkmet is too much of nothing to be a part of the Aurora Contingent, and too much of something for them to come in with their machines and make it viable. If I can change that, if I can make this planet desirable, it will become a part of the collective. It will be safe for families again. Good people can come home, where they belong."

"Why do you care so much about this place? You might have grown up here but, you haven't lived here in years."

"Hey!" Merrick called from the cockpit, interrupting any answer Colliers might have given. "I've got a guy on the radio here who wants some codes or he's going to have us shot out of the sky."

"Excuse me." Colliers stood. "I need to handle this. I don't blame you for hating me." He disappeared through the sliding door.

Avery had never put much thought into what was in the box he was protecting, but she'd always figured it was something... else. Something sinister or something that would do nothing but add to Colliers's already huge bank accounts. It never once occurred to her that his cause could possibly be a noble one, however destructive its initial phase.

"Dad never once shied away from a mission because it was dangerous." Without fully realizing it, Avery began talking to Leiurus who had crawled up onto her shoulder. "He would never have agreed to take the job without knowing what the cargo was. He knew what he was getting into. I just wish he'd told me."

"Would it have changed your opinion of me if he had?" Colliers was leaning against the doorframe, the smile on his face less smug than usual, almost ironic.

"No, but I would have been better prepared for combat." She looked away. "He didn't tell me because he thought I'd back out if there was a chance for combat. He didn't trust me to be able to handle it." She couldn't stop the tears from falling.

"I doubt that, Brinna." He lowered his muscular frame onto the bench next to her. "When I first hired Madison for this job, he made me promise not to tell anyone what the cargo was. Not because he didn't trust you, but because he wasn't sure that you trusted yourself. He said you'd lost faith in yourself. He didn't explain how or why but it wasn't that he didn't trust you."

"Thanks. Even if you *are* lying." She wiped her nose on her torn sleeve.

"I'm not. I swear it." He held up his hand as if taking an oath. "I really am sorry. I can't tell you how much." His hand came down over hers.

She pulled away. "I know you are."

"I'd like to replace the *Griffin*. If you'll allow me to. If you're serious about continuing your father's business."

"I don't think that would be a good idea. She was insured and I really don't think I want to be indebted to you. To anyone."

"I wouldn't hold that over you." He reached out to touch her again but stopped.

"Not now, maybe. But what happens next time you need a transport?"

"All right. You have to let me do something for you. Let me give you something that might balance the scales a little."

"You think you owe me?" She laughed and petted Leiurus. "You've only got one thing I want. If you can bear to part with her."

"Leiurus? You want her?" Colliers looked at her strangely. "I thought you didn't like her."

"I didn't. But she saved me. And patched me up." Leiurus chattered quietly in her ear.

"You promise you'll take good care of her?" Colliers pulled three small controls from his pocket and handed one to Avery. "She'll tell you what she needs when she needs it. It's a good thing you asked for her. I don't think I could have convinced her to leave you without reprogramming her."

"We'll be fine." Avery strapped the monitor to her own wrist and smiled to the bug on her shoulder. "You good with that Leiurus?" The bug ran a thin leg over her cheek. "Good."

The ship jolted to a hard stop, sending Avery almost into Colliers's lap. "I'll arrange for you and Merrick to be taken back to Lorn."

"Thank you." Avery moved quickly away from him, picking up her pack. "I appreciate that. You never did answer me. Why do you care so much about this planet?"

"Because it's mine. My ancestors were the first to arrive here. The first to settle here. According to our laws, and the deed filed with the Aurora Collective, this planet is mine. I want to do more with it than my parents did. I want to build something good here." He smiled again, the distance between them multiplying rapidly. "For three generations, my family has allowed our planet to fall to ruin. They encouraged outlaws and criminals to seek refuge here. I decided when I was just a kid that I was going to change things."

"I would never have figured you for the noble type." Avery knocked on the sliding partition. "Come on Merrick! Colliers here is going to get us a lift home."

"I think that might be a little difficult." Merrick pulled back the partition and Avery looked past him to the men that had surrounded the ship, guns drawn.

"Please, please tell me those are your people." She looked back to Colliers.

He peered out the windows and grinned. "They are. Let me go out first and get the weapons lowered."

"You do that." Avery stared at a boy, no more than eight, holding a blaster like he was trained to use it. Maybe, when the terraforming was done, kids could be kids for a little longer on Ehkmet.

Colliers stepped out of the ship and immediately every gun was returned to its holster. The people swarmed around him as though touching him could give them something. Could bring them a step closer to greatness.

"What happens now?" Merrick asked.

"We go join the party." Avery cocked her head toward the door, Merrick gathered his pack, and they exited the ship together.

The town was small, a few square kilometers situated where the sand met the irrigated lands of the hospitable region of Ehkmet. Everything was dry, dusty, and rundown with dirt streets and sunbleached buildings of chipped brick walls and white metal roofs. The street in front of them was full of people, dressed in long robes with sunburned faces and lengths of fabric wrapped around their heads to keep the sands at bay.

The people around Colliers stepped aside to let him pass as he made his way toward them the moment they exited the gunship. "I still have work to do, but the two of you should go on and get aboard one of our ships. My friend here, Ash," he motioned to a young woman with a wide smile, "she'll take you to the cruiser and get you settled."

"Thanks." Avery nodded.

From her pocket, Leiurus started chirping at the same moment that Androc shot up out of Colliers's pocket and up onto his head.

"Incoming," one of the men in the crowd yelled.

The people in the streets scattered, blind with panic, running away from Colliers and his box. Avery stayed with him and Merrick followed her. She could have run toward the ships with the others. She should have left him to his own.

Six hover-tanks rose up over the village, their laser-cannons firing at people indiscriminately. As the ships got closer, Avery ducked around a corner and checked her rifle. She used up the last of her father's handmade ammunition, but when she was done there were only five hover-tanks and Colliers's people had their fighters off the ground.

"Let's get your Medusa running and get out of here!" She caught up to Colliers. Merrick wasn't with him. She looked frantically around them, at the streets, until she found him, sprawled on the ground, singed by laser fire, his body smoldering and smoking from the hole in his gut.

Avery cursed through a sheen of tears. "We need to take cover. Now."

Colliers nodded and took off running through the town. He kept them in the shadows of the low buildings, trying to give them as much cover as he could until he reached his destination. Avery knew what he was doing, understood the tactic and wondered what army had trained him.

The building he ducked into was small and unassuming, painted up like any other house in the village. Avery was certain it was just for a moment's rest or cover. Until she got inside. Control panels and monitors covered the back wall of the building and a metal hatch in the floor, accented with wood planks to conceal it, opened to reveal a large underground bunker.

"I'll cover; you do what you have to do." Avery slung her rifle over her shoulder and took her blasters out, taking position in the doorway.

"You don't have to do this." Colliers looked at her as he stood at the edge of the hatch. "You should go get on one of my people's ships. They're going to be hard to come by here, now that my people are scattering."

"How do you intend to get off this place once Medusa is running?"

"I'll figure that out when I need to. You should go." He dropped down into the hatch.

Avery knew he was right. She should leave him there to his mission. Except that she couldn't. She'd lost everything but him already. If she left him there to die when the nanobots were given their orders and released into the atmosphere, the core, and the upper crust of the planet, she'd be left with absolutely nothing. Her father, her ship, her crew, they were all gone. For what? It was up to her to get their passenger to safety. It was up to her to make sure that something good came from it all.

A gunship cruised overhead, moving steadily toward the south end of the town, toward the airstrip. They would destroy any ship capable of leaving the planet. They would doom as many people as they could just to spite Colliers.

Avery moved to the edge of the hatch and called down, "Do your people keep ships anywhere besides the southern airstrip?"

"No." He called back.

"Then we may just be stuck here." She started laughing. The hysteria in her own laughter sobered her. "How about a short-range vehicle? You got something that can get us to a different airstrip where I might be able to hotwire something?"

"Yeah. There's a little fighter across the street and four doors down. It's a little hangar."

"Great. You wait here. I'm going to go and get us a ship. Can Leiurus talk to Androc from a distance?" She yelled down into the hole.

"Yeah! Do what you've got to do and let me work!"

"How long do I have?"

"It's going to take about half an hour to get this up and running." His voice was distant, muffled by the bunker.

Avery dropped her pack at the door, crept out of the building, and ran as fast as she could, across the street and four doors down. She pulled open the bay doors and squealed with delight at the sight of a standard fighter. Just like the ones she'd flown for Lorn. Just like the one that nearly killed her.

Without hesitation, she climbed up the ladder into the cockpit and pulled the top down. The engines fired without a problem and she flipped the laser-cannon's charger on. As she lifted off, a gunship spotted her and turned in her direction. The controls felt familiar beneath her hands, instinct and her training taking over. She maneuvered fast and uneven, dodging cannon fire even as she took aim. The gunship never stood a chance. She'd trained for years for situations like this.

A steady stream of long distance cruisers were lifting off to the North. There had to be an airstrip or something there large enough to accommodate the number of ships she saw taking off. It was a good bet there was one there, just waiting to be stolen.

She pushed the fighter as fast as it would go, the gunships behind her were more concerned with destroying the village in hopes of stopping the Medusa altogether and ignored her completely, allowing her safe passage to the city.

As she landed, she took stock of the ships being prepped for takeoff. Six cruisers were being loaded up with crates and people. Anything and everything they could carry. In the center of the field was a small fleet of a different kind of ship. Long-range fighters, their original markings painted over with insignia Avery didn't recognize. Not very big, enough for two or three people and the massive amount of fuel it took to go any great distance. She prayed one of them was ready to go.

Avery leapt down out of the fighter and allowed Leiurus out of her pocket. Immediately, Leiurus cast her laser-web over Avery's back. Without a partner, the shield only covered one side, but so long as her rear was covered and no one could shoot her in the back, she'd be okay. She didn't bother trying to remain unseen as she inspected the nearest fighter.

There was a man near it, checking numbers and gauges, obviously prepping it for flight. He was older and graying but fit. He took care of himself. She crept closer to him as he topped the fuel tanks from the hoses coming out of underground tanks. She had to duck behind crates every time he looked over his shoulder. Like he was waiting on someone. Just her luck.

She glanced around the field. It was chaotic. People running in every direction, hauling crates, scurrying for their ships. All of them too busy to notice her.

Someone called out to him from the other side of the field and the moment he was distracted, Avery sprinted the remaining distance and wrapped her metal fingers around his throat, bearing down with the full force of her prosthetics. The snap of his spine was loud, echoing in her head as blood gushed over her hands. She dropped him to the ground and pulled herself into the ship as voices and laser fire erupted all around her.

The cockpit was blessedly empty as she fired the engines and lifted up off the ground. It took her a moment to get her bearings and find Tullura again. She was pushing her time limit now, that half an hour had disappeared like nothing. She wasn't leaving Colliers behind. No way.

As soon as the ship neared Tullura, Leiurus started beeping and chattering. "That's right girl, tell them we're coming." She smiled as she searched the village for the little unassuming house. "I can't put this down in the street. He's going to have to run." She spoke into the control on her wrist, which translated her words into something Leiurus could understand.

She spotted Colliers, running with both of their packs toward a small crop field. She lowered the ship easily into the field and lowered the ramp.

"Who did you have to kill to get this beauty?" Colliers set their packs on the floor and strapped into a seat.

"I don't know. It's not like I stopped to ask the guy." She lifted the ship back off the ground and took off. "How long until it starts working?"

"It's already started. It'll be about half an hour before the first digger hits the core and the quakes start. A lot of these good-for-nothings will get away, but at least they won't have this place to come back to. By the time it's habitable again, I'll have the deals in place with the Collective."

Avery plotted the course for Lorn and watched as Ehkmet dropped away. They were well on their way, far enough that the rumbles of the planet's core wouldn't spike the gravitational fields and pull them back in, before it started. A few ships, not far enough from the surface, were pulled back in. She watched with horrified awe as the planet began swallowing landmasses and volcanoes erupted, their black clouds of rock and ash visible even from space.

"Do you want to ride all the way to Lorn, or would you rather I drop you off somewhere else?" Avery didn't look away from the planet when she spoke.

"Lorn is fine. I can get a ride to Aurora Prime from there."

Silence stretched out between them as they watched the first phase of the terraforming machines from a safe distance. Ehkmet faded into the distance, not fast enough for Avery, but soon there was nothing but white speckled blackness and fleets of fleeing ships headed for the Collective and the nearest hospitable station.

Avery dug into the bottom of her pack and pulled out two of the bottles of vodka. "Snagged these back on the *Griffin*. Figured I'd be drinking to our health and safety with Merrick." She shook her head. "To your health, Mr. Colliers." She lifted her bottle.

"It's Scott. And I'd rather drink to you. If you weren't so frustratingly stubborn, I'd be waiting for the nanobots to rip my atoms apart instead of sitting here watching the stars." He touched his bottle to hers.

"To the *Griffin* and her crew." Avery whispered, and they drank.

Author's Note:

Terraforming probably won't look anything like this even in the farthest flung futures but the idea that we could manipulate the structure of a planet at the molecular level is interesting to me. But it's also a terrible, violent weapon. Perhaps the idea would start out as a way to extend humanity's reach, but it would only be a matter of time before a despot, a fanatic, a man bent on vengeance would get ahold of it. Make no mistake, no matter how justified, Colliers isn't a good guy here. He straight up murdered people.

Leiurus was something of a happy accident stemming from a little too much television and a desire to write about the things I'm afraid of. Little bugs that can kill you are not my thing. I like the idea of personal security in the form of little mechanical sentinels in this case, scorpion shaped. And I very much liked the idea of like meeting like and having one artificial life see sameness and kinship with a woman with artificial parts.

POETRY

The Miracle Disease

Little
Fingers of steel
Tracing a path through blood
Memorizing the patterned code
Of life.

Fixing
Small injuries
Broken skin, fractured bone
Knitting flesh with pins and needles
No scars.

Hive mind
Collective dream
Swarming in schools like fish
Reproducing too fast to stop
To control.

Unseen
Infestation
A miracle turned curse
No cure for the medication
New plague.

Death knell

Necessity
Programmed execution
Viral vaccine shot into veins
Hope lives.

FIRST PUBLISHED IN THE FIFTH DI.

Perfect Man

Words spoken, calculated for maximum effect
Pseudo-eyes glisten with clear oil lubricant
Tip of synthetic tongue playfully peeking
From sinful mouth to dampen flesh-rubber lips
Laboratory pheromones, unadulterated masculinity
Oozing from manufactured Kevlar pores
Tricky fingers performing choreographed
Ministrations too complex to be possible
Rented out by the hour, by the night
Worth every saved, hoarded, stolen cent
For a woman to whom no one listens.

FIRST PUBLISHED IN 2008 SAMSDOT CALENDAR.

Future of Medicine

Hole punched in soft flesh
Blood staunched on impact, skin healed
Knitted by machines.

FIRST PUBLISHED IN SCIFIKUEST.

Author's Note:

Poetry is a great love of mine. I don't know that it speaks to everyone and I know it means something different to everyone who reads it or hears it. Poetically, my heart belongs to Cohen and Rollins.

EVOLUTION OF A SHADOW

Section One: Coming Full Circle

The slick, wet sound of steel through flesh resounded through her head as if amplified. Hot, red warmth gushed down her face, the pain bit into her with a ferocity that threatened to push her under the ice of her mind. Instinct, drive for survival, took hold of her and forced her to fight back.

A white flash to her left shone like a star just before an angry hole ripped open in her thigh. Her tiny fingers grabbed hold of the man behind her, the knife-man, pulling his jaw as she fell. The crackle-pop of breaking bone exploded beneath her trained fingers. One moment of shock and pain and the blade that had cut her face belonged to her. The gun-man fired again from the doorway but she used the knife-man as a shield, covering her body with his, the silenced bullet burrowed into his flesh instead of hers.

Gun-man lunged at her, and she spun on her heel, turning so that his hand came down over her right shoulder. She grabbed his hand by the meaty part and twisted, turning his arm behind him, bent at a weak angle. With all her strength, she slammed her elbow down on his forearm and he screamed as it snapped.

Her blood roared in her ears like the tides of the Pacific below her home and she shoved his broken arm into Gun-man's side. The ragged edges of bone ripped through his skin like a blade, through his arm and deep into his flesh, into his lung.

Shade lurched awake, the last tendrils of memory clung to her, still staining her hands red. She shook her past away and opened her eyes to the morning. A glance at the flashing time display on the wall spurred her out of bed. She was going to be late. Every advantage she would have had was lost.

"He knows better!" Shade muttered to her empty apartment as she pulled on her clothes. Rado, in his overwhelmingly obnoxious need to take care of her, had slipped a sleeping pill into her coffee again. She couldn't get through to him that it wasn't insomnia that kept her from sleeping; she just had a different cycle. She didn't need as much sleep as he did.

She pushed aside her frustration and double-checked her weapons. A 9mm in a pancake holster in the small of her back, a small taser in her jacket pocket, and an assortment of knives in various pockets and hide-a-hilts on her body. Shade wasn't thrilled about being the last one to the party, but she had to make do. It wasn't like it hadn't happened before.

Rain caressed her cheek as she stepped out into the chill of a Seattle dawn. The flame of her lighter flared in the waxing light. She moved with purpose, long strides eating up the street as she cupped her hand over her cigarette to keep it dry. Standing beneath an awning across the street from the meeting site, she surveyed the layout with a practiced eye. Easy up and easy out, ideal for a woman in her line of work, one that often strayed very close to death.

Shade bolted across the street, cutting in and out of traffic. She climbed up the fire escape shrouded in deep, fogged shadows, leather whispering softly against metal, her boots grasping the slick, coated steel of the old ladder.

Swinging herself up onto the roof, Shade searched the shadows for any sign of her prospective client. "You called this meeting, not me." She called to him, certain he was already there, as she stepped into a clear, well-lit space in the center of the rooftop. Shade tuned her ears to the shadows, listening for him, his movements, his voice, his breath.

Two shuffled steps and he stood behind her. "All right." He said as the barrel of his gun pressed into the back of her head. "Did you come alone?" His voice sounded raspy and forced, as if he pressed a voice changer to the roof of his mouth. It was slightly more human than sound of speaking through a fancy kazoo.

"That was the arrangement." His breath brushed against her neck, warm and traced with mint. She expected the gun and precautions of her would-be client, but fear never claimed her. He had a job for her and her team to do. They couldn't very well do that if she was dead and wouldn't do it if she were injured in any way. It was nothing more than posturing. "What do you want?" As she moved to reach into her jacket, she felt the barrel twitch as she tested him. "I'm just getting a cigarette." His hand trembled, as if possessing the gun made him jittery. "Keep me or kill me, it's up to you. If you do choose to shoot me, you'd better make sure I never get back up." Shade laughed without humor.

"I want you to find someone."

"I can't very well do that if I'm dead. Why don't you put that gun away?" She put her cigarette to her lips and lit it. A smile crept over her face as the gun dropped away, the pressure on the back of her skull disappeared. He'd passed his first test. "Who is this someone you'd like to hire us to find?"

"Just a girl. All the information is on the disc." He coughed and she heard the whistle of the changer as it fell out of place.

"And the offer is what?" She inhaled and blew smoke into the morning.

"Not up for negotiation." A large hand clamped down on her shoulder. "Ten now and a hundred more when you bring her to me." He tossed a fat envelope at her feet. "The cash and the disc are in there. It's everything you need to know. From what I've heard, if you and your team can't find her, no one can."

"Very true." She smiled at the empty compliment. "How do we get in touch with you when we have information?"

"You don't." Shade listened carefully as he moved away from her. "I'll be contacting you daily for progress reports. I don't want this slipping through the cracks or getting forgotten about."

"It won't be. I can promise you that." Silence spread for a moment, then the sound of shuffling feet filled the tense morning, the door clicked closed and it was done. He had retreated into the hotel below.

Shade waited for a moment in the rain and finished her cigarette. She picked up the envelope. $10,000 cash with a good bit more to come. It wasn't bad at all. She'd worked harder for less. Her first finder's fee had been a paltry $1500. She'd come a long way in fifteen years. Overall, it had been worth it.

Meeting Andre, her friend and business partner, had changed everything. Before she'd tried to steal his wallet, she'd survived by fishing through dumpsters and stealing what she needed. Andre had taken her in, treated her like a protégé and not a daughter, even though she was young enough to be his. Together, as their operation grew, they'd handpicked their team of specialists. They were finders, thieves, and hackers. As long as the dollar amount matched appropriately with the job, it was a go. 110 grand for finding some lost little girl was a bit on the high side, but the CEO of the shipping company they contracted with had paid more than twice that to find his underage mistress.

Flicking away the butt of her cigarette, she went back down the fire escape. The sun chased away most of the shadows in the alley, burning off the salt-laced fog. Her restaurant was only a few blocks to the south. It was a convenient place; it provided a legitimate front, a good meeting place for her team, and a second home for her.

The scent of steamer buns made her mouth water. Chen,

the soft-spoken, unassuming chef, was already working on the lunch special. It took most of a morning to steam enough of the pork and dough balls to feed the crowd that had come to expect them every Tuesday. Chen had been her biggest coup. Recruiting a chef who also happened to be a wanted killer and fancied himself a bit of a samurai had its advantages. She could trust him to keep her secrets and, when she needed to, she could trust him to take care of certain . . . obstacles.

Waving to Chen as she passed through the kitchen, Shade let herself into her office. It was simple, a desk, chair, couch, and closet of costumes and weapons. Apart from the weekly tour of the books, she didn't spend much time there. She stripped out of her leather, tossing it on the couch. Ripped up fatigues, a red wig, and mirrored glasses made up the costume she always wore when she went to visit Alec, one of her parts dealers. That was the key to her survival. None of the people around her contacts ever saw her out of costume.

Shade stepped into the closet, closing the door behind her before she opened the small panel behind the coats and wigs. Pressing a quick code, *5388,* she listened for the click of the lock and pushed the back of the closet open. When she'd refurbished the restaurant, she and Andre had built in the secret passage so she wouldn't be seen leaving in a hundred different costumes. She had a plain face, but if used day after day, even her best costumes would be recognizable. The passage opened into a supply closet in the cheap motel next door. Owned and operated by Andre, and since he occasionally rented rooms by the hour, no one paid too much attention who came and went through those doors.

Seattle's criss-crossed alleyways and cluttered skywalks were as much a part of her, as familiar to her, as the tattoos she wore. Every taut thread of pavement had felt her presence at least once. The route she took was not a straight one, cutting over, doubling back, taking steps to ensure she was not followed. A healthy dose of paranoia was a good thing. Especially for Shade. It had saved her life more than once.

When she reached the bar, the boy wiping down the tables smiled and waved at her. Shade nodded curtly and headed for the back. "I heard my parts came in!" Anticipation draped over her, taking control of her fingers. It was one of the last pieces of the puzzle she'd been putting together for nearly fifteen years.

"They did." A short, broad-shouldered man stepped into view. "I'm afraid I'm going to have to charge you extra though. It's going to be ten now."

"That's ridiculous, Alec!" Her fingers itched for her gun. She did not like changes.

"Seems you have a stray using your name for credit with the local Phire dealers." Alec motioned to the shadows and Shade heard a girl's voice, unintelligible and angry. "She offered to dance for it but I'm not that stupid, not if she really is connected to you."

A man came from the kitchen, shoved a half-dressed girl at her feet and handed her a heavy black suitcase. "Do me a favor," Alec stepped closer, "keep her out of here. I can't control everything, and next time she's liable to get a lot worse than a pity hit and a drunk groping her at the bar. I don't want to see her back here."

"Sure." Shade handed him the envelope. It'd been nice while she had it. The girl at her feet giggled and cried simultaneously. "What are you doing, Lonna?" Disappointment flooded her voice. "Thanks Alec. If you see her back in here again, she's on her own. I'm done." Alec nodded curtly.

Suitcase in one hand and the bleached blonde, strung out waif in the other, Shade dragged Lonna, protesting, from the bar. They went two or three blocks in relative silence, getting more than a few dirty looks from pedestrians and onlookers. They veered off into a nice dark alley and Shade let her go. "What on earth do you think you're doing? If you ever pull another stunt like this again, I'll let you find your own way out. Do you want to end up dead in an alley? Left for the rats and the junkies? Do you really want to put your father through that?"

"I'm . . . sorry, Shade." The girl looked down at her feet as she rocked and hiccupped.

"I don't believe this. You're still high aren't you?" Shade lit a cigarette. "Andre is my friend and a important part of my team. He can't function right when he's worried about you. You're all he has left, Lonna. What about that don't you understand?" She put her hands on the girl's shoulders and shook her. "You've gotten yourself in way over your head for this poison. There had better not be a next time. I meant what I said to Alec. You do that again, and you're on your own. Do you understand me?"

"Y . . . yes." She nodded and bit her thin lip hard enough to draw blood.

"Go home and get cleaned up. If I hear word one about you on the streets looking for that stuff, and I'll be asking around, you aren't going to like what happens."

"You aren't my mother, you know." Lonna whispered, her voice almost level.

"I never pretended to be. I thought we used to be friends. I thought we used to be like sisters. When did you get so screwed up?" Shade shook her head and turned to walk away.

"He likes you better. Did you know that? You make a better daughter than me."

"Bullshit. Go home and sober up." Shade walked away.

Shade made a quick stop at the restaurant to change her clothes and filch a few steamer buns for her own lunch, and then hurried back to her apartment. It wasn't much, a two-bedroom affair with two large leather recliners and a television the only furniture in the main room. The kitchen, a long counter on the back wall of the room, was sparse and held only the necessities, its one spot of elegance being the chrome and black coffee maker on the counter. Down the short, stubby hallway, there were two bedrooms—one of them a very cluttered computer room and the other crammed with two beds and mountains of laundry. She wasn't much on cleaning. Ever.

The parts in the briefcase screamed for her attention. She checked the case first, inspecting the new units, black market super servers, sticks of DRAM, integrateable hard drives straight off the manufacturer's belts in Japan, and a matte black metal box. The box contained a thousand nanobots, made to order by a tiny company in Okinawa. So long as they made them to her specifications, they would multiply if given the proper materials. She'd gone to see them and donated the starter pair from her own blood. She was ill-equipped to foster a new colony and didn't want to take her attention away from other facets of her current project to build the equipment she would need for that. The company in Okinawa fell over themselves to donate their time and effort, so long as she allowed them to keep a colony of their own.

Cradling the box of nanobots, Shade stepped into her office. A room filled with her computer. Technically, it was several computers networked together and firewalled with more protection than the Feds used on their network. She knew that for certain. Rado had on more than one occasion hacked into Quantico to get information, or into the IRS system to do some creative re-accounting. One unconnected computer sat tucked into a corner, and she took the mini disc her new client had given her and laid it in the tray.

The system ran a complete check on the disc for viruses, hacking codes, back doors, explosive residues, tracers, the full gambit. A moment later, her first line of defense proclaimed the disc clean. Shade took the disc and put it into her main system, downloaded and saved the files. She'd keep the disc for a little while; see if Rado could find anything of interest on it somewhere, a name, an identification number, anything that might come in handy to have.

She was just getting ready to have a look at the data when someone started knocking on her door. The knock didn't so much startle her as annoy her. It never failed, the moment she sat down to really get to work, somebody wanted something. "What is it?" she yelled at the door as she neared it.

"I hear I owe you some money!" A familiar, graveled voice called out.

"Andre!" She threw open the door and wrapped her arms around the older man. "I take it Lonna made it home."

"It didn't hurt that you dropped her at my door." He sighed deeply, the lines of age deepening in his sorrow. "I don't know what to do about that girl."

"She's just going through a phase. She'll get over it soon enough. Especially now that Alec is putting the word out that no one is to give her anything." Shade pulled him into the apartment and shut the door, listening to the creak and click of the automatic lock.

"Thanks for that, too, then." He nodded, running a hand over his gray, high and tight buzz, the last remnants of his days as a Marine. "How'd it go this morning?"

"I'm not sure yet. I was just sitting down to look through the files." As she spoke, she started a pot of coffee. "The guy was strange, too nervous. It just felt off a little. Not enough to have me reaching for my gun, but not right either."

"What do you mean?" Andre leaned the bulk of his muscular frame against the counter, concern coloring his gray eyes darker than usual.

"For one thing, his hand was shaking when he had the gun to my head."

"Are you sure it was a man?"

"I think so. He smelled like a man, not just the soap but under that. And his hands were big, too big to be a woman's, I think. I don't know. Anyway, the disc was clean. I guess I'm just getting paranoid in my old age." Andre followed her into the workroom. "Let's bring up those files and take a look at the target."

She sat down and pulled on a pair of thin, silk and wire gloves. Her fingers moved quickly through the air in front of the line of monitors, pulling up files and opening them. The name, Marron Buchanan, made her blood run cold, a chill of the ghosts in her past running through her. A photo popped onto the center monitor and she stared into the face that had once belonged to her reflection. "We're in trouble, Andre."

"I see that." Andre watched from over her shoulder as she pulled more pictures to the surface. All of them were old, fifteen and twenty years old. All of them were from before the surgeries, and facial implants, that had given her a new life. All of them were from before that horrible night when she'd watched her family die. Before the night she became a killer.

She hadn't meant to call up the memories, but they came, clawing and screaming back to the surface. One moment, it was a quiet night. She and her mother were looking over the latest test results from one of the rats in the lab her mother ran. They were talking about a new computer chip, a tiny little square of carbon transistors and circuits. Shade had been holding the chip when the door exploded and the two men started shooting. Her father fell first, running to protect his family. Her baby sister had only been four years old, and they shot her in the head. Then her mother. All the time, Shade watched and did nothing. She hadn't been able to move, and then it was just her and them. Then, they were dead, too. Blood was all over her hands. It never washed off. Not completely.

The newspapers had said that she killed her family. That there was evidence. And there was evidence at every crime scene of the eight murders of the OriqualTec research and development team. Someone had come, after she'd fled, cleaned up their men and planted her hair, skin, and prints at eight other crime scenes. They hadn't wanted her dead, or she'd have been dead. For a while, she believed that they just wanted a scapegoat, but with time and perspective, she thought it might have been more complicated than that. Now, seeing her former self, all wide-eyed innocence and youthful beauty, she knew it was. No one else would care about a girl who had died, at least on paper, so long ago.

"Why now? It's been years. Either they already know who I am or this is just coincidence. Or maybe they think they know and want to be certain. But why not just kill me on that roof, at that meeting?"

"I don't know. I don't believe in coincidences, Shade, and neither do you." Andre patted her on the shoulder, trying to lend a little comfort.

"All right. I have a lot of work I need to get done right now and figure out just what I'm going to say to these lowlifes. I don't know how much time I've got."

"What do you want me to do? Anything you want, you've got it; you know that."

"There's nothing you can do for me." She shook her head and leaned back against the wall. "You'd better get back to Lonna. Spend the day with her. Spend as much time with her as you can. Hopefully, she'll detox fast."

"If you need anything, call me." Andre turned toward the door. "Thanks again for getting Lonna."

"I was just in the right place at the right time; it was nothing major."

"She should have called me."

"You couldn't have done anything more than I did. But, as I told her, I won't be doing it again. Next time, she's on her own. I've done everything I know to do for her except let her hit bottom. Maybe it would be better if we did." Shade walked back to her computer and got to work. She didn't hear Andre leave.

Shade was lost in her research, pulling the file on her 'death', gathering up the evidence that Marron Buchanan was not only dead, but also cremated. The plastic surgeon had done wonders on the corpse in Philadelphia to make the poor hooker look just like her. A second surgeon, one she'd found through a former assistant of her mother's, had given her a new face to match her new name. Sure, she'd been prettier as Marron, but it was so much easier to do her job with a plain face, a sterile, unrecognizable face.

She was in the process of downloading the death certificate, doctored DNA profile, and photographic image of the dead girl when Rado let himself in. She didn't hear him so much as smell him. His cologne was nice, but it carried. He said nothing to her, getting straight to work installing the servers. Out of the corner of her eye, she saw his bare shoulder, dark like fresh earth and muscular, familiar. In a small way, it was comforting to have him there.

Her thoughts swirling, her guard down just a little, Shade jumped when she felt his breath on her neck, his long, black braids falling over her chest as he turned her to face him. "She's all set up. Test the connections for me." He turned her back to the computer and let her get back to work.

"Could you get me another cup of coffee?" Her voice echoed through the small apartment. "Without the sedative, thank you very much!"

"You need your sleep." He scolded as he handed her the cup. "I didn't put anything in it. But I should."

"I don't need as much sleep as you seem to think. In fact, I function better on four hours than I do on eight." She smiled at him and looked at the monitors. "Diagnostics checked the connections and it looks good. You can go on to bed if you're tired."

"Right. Not a chance." He crossed his arms over his chest. "You first. I'm going to watch a movie or something until you're ready."

"I don't need a babysitter."

"That's good. I'm not one." He walked away.

Shade sighed. It had been Andre's idea for Rado to move in with her since she wouldn't move in with him and Lonna. She needed backup, he said. Like she'd had when Claude was alive. Like he had in his brother and nephew. The moment her thoughts circled to Claude, her late husband, she stepped away from the computer. Shade dumped the last of the coffee down the drain and went to bed. Rado followed soon after, settling into his low bed on the other side of the room from hers. Comfortable. Easy. Uncomplicated.

"Do you have any information for me?" She was not at all surprised to hear the distorted voice of her new client the next morning. "Have you found her?"

"There may be some difficulty with that. What do I do if she's dead?" Shade lit a cigarette with fingers that still trembled from her nightly tour through her darkest moments.

"Exhume the body. Bring me actual proof that she is dead."

"Exhumation changes things. That's a far more traceable illegal operation than I am accustomed to. I don't like the idea of being a grave robber. I think I had better get my full fee up front, to cover my costs and my skin." *And cushion my accounts for what could be a dry few years.*

"You must really believe she's dead." She thought she heard a faint laugh. "How shall we make the transaction?"

"Same roof as before, all cash. Leave it there and I'll get it." She strained her ears to hear what was going on in the background but there was very little, as though there was something hiding just below the surface of the static, something important.

"Give me three hours." The line went dead.

If they didn't already know, they suspected and were looking for proof. All she had to do was buy some time. She wouldn't need much, just a few solid hours for the download and then, then they could take her. Maybe it would be better if they did.

"Rado." She shook him gently. "I've got to go out. Run a few more diagnostics, and send me the specs on storage and speed. Okay?" He nodded, eyes still closed. "Thanks. I'll be back in a few hours."

Shade took a quick shower and dressed in old jeans and a loose, wide-necked sweater. Tenderly, she ran a finger over her face, near her hairline, feeling for the bump, the perfect square of plastic beneath her skin, the tiny chip inside it nearly priceless. It was there, always there, as if she'd been born with it. She wondered if she'd feel different without it. Naked.

The sun was shining over the city, too cheerful for her mood, as she headed for a refurbished warehouse on the pier. As was her habit, she took note of every face she passed, every potential hiding place for a threat. She'd been chided in the past about her paranoia, but it proved to be well served now that they were looking for her again, probably even knew who she really was.

She stopped at the side door of a warehouse and punched the code into the lock, the door swinging open to allow her entrance. She pressed the button on the intercom system. "Corinthian!" Her voice boomed over the speakers. "We have a problem."

"Shade?" A young man with brown hair and a concerned look on his face opened the door to Corinthian's office. "He's in surgery right now."

"What's on the table?"

"A muscle implantation for one of our biggest clients. Can you wait?"

"No. You can do an implant in your sleep. You did mine." She pointed to her face. "Scrub in and kick him out. I need him."

"All right," he held up his hands in surrender, "but you take the blame, got it?"

"Anything you want, Gregg. Just go get him."

"What is going on, Shade?" A figure appeared at the top of the steps a few minutes later, still in a blood-smeared apron. "This better be important."

"It's about as important as it gets." She smiled and tapped her head, her finger connecting with the hard plastic case at her hairline. "It's time."

"What do you mean, it's time?" He stepped out of the shadows as he pulled the apron from his bony frame. "No. Please, tell me you're kidding. Shade, this process can't be rushed. We have to run tests and diagnostics on the machine still."

"We don't have time." She met him on the stairs and pushed his long white hair away from his face. "They came looking for me. It has to be Jacob. No one else would care about a girl who's been dead for so long. They're paying me to find myself. I have to go and pick up the payment in about two hours. I think they know who I am."

"He wants the chip. Does he think you'll lead him to it?"

"I'm not sure. I think he's trying to push me into doing something stupid. Even when we were kids, he underestimated me. He knows what we are, that we should be equal, but he always treated me like a fool. Maybe I should play into that. Maybe I should play on that assumption."

"No way. It's not worth your life."

"Maybe, maybe not. Maybe it isn't just the chip he's after; maybe it's my body, too. Maybe he thinks the answer is there." She sat down on the bottom step. "I think they were always supposed to take me to him. The night the men came and killed my family, they could just as easily have killed me, too. But they didn't. They fought with me, but they didn't aim to kill. I'd be dead instead of them, if they had."

"Maybe Jacob didn't want you dead. Did you ever think about that? The two of you were always so close, maybe he thought you'd help him if you knew it was him."

"Doubt it. He killed his own parents, Corinthian. Or at least, had them killed. There is no reason for him to let me live. None. We may have grown up together, but we were never really friends. As for helping him, what good would that have done? I knew nothing about myself until that night. How did he?" She shook her head.

"Whatever the reason, you're still alive. And I would really like to keep it that way." He held out his hand and helped her up. "Come on. I'm going to need that chip now." He led her up the stairs, deeper into the building, where the sterile operating rooms were.

"We've been expecting this for a long time. Maybe we've just been lucky it took them this long get so close."

"Is your computer system even ready for this?" Corinthian asked.

"I think so. There's no telling until we install the chip, but the last of the components have been installed. We have to take this step now."

"If it isn't ready, all that we've been working for could be for nothing."

"That has always been a possibility." She sat in the long chair, as still as she could. Corinthian gently leaned the chair back as far as it would go.

He turned on the hot, bright light, his impish lips curling back from his too perfect teeth. "Want the anesthetic? This is going to hurt."

"Novocain only. I need to have all my wits. Besides, it hurt before." That night flashed in her head again, standing at the bathroom sink, bleeding everywhere, she'd taken the chip in its plastic shield and tucked in under her skin, shoving it as far in as she could, toward her hairline. She'd used a needle and thread to stitch the skin closed, crying, not at the pain, but at the thought of the wicked scar she'd have all the way down her face. She could afford vanity then. At least, she had thought she could.

She felt the pinch of the needle and the pressure of his fingers as he sliced a two-inch line even with her hairline. It took him a few moments, hacking through the tissue that had grown around the plastic case, claimed it for a part of her, but soon the chip was free. He didn't bother stitching up the wound.

That night, when her family died, Shade had learned quite a lot about herself. She had it in her to kill without mercy and without much thought. And she healed fast. Wicked fast. There had never been a scar where she'd been shot. There had never been a scar where the blade tried to remove her face. That was when she knew that her mother was a liar. A crafty, too smart for anyone's good, hypocritical liar. Shade hadn't been just an observer, just a witness to the OriqualTec's projects, she was one. Genetically engineered, tampered with, infected with machines, and trained to kill. She was a product of a war-machine like none that had ever existed before. So was Jacob. But she had two things he didn't. The chip the team created, and the paperwork from the department of defense that outlined the project's complete purpose. Individual soldiers were only the first phase.

"How long will that take to heal up?" He helped her to stand.

"Not long. A couple of hours maybe." She shrugged, mopping at the blood with a bit of gauze.

"That's incredible, you know."

"Yeah, I do." She sighed. "No matter what happens in the next few days, you can't tell anyone about it. No one can know just how fast I heal. Even if you think they already know or that they deserve to know, you can't tell anyone."

"Why?" He looked at her, suspicion filling his eyes as he pursed his thin lips. "What are you going to do?"

"You have work to do, Corinthian." She touched his arm, squeezing just slightly, just enough to say what needed said. "And so do I. I'm going to go get the money and then I'll be back for the download."

"I'll need at least an hour before I'm ready, so take your time. When you get back, you'll need to do a little bit of prep work. I need you to shave your head."

Rado was waiting for her when she returned to the apartment. He was jittery and nervous, obviously worried about her. He didn't say much, no pointed questions about where she'd been or what she'd been doing. He was like Claude in that way, keeping everything bottled up inside. She knew how he felt for her, knew how hard he would take all that was to come. It had to go down her way to be successful. She set the terms. It had to be that way. Unfortunately, that didn't mean it was going to be easy on anyone. Especially not on the people who cared so much for her and got so little in return.

They spent the day together. No talk of work or the past or the future. Shade was surprised how much she enjoyed his company. She didn't feel the way he wanted her to, but her emotions weren't as dead as she'd always hoped.

Whatever was to come, she felt the need to say goodbye to him, but she didn't know how. All he had ever done was love her, and she had pulled away. Rado had never budged. He had stayed by her side, never straying. It occurred to her that he was as devoted to her as Claude had ever been.

Late in the evening, after a great deal of wine, Shade's thoughts circled back to Claude, to her husband. Her dead husband. All she had left of him were her memories. She often found a strange peace in the dead of night as she remembered what it had been like to lay next to him, to feel his arms around her, to feel him inside her. She longed for him deep in a part of her she refused to acknowledge. A part of her she silenced with a liquor gag.

Drunk and laughing, Rado and Shade stumbled back into her apartment. Shade looked up at him, not seeing Rado, but Claude. She put her arms around him. "Thank you." She pressed her lips to his.

"For what?" His eyes were wide and his smile real.

"For loving me the way you do." She kissed him again. He didn't ask any more questions, didn't say a word, as if he was afraid of breaking the spell. It was Claude's touch she felt as Rado's fingers traced her body. When they kissed, Shade felt Claude's lips against hers. Only when Rado's hair danced on her skin was she aware that he wasn't Claude, didn't even resemble him. It was close enough. Close enough to being human. Close enough to being real.

The next morning, as they lay entwined in sleep, the phone rang. Rado lay still, listening to her, feigning sleep. "I got the information you wanted," she said to the caller. He assumed it was the client. "I have as much proof as there is that she is, in fact, dead. Do you still want to see it for yourself?" There was a pause as the client responded. "I'll meet you back on the roof in an hour." She hung up and started pulling on her clothes.

It took every bit of self-control he had not to leap out of bed and beg her not to go. It didn't feel right. Nothing about it felt right. And he knew that she already knew that. Which scared him. He forced himself not to move as she laid an envelope on the pillow where her head had been only moments before.

He waited for the click of the lock and dressed as fast as he could. He followed her out of the building. At a reasonable distance. She was an expert at catching tails, eluding them, but she never once looked back. No. This meeting wasn't right at all.

They traveled through the alleyways that connected the legitimate world to their world. Through a maze of vendors in the square and past the dealers in the shadows. Past structures of plastic, metal, and concrete. He followed her, noting all the times she should have looked over her shoulder. Shade would normally have kept one hand in her pocket on the taser and the other not too far out of reach of her gun, but her hands were swinging at her sides like she wasn't going somewhere dangerous. Or like she had already resigned herself to a fate that turned Rado's stomach in on itself.

When they reached the hotel, he wasn't surprised to see her climbing the fire escape. She had a thing for rooftops. Something about vantage points and who had the stronger ground. There was nowhere higher on that block. Nowhere he could watch over her from. When Shade was on the roof, he jogged over to the alley and started the climb up after her.

He was halfway up the building when a gun went off on the roof. Rado pushed aside his fear and charged up the remaining floors as fast as he could, no longer caring about how loud he was, clumping up the steel ladder. When he reached the roof, one look over the edge told him everything he needed to know. Shade lay on the roof in a pool of blood, spreading out—so much blood, too much blood. A man in a dark coat stood, leaning over her, talking into a phone.

Rado didn't think, didn't hesitate, pulled his gun from inside his jacket and fired. One shot, straight into the man's right eye. It would have gone into his temple, but, at the last moment, he turned his head and saw Rado kill him.

Rado threw himself over the lip of the roof and ran to Shade's side. Her face was as perfect as it had ever been, but an ugly red flower bloomed over her heart as her blood ran out. He lifted her in his arms and pressed her to his chest, rocking her like a baby, tears pouring down his face.

From a distance, the che-che-che whir of chopper blades caught his ear. News or cops. Some do-gooder must have called 9-1-1 after the first shot. Either way, he'd be screwed. He had sixteen warrants out for his arrest.

"I have to go now, Shade." He kissed her lips. "I swear to you, I'm going to find the people responsible for this and make them pay."

Rado set her gently on the roof and ran for the fire escape. The chopper was closer now, but still far enough away that he figured he'd be on the ground before it got there.

The walk back to the apartment was long and lonely. He held his jacket tight around himself, as much for support as to cover the blood stains. Her blood was all over him. If he'd been faster, she wouldn't be dead. He barely made it inside before he broke down. Sobbing, he grabbed a bottle of Scotch and slumped to the floor, his back against the door to the bedroom. By the time the bottle was empty, he'd calmed down. Rado rummaged through the cabinets until he found more whiskey and retreated to the bedroom.

He lay down on her bed, her smell filling his head. He remembered the feel of her skin, the sound of her voice, the beating of her heart. Swallow by swallow, memory by memory, he got drunk enough to pass out.

The sun was still not up when Rado opened his eyes. He had hoped it had all been a dream. That he would wake up to find her lying next to him. She wasn't there. It hadn't been a dream. Where her head should have been, the envelope laid. Inside was a chip, a disc, and a note.

"Rado. Install into main unit of system. Instructions on disc. Top priority. Shade." That was it. No prophetic goodbyes or declarations of love. Just instructions.

Still not quite sober, he did as he was asked. If he could do his job and get it right, maybe it could all be reversed. Maybe she'd walk in any moment. Part of him wanted to dismantle the whole system and destroy it. It was too much a part of her.

Closing his eyes, he saw her in a pool of blood. Dead. Rado opened another bottle of whiskey, the only liquor she'd ever liked, and stumbled into her bedroom again. She had never loved him the way he wanted her to, but she had loved him enough to let him in.

Section Two: Resurgence

Unable to find sleep in her bed, Rado and his bottle returned to the computer. Maybe, if he could figure out what she'd been doing just before she was killed, what she was up to in those missing hours of silence, he could understand what happened. "What on earth am I supposed to do now?" He asked himself.

"Hello Rado." Words appeared on the center monitor. He hadn't typed them, hadn't been near a keyboard or Shade's wireless gloves. He couldn't imagine anyone hacking the system, not with all the ice and fire he'd built into it. "It's me, Rado. Shade."

"What the . . ." He stared blankly at the screen and then the bottle on the desk.

"Don't be so shocked. If I could figure out how to talk, you'd be hearing me instead of reading me. I can hear you. I can see you. I just can't talk yet. Please, say something."

"Jesus. I didn't think I was this drunk." He put the bottle to his lips and swallowed a mouthful, then a second.

"You aren't that drunk. You've just been the midwife to the project I've been working on, working towards, for my entire life. What you are seeing now is the culmination of my mother's research, Corinthian's ingenuity, and my determination. What is my physical self's current location?"

"No. This is just a hallucination." He took another drink. "This is impossible. You're dead. I watched them kill you."

"Great. I was afraid that might happen. I suppose we were just damned lucky it didn't happen any earlier." The words appeared on the screen and Rado wanted desperately to believe it was real, that some small part of her had managed to survive. In any way.

"How much of your real life do you know, do you remember?" He leaned forward in the chair, reaching toward the monitor.

"Everything up until the moment of my upload."

"When was that?" Rado touched the screen, running his fingers over her words as he had her body. It wasn't the same.

"If my system has the right time stamp, about forty-eight hours ago."

"Then you don't remember." His shoulders sagged.

"Remember what?" The words asked.

A light knock on the door shut Rado's mouth. He stumbled toward it. "Hello?" His voice, drained and shocked, barely made it through the door.

"Rado? Let me in already."

As he opened the door for Andre, he felt tears welling up in his eyes again. "She's dead."

"What?"

"They killed her." Rado shut and locked the door behind them. "The client, he shot her."

"That's impossible. I got a message from her this morning." Andre shook his head.

"No, you didn't. You got a message from a computer."

"Excuse me?" Andre leaned closer, sniffing the air around Rado. "Just how much have you been drinking?"

"Not enough. Come on, see for yourself." Rado led him to the computer. "Have a seat. Pay attention. She types fast."

Andre sat down in the chair. "Hello, old friend." The words appeared on the monitor. "This is everything, the project I would never tell you about. This is my life's work, what was always so important."

Running his hand over his face, Andre leaned forward. "Is this some kind of joke?"

"No. I hope you got my message this morning and I hope that it makes sense to you now."

"What the . . . What's going on?" Andre looked from the monitor to Rado and back again.

"Rado says he watched them kill me."

"You don't remember being killed? I would think something like that would stand out." Rado's voice had an edge, a bitter blade that gave away more than it concealed.

"I am trying to explain this to you. I am not a ghost. I don't remember anything between the moment I was downloaded and the moment I was booted up. I am a copy of my physical self, imprinted on a chip, made digital."

"I don't understand." Andre shook his head.

"It's simple. When I first met you, I told you I was working on something that would be bigger than any one of us. I know you didn't believe me then; I was so young and so arrogant. But here we are. What you see now is the first phase of that project. The night my family was killed, I escaped with a large quantity of the research and, more importantly, a chip my mother designed. It was designed to hold about 12 terabytes. The nanobots that created the transistors were able to make them small enough, complex enough, to store most of the entirety of a human mind. About eight years ago, I managed to track down one of OriqualTec's interns who helped create it. Corinthian and I have been working on it ever since. We had to push our timeline up, jump before we were ready, when I realized that Jacob, the one who has been looking for me, had to know about the chip. If I didn't deliver the chip, I figured I'd be killed or captured and, if something happened before the download, we'd lose everything we've worked for."

"This is crazy, impossible," Andre whispered in disbelief and awe.

"Aren't I proof that nothing is impossible?" The words paused for a moment. Neither man spoke, at the same time awed and distraught.

Rado pulled Andre into the living room. "I don't know if I can do this. Sit there and act like it's normal to talk to a dead woman."

"I warned you when you signed on not to fall in love. You didn't listen." He put a hand on Rado's shoulder.

"But this, whatever she is now, how can I stay with that kind of reminder? How can I stay with this thing that's not real, and too real?"

"I don't know. You'll have to figure that out."

He shrugged out from beneath Andre's hand and grabbed his jacket. "I'm going to take a walk."

"Good. Go clear your head." Andre watched him leave and walked back to the system. "Okay Shade, explain just what you think you're doing."

"I had to let them take me. I should be inside now. We have to give my physical self one year to gather information and get out on her own. If she's not home by the end of that year, then we can go in and get her out. We need to know how far he's come; how close he is to creating his army. The real Shade can find that out. Besides, she can point them in the wrong direction, keep him off our tails. Hopefully, when it's all over, we'll have the answers, control of the technology, and Shade back to boot."

"You should have told me what you were doing." Andre sat down in the chair.

"There wasn't time. Besides, you would have tried to stop me. Her. Us. Whatever."

"Why can't I tell him that you aren't really dead?"

"If he knew the truth, he'd go in half-cocked and destroy any chance of getting the information we need."

"He deserves to know."

"He deserves to live more. I've worked too hard to lose it all now. Promise me, Andre."

"Fine. But you know how I feel." His tone was curt, but he doubted this mechanical Shade would feel the cuts.

"So noted, old man."

"What do we do now?" Andre rolled his shoulders, wincing at the pop and whine of old bones.

"I need you to put a disc in the tray, the one the client gave me. It's the top one on the stack. A mini with no label." Andre slid the disc in. "Get online; spread the word that I am dead. Make it believable. I'm going to dig into this disc, see if I can't find a few shadows, a line on the alias that hired the middle-man."

Rado returned to the apartment after a few hours of walking aimless around the streets of Seattle; he'd even gone down to Pike's Street Market, just to be one among many. To be surrounded by real, live, breathing people for a while.

"Rado." Lonna put her slender arms around him as he stepped through the door. "I am so sorry."

"Thanks." He held her for a moment. "Where's your dad?"

"In there, with it." She twirled a chunk of her hair around her fingers. "Rado, would it be all right, since the team is a member short now, do you think maybe I could join you?"

"I don't know, Lonna. I'll have to think about it. You'd have to stay sober, permanently."

"I can do it. I swear I can. Just give me a chance." Her fingers clung to his jacket, desperation a little too clear in her eyes.

"Prove it first and we'll see." He walked past her into the computer room. "Sorry about that. I just needed some time."

"I can understand that." Andre nodded. "We've learned a few things while you were gone." He smiled. "Shade hacked the disc the client gave her. He'd done a decent job erasing the traces of the original, but some things are really hard to erase."

"One of the documents," a mechanical monotone voice filled the room.

"What?" Rado looked around.

"I loaded a reader program until we can write something better. At least she can talk." Andre shrugged.

"As I was saying," the voice continued, "one of the documents contained a digital watermark. Quite convenient for us and probably just a stupid mistake on their part. Though there is always the possibility that it's a set up, I don't think it is."

"And the watermark was from where?" Rado leaned against the door, promising himself to write her a better speech program if only so she wouldn't sound quite as mechanical.

"We traced the watermark back to a conglomerate company, Fumetsu Kokoro. On paper, it's based in Japan, but it isn't really. We dug up everything we can on them. The company has its hands in everything. Cellular reanimation, genetic engineering, biotechnics, gene therapy, gland replacement—you name it, they're in on it."

"And that means what? That they're a research firm?" Rado almost took a step toward the machine.

"Sure. That's always a possibility." The voice said.

"Except for one thing." Andre interrupted. "There is no record at all of Shade's body being found, of a shooting at that building at all."

"What?" Rado covered his face with his hands. "But I heard the chopper. Airspace is restricted; it had to be cops or news people. I heard the chopper."

"And they probably paid someone off to let the chopper fly. There are a dozen ways it could be done and you know it. We've paid off some officials before, too. It's not like it's hard," Andre said.

"There is no record of my death." Shade's false voice filled the room, filled Rado's head. "They have my body."

"What could they possibly do with that?" Rado pressed himself against the doorframe.

"Nothing good."

A knock at the door jarred them back into real time. Rado stepped into the other room as Lonna opened the door. The man in the doorway was strange: long white hair, pale sallow skin, eyes sunk into his head so far he looked skeletal. "I'm here to see Shade."

"You're a bit late." Rado filled up the entry to her mausoleum.

"No. I'm right on time. I need to run the diagnostics, and I have a new piece of hardware for her." He dropped his bag to the floor.

"What?"

"My name is Corinthian. You must be Rado." He stepped forward with a hand outstretched.

"Come on in. Maybe you can answer a question or two." Rado folded his arms over his chest, ignoring the peace offering.

"I can try."

"How did you do this? Why did you do this?"

"Let's sit down. This could take a while." Corinthian stepped inside and sat cross-legged on the floor in the middle of the main room. "The chip you installed on the motherboard is special. It has special transistors that are smaller, more precise, and much faster than what is currently available, anywhere. Shade and I spent months mapping the chip and her brain. Using a variety of medical scans, deep probes, and finally a machine similar to an EEG, except it does more than just measure activity. We were able to download her persona, it seems to me, rather successfully."

"Artificial Intelligence?"

"No. Duplicated. It really is her mind embedded on that chip."

"You had to know what was coming. You let her go unprotected into that mess? You allowed her to be killed?"

"Killed? What do you mean?" Corinthian's eyes went wide.

Andre walked into the room before Rado could speak. "You must be Corinthian. I'm Andre."

"What's this about Shade being killed?" His words tumbled so fast from his mouth they were nearly unintelligible.

"When she went to that meeting, they shot her; and after Rado left, they took all the evidence with them."

"You were there?" His voice rose a few levels, anger and panic filling his pale eyes.

"I wasn't fast enough. There was nothing I could do." Rado ran a hand through his braids, tugging at them.

"And you left her there?" Corinthian covered his face with his hands and took a deep breath.

"That's enough." Andre stepped between them. "Both of you. We need to figure out what comes next."

"First, I need to get in and see her. We have a few things to go over before we can even begin thinking about next steps." Corinthian glared at Rado, stood, and grabbed his bag.

"Well, get to it then." Rado didn't move but watched closely as Corinthian went through the door to the other room.

"Any problems yet, Shade?" Corinthian leaned toward the monitor. "We're going to need to add to the system. Last night, I did it. I replicated the chip."

"That's a great way to start the day! That's wonderful!"

"Once I get this chip installed, you'll have somewhere to grow into."

"Do you think that's possible?"

"If you evolve, you grow. I think it's inevitable." He said. "You don't stem from an artificial base. Your foundation is organic. If the research was right, if the theories are correct, you will continue to behave on the basis of that organic foundation and then, of course, you will grow and learn. We have to come at this from the most optimistic angle. If we don't need the chip, then we don't need the chip. I'm betting we do."

"You are not a gambling man."

"Ha. You don't know everything about me, Shade. Not by a long mile." He laughed.

"Before you get to work, I think it's time for all my teams to get together and combine efforts. Talk to Andre. We need to move everything to a new warehouse. It can't be too far from this part of the city. We'll still need access to my armory. They'll be here as soon as they realize I don't have the chip. Shut me down, dismantle me, and reassemble me in the new place. I'll be fine. Just move fast."

"No kidding." Corinthian turned to Andre who'd been listening. "Well?"

"Let's go. Shade, before we shut you down, can you find a new warehouse?"

"Give me ten or fifteen minutes," Shade said.

"Rado!" Andre called out to him. "Pack up everything you don't want to leave behind. We've got to move before they show up here looking for the chip."

"Right." Rado shook himself out of his slump and started tearing through the apartment, looking for anything that might be worth keeping. Lonna helped him load the weaponry into cases and maps into their tubes. Corinthian and Andre worked in the computer room, packing every last shred that could be useful. In the midst of it all, Shade found them a new warehouse.

Corinthian stepped out of the computer room and flipped open a tiny phone. "Gregg. Get the team, pack up everything. I'll be along shortly to explain. We've got to move. You have two hours."

"Who was that?" Rado paused for a moment, glaring.

"My research assistant." Corinthian smiled. "My team will have everything ready to go before I get there."

"What is it you do?"

"Cosmetic modifications and enhancements mostly, but I've been known to walk the fine line of legality a time or two. I do what I'm paid to do. I didn't feel right letting Shade finance the whole project on her own." Corinthian disappeared back into the new Shade's room.

Rado and Andre set to work on the security of the new warehouse while Corinthian and his small group of technicians set up Shade's system in a large office on the main floor. The motion detectors and cameras, both inside and outside the building, were all wired directly into Shade. The security was online in less than half an hour, even before Shade was.

Every safe house in the network was moved; all essential personnel were brought to the new warehouse. Without a word, both teams melded together and prepared for some level of war. They evacuated Andre's munitions bunkers. Everyone was on edge. For the first time in a decade, they were without one of their leaders. She had shared that position with Andre and Corinthian and their respective teams, and the loss was keenly felt.

Corinthian stayed his anxieties by focusing on his new laboratories. He bleached every surface before coating it in a sterilized latex paint. He spent long hours at work with Shade, adding to her, going over data simulations with her.

Rado kept to himself. He did his duties; he followed orders, but that was all. He couldn't stomach being in the same room with the new version of Shade. He wanted her back, and felt helpless in the only world he understood and knew how to maneuver through.

They had only been in the new warehouse for a week when word came that Shade's old apartment and Corinthian's warehouse had both been destroyed. Someone had linked them together. The enemy had far more information than they were supposed to. Somewhere there was a leak, and it was close.

Corinthian and Andre sat huddled around Shade late one evening just after the explosions. They had to find the answers soon, before they were left on the run with nowhere safe to go.

"This is what I want." Shade's voice was getting better with each tweaking of the program Rado wrote for her, but it still was not a replication voice, she still did not sound like herself. "We know the leak is on the inside. No one leaves the compound alone. No one is on watch alone. I want cameras in every bunk. It has to be coming from somewhere."

"Rado and I will install the cameras ourselves." Andre leaned in close.

"I'll double check the connections so that every cell, every headset, and every computer is routed through you." Corinthian said.

"Good." There was a small pause. "We need to move again. Our leak may have compromised our current location as well."

"That's a shame. This is a good place." Corinthian sighed.

"It has to be done."

"You're right." Andre turned from the computer. "Corinthian, I'll get Rado and get to work. I don't care if I have to drag him by his hair, we'll meet you back here in three hours."

Neither man heard the footsteps leading away from the bunker door and up the steps. A small screen lit up and slender fingers went to work. "My position is compromised. Communications must stop. Will get in touch with you when there is news." After the message was sent, the small phone was thrown in the bottom of a bag, to be disposed of later.

Corinthian ushered the core of the team into Shade's bunker at three AM, four months after the second move. The meeting was more secretive than usual, their nerves still rattled, having found no sign of the traitor in their midst. Chen was trusted to guard the door. Part of his personal code of honor, once he'd taken his oath to Shade, become part of her team, he would have given his life, his soul, to keep his promises.

Andre started the meeting. "We have a leak. One of our own gave up the locations and the connection to Corinthian. We have found no sign of them since we installed the surveillance system. We've reached a point where we have to get back to work. We can't put everything on hold any longer. It's already been too long. We will remain cautious and watchful, but we have things we need to do."

Corinthian stood up. "Rado, you and Duncan will each take a squad to visit the survivors of the OriqualTec research team. Be sensitive, but quick and thorough. We are already behind schedule, thanks to the leak. Andre, you and Kathleen will take squads to OriqualTec and do a paper search. Take anything and everything that looks like it might be useful. Gregg and I will stay here and work on the analysis. We'll meet back here in exactly two weeks and compare notes."

Rado nodded. "Do we have anything specific we're looking for?"

"At this point, any information you can get will be something we need. Do whatever you have to do to get your hands on old notes, files, computer discs. We need all the information we can get."

"While we're all here," Andre stood up, "do any of you have anything you want to ask, to say, or any other business you need to discuss?"

"Yeah." Duncan shifted in his chair. "We know they killed her; are we ever going to get them back? Are we just going to let them get away with it?"

Andre tried to smile. "I swear to you, Duncan, they will pay dearly for what they did to Shade. There is no one who wants that more than me."

Kathleen cleared her throat. "I think there's a lot more that you and Corinthian know than you're telling us."

"If there is, you are just going to have to trust us. I think that about sums everything up. We break in the morning."

As the team filed out of the bunker, Rado dropped back and stood in front of Shade. "How can you stand it, being trapped in a machine?"

"Rado, I've been preparing for this for so long. Even before I knew about the program, my parents were preparing me for this. I'm not trapped. I've spread farther than I ever could have physically. I'm faster, stronger, smarter. I get to be my life's work. How often does something like that happen?"

"Not often, I guess." He sat down in front of her. "I want to ask you something, but you don't have to answer."

"Okay."

"How did you get past Claude's death? How did you move on?"

"I'm not the one to ask about that. I didn't move on. I still love him more than ever. Rado, if you're asking how to go about getting over me, it's simple. Someday you'll meet a woman who deserves you, who can love you like you need her to."

"You could never have done that, could you?"

"No. I'm sorry. I do love you Rado, as I do Andre and Corinthian. You three are my family. I wish I could have given you more. I'm glad you're talking to me again."

"It's taken time for me to get to this point, Shade. I really am trying to accept it."

Section Three: A Deceiver's Heart

Watching the members of the squad carefully, waiting for the men and women to scatter in different directions, the figure in the shadows saw her chance and slipped out into the night to a pay phone. Dialing the familiar numbers, she waited anxiously for the answer. "Hello?"

"Jacob, it's me. I'm at OriqualTec's storage facility. They have us going through old files while two other groups are questioning the families."

"The families?" He asked.

"The survivors of the OriqualTec team. I guess they think there might be something in their stuff that might be important."

"Really? After all this time?" Jacob was quiet for a moment, thoughtful. "Have they found anything useful?"

"I don't think so. I don't think they know she's still alive."

"Then they're stupid." His voice made her knees tremble. "I miss you."

"I can't wait until all of this is over and we can be together."

"Patience my love, patience. The time will come. You've done a wonderful job so far. We're getting closer."

"I don't know when I'll be able to contact you next. I'll try and make it soon."

"No rush my love. We will have forever when this is done."

"I've got to go, Jacob. I love you." The line went dead and she placed the receiver on its cradle. On her way back to the storage center, she was nearly caught by a guard, barely slipping through the back door before he turned the corner.

It was dark when Rado pulled into the warehouse. The guard called for Andre and Corinthian. Rado was unloading the van when they appeared. "Did my squad make it back all right?"

"Yes. You're the last to get home. We've got a lot to go

through." Andre climbed up into the van and handed the last of the boxes out.

"I ran into some trouble out there. I think Jason Kuo's brother knew something. When I got there, he was already dead. I don't think he'd been dead for more than an hour. The place was a disaster. Anything that might have been there was long gone. I just got myself out of there as fast I could. Who knows who was watching? That's why I didn't contact you. I drove all through the night and got to Mark Lawrence's parents' house in time. I talked to them for a few minutes and they gave me every-thing they'd salvaged from his apartment. Before I left, I told them to go into hiding."

"Do they even know how to go into hiding?" Corinthian looked up from one of the musty boxes.

"That's not my job. I sent them to an old friend of mine who can help them. Hopefully, they made it out in time. How did everyone else fare?"

"It's hard to say yet. It's going to take weeks to go through everything, but you aren't the only one who was beat to the families."

"What?"

"Two others were found dead. If we're lucky, they didn't have anything we need." Corinthian shook his head. "I think this points back to our traitor. We need to figure this out. We aren't meeting tonight. Any meetings we have will now be just us, down in the bunker, with the doors closed."

"God, this sucks." Rado picked up a box and headed for the bay where they were compiling the data.

"Gregg, we need to find a willing guinea pig, a living body." Corinthian sat in Shade's bunker. "We need a healthy, drug-free woman."

"For what?" Gregg asked.

"The construct. We've come so far that we can't stop now;

we have to take it all the way."

"And it has to be a female?"

"For this first one, yes. They're easier to manage and treat. I need to have someone who won't be resistant to the implant. I think I have most of this figured out. We found schematics for a suit; sort of a cybernetic, kinetic fabric. Something like a wearable power station. I've got Kathleen working on the prototype now."

"Power station for what?" Gregg asked.

"The suit powers a series of chips implanted inside the donor body, designed to run a smaller, internal version of Shade."

"How fast do you need a donor?"

"As soon as possible. There are a lot of things we haven't got figured out, but for this first prototype we need to use a structure as a model."

"This construct, does it connect to the mainframe?" Corinthian nodded. "At all times?" He nodded again. "Lord. Do you have any idea what that means? Do you have any clue what you're doing?"

"I've always known. We're designing the perfect army."

Gregg shook his head in disbelief and walked out of the bunker.

"What is it we're missing, Shade?" Corinthian turned to the computer. "I feel like there's something right in front of me that I just can't see."

"There is an answer somewhere." Shade insisted. "There has to be. The OriqualTec people wouldn't have started this project unless they were certain they could at least come close to perfecting it. They'd been working on it for ten years before they created Jacob and myself. They wouldn't have taken that step without some understanding of how to take the next one."

"I only pray we find the answers before they do. If they have no use for you, they could find a way to really kill you. I pray we get there in time."

"Anybody down there?" Rado called from the top of the

steps.

"Yeah." Corinthian yelled back.

Rado came down the steps. "I just got a call from the friend I sent the Lawrence's, too. He says he has something for me."

"Can you trust him?"

"We've done a lot for each other over the years. I would trust him with my life."

"Okay." Corinthian rubbed his neck. "How long will you be gone?"

"Three or four days. I need to go on my own."

"You need to talk to Shade about that."

Rado moved closer to the central monitor. "Well?"

"I have monitors in all the vehicles now. It'll be all right. Just be careful." She answered.

"I will." Rado nodded curtly and left the room.

"Corinthian. How is Gregg coming along?"

"He thinks he may have found a donor. He's got her sequestered at a motel until we figure out where to begin. She's willing to do this, for the right price, but I'm not sure she's capable."

"Why?"

"She's not testing well. I'm not sure we'll get past the first stages of the process."

"I say we wait and see what Rado brings back with him, and then we'll make our decision. It may be worth doing just to iron out the kinks. If it doesn't work with her, we know to be more selective the next time."

"I've got Kathleen at work on the suit anyway."

"Good. So, does this donor have a name?"

"Natalia."

Section Four: Sacrifice

The moment Rado pulled his van into the warehouse, Corinthian was opening his door and battering him with questions. "Who was it about? What was it? Will it help?"

"Hold up. Give me a minute!" Rado shook his head as he

stepped out of the van. "Fate is smiling on us. Or whatever. Mark Lawrence's mother ran into a familiar face at the safe house. Jason Kuo's half-sister has been in hiding for all this time. He gave her a set of discs and some money and sent her into hiding two months before the killings."

"He must have known something was coming." Corinthian shook his head. "If he knew, why didn't he warn anybody?"

"I don't know the answer to that. Maybe these will help." Rado pulled a small black case off the front seat. "There are seven discs here. I skimmed a little but haven't watched them all. There's some interesting stuff on there."

"Like what?"

"There's a video of a surgery performed on Shade. She was just a kid. They wired her up like a bomb and she was just a baby." Anger poisoned his words.

"Wired?" Corinthian's head shot up, his eyes wide and intent. "I've been so stupid! That's the key!" He grabbed the case of discs and ran for the bunker.

"What key?" Rado chased after him. "What's going on?"

"You just found the one element I've been missing." Corinthian sat down in front of the mainframe and inserted each disc into a separate drive. "I was looking for something more advanced, something spectacular. It's going to take more than one implant. That's why she was pumped full of wiring. Synaptic receptors aren't going to be enough. The answer was there the whole time. I'm such a freaking idiot."

"If you are an idiot," Shade's manufactured voice filled the small room, "what am I? I knew nothing of this. And it was my body they wired!"

"What do you think?" Corinthian asked.

"I think we've just jumped to making the construct a reality instead of a possibility."

"Construct?" Rado sat down.

"We're going to implant a piece of Shade inside a donor body."

"You're going to what?" Rado was nearly shouting, the vein at his temple pulsing in time to his bitter heart.

"We're going to take a special chip and install it into our living volunteer. If it all works the way we think it will, our volunteer will become an extension of Shade with some added benefits."

"You're kidding me, right?"

"No, I'm not." Corinthian smiled.

"That's impossible."

"It certainly was this morning." Corinthian said with a broad smile.

"I'll believe it when I see it." Rado shook his head. "I don't know if I like this idea."

"Get over it Rado. This is not an affront to your feelings, but this is bigger than you or me or even Shade. Do you have any idea of the ramifications of this kind of technology?"

Rado stood and left the bunker. He didn't want to know any more. He didn't want to hope for the impossible. He didn't want to risk losing another piece of the woman he'd loved for so long.

The operating room fell silent, listening to the strange, uneven rhythms from the machines that monitored the woman's heart, brain, and breathing. The heart monitor bleated with surprising regularity. The brainwave tape kept its squiggle, even if a different pattern was emerging, one that had sudden leaps, playing hopscotch as if it had nothing better to do. "There is no way to tell just how much we've damaged." Corinthian shook his head sadly, peering into the pretty face of his patient.

"What went wrong?" The mechanized voice of Shade drifted down from the speakers.

"I won't know until the anesthetic wears off. We had better keep this to ourselves for now." Corinthian, Gregg and Kathleen slipped out of the clean room and dropped their surgical scrubs in a can.

"Is it possible to keep this quiet, Cor?" Kathleen's eyes

searched his, trying to glean the truth from them.

"We have to." He closed the door tightly behind him and re-programmed the lock. "No one can know about this. We have to go along as if it all ran perfectly."

3

"Jacob, I had to write. There's no other way to get in contact now. I hope that this letter reaches you in time. The construct program has succeeded. They're coming in. The mission is scheduled for June 20th or 23rd. Be on guard as best you can. I'm going to need a scapegoat. If I can pin the leak on one of the members who go in to your compound, my movements may be less restricted and my access to information will be greater. I love you. I want this done."

With a sneer, Jacob refolded the letter and slid it into the inside pocket of his suit jacket. "You see, Marron? My nets reach very far and very wide."

"It won't matter, Jacob. Not in the end. My people have come a mighty long way in just a year." Shade shook her head, sadder than she wanted him to see. "They're further than you ever got."

"But my darling," his slick voice filled her with disgust, "I have you."

"Only because I have allowed it."

"I've heard that one before." He laughed cruelly.

"You don't think I knew how hard it is to kill me? I have tried to die. I lost everything twice; I was begging to die, but I'm still here. I'm still alive and kicking."

"They weren't really your family. I am your only family. The only other member of our species."

"You killed my family, my parents and my sister. You killed my whole world and framed me!"

"How did you lose everything twice?" His eyes narrowed and he leaned toward her.

"That's not important." She shifted slightly in the hard chair. Her emotions hadn't gotten the better of her during her entire imprisonment until that moment; she didn't want to allow

Jacob into that place, that memory. The only one she had left that wasn't tainted by the project. "Do we always have to talk about me? Why don't we talk about you for a change? Why didn't you just wait until OriqualTec finished the project?"

"Because they chose you."

"They chose me?" Shade ran a finger over the glass that separated them.

"When the project began, I was supposed to be the mainframe and the soldier. You were just my mate. You were a baby machine. I was supposed to be the leader and then you started to develop. You were more stable than I. You were better suited to handle the sensory deprivation. You were smarter." His voice ridiculed her, mocked the scientists that created them both.

"So what, Jacob? That gave you the right to slaughter everyone who cared about you?"

"They didn't care about either of us, Marron." He pressed his forehead to the glass, staring into her eyes. "This world needs us. Needs me. I can take control, bring order and stability."

"Don't try and tell me you're doing this for humanity. You want the power."

"And you're any better?"

"I never said I was. But my people—they're good enough to keep me in line." She turned her back on him. "And my name is Shade."

"Oh yes, so little is left of Marron now. You were so pretty then, but maybe I'll get a surgeon to give you back the face that suited you. So beautiful. And you gave it up for what? A life of danger, death and misery?

"I gave it up to survive. Something I had to scrounge to do, thanks to you." Shade turned her back on him.

"Natalia?" Corinthian spoke into the microphone.

"Natalia?" The empty shell of a woman spoke back to him, mimicking.

"This is as good as it is going to get." The monotonous tone of the new voice could not convey Shade's frustration amply enough. "We have to run with what we've got. He'll be expecting us by now."

"I'll take her to the meeting, you take over the mic." Corinthian positioned the microphone near her central speaker and took Natalia's arm. "Come with me." There was no resistance, no sign of comprehension. He walked her slowly to the bunker and called the meeting. He spoke softly to her as the others filed in to keep them from trying to talk to her, from learning the truth.

Corinthian stood at the head of the conference room flanked by Rado and Andre. "We are now ready to go in."

"Kathleen," Andre spoke, "you, Natalia, and Duncan will go inside Fumetsu Kokoro's compound. We'll have two teams waiting on the perimeter." He spread an enhanced satellite image out on the large table. "Kathleen, you will handle the explosives in the west wing of the central building. Duncan, you will handle the retrieval of Shade's body, which we think is here, in the east wing. That's mostly refrigeration, so be careful with the explosives. Natalia, you will go here, to what we believe are the labs." He pointed to a building set fifty yards from its nearest neighbor. "Retrieve any information you can get your hands on and set your explosives. You have thirty minutes at most to break in, do your jobs, and get out."

"I'll be waiting at the rendezvous point." Rado nodded at them. "If anyone other than me is in the driver's seat, run."

"Are there any questions?" Corinthian looked around at the faces of the men and women, seeing only concern. "That's it then. Natalia, I want to run some last-minute diagnostics." Corinthian waved everyone away. Once they were gone, he took her arm and led her back to the clean room.

"Are you sure this is a good idea?" He laid Natalia down on her bed and gave her a dose of tranquilizer.

"We have no choice." Shade's words came at him in stereo, through the speakers and then mimicked by Natalia, the vegetating girl's voice lending a new timbre to her words. "We haven't found the leak. Mark my words, they'll be expecting us. Only we know that the chip she holds is a farce. When she goes down and the neurotoxin goes through her system, they'll tear her apart to get to it."

"I hate to think we're sacrificing these people for nothing."

"It isn't for nothing. It's recon. Kathleen, Duncan, and Natalia are all wired with receptors. The three of them will get us the information we need, and that chip will lead us to me."

"God, you're cold now, Shade."

"I was always this way. It isn't anything new. You're going to have to trust me."

"How is the search coming?" He asked before the truth started to weigh too much.

"I believe I found her. I'll be sending Gregg to monitor her after today. I think this may be the right one."

"And we thought Natalia could handle it, too. We fried her."

"Now we're smarter. Now we have Kuo's journals scanned in. Now we have the genetic markers to look for, the fertility clinic's records. This time will be different. Natalia was a practice run, a good learning experience. We were bound to fail the first time. We didn't have all the facts. It will all go smoothly this time." Shade paused. "Could you move the microphone please, I don't think I care much for the parroting."

He did as she asked, and then Corinthian placed a series of monitors on Natalia's body. "She's ready to go. We have visual and audio transmission." Corinthian smiled a dark smile.

"I know it seems heartless of me, Cor, not to factor in the lives of our friends, but we both know it has to be done this way. We have to give them a false start and it has to be believable. Jacob is a smart and cunning man. I need to give him reasons to keep the real me alive. The odds are good that our leak is still filling him in with the information we're feeding the bulk of the team. The odds are good that he'll keep the real Shade alive long enough to gloat, but once he has no use for me, he will kill me."

"Most people think you're dead already."

"It doesn't matter. I know I'm not. The me that is in that

compound is far more capable than the me in this computer. She will always be able to do things, to get places that I can't. When we get her home, we will be unstoppable."

"What do you know that I don't?" Corinthian dropped his exhausted frame in a chair.

"I've run the simulations, I've calculated all the possible outcomes and we have to keep pressing forward. If Jacob somehow succeeds, this whole planet will be destroyed. He must be stopped. For civilization to continue as it is, as it should, he has to be killed."

Rado inched further into the heavy brush on the hill overlooking the compound, careful not to cause too much of a disturbance on the off chance that someone was watching. He put his binoculars to his eyes and focused on the fenceline. Corinthian's voice over the radio kept him up to date.

"They've split up." Between updates, Rado fidgeted, tapping the dirt beneath his fingers or playing with a leaf on the bush that hid him. Part of him wanted to storm the place and kill everybody. The thought of Shade's killers being so close made him want to crawl out of his skin. He had fought tooth and nail to take Kathleen's place, but Shade and Corinthian wouldn't let him. "They have company. They seem to know Kathleen. They really did know we were coming. They tranquilized Natalia and they're blocking transmission. Rado, pull out now. Get the squads out of there!"

As Rado climbed into the van, the explosion rocked him. "Corinthian! What just happened?"

"I set Natalia's explosives. The neurotoxin killed her first. She didn't feel a thing and maybe, just maybe, she took some of the trash out with her."

"What about Kathleen and Duncan?"

"We'll rescue them when we go back. They're both still alive."

"After this, there's a next time?"

"Rado. Calm down. Get back to base and we'll discuss it."

"Yes, Sir." Rado started the van and drove off into the night for the four-hour drive home.

"It went well, Corinthian." Andre came down the stairs into the bunker.

"All according to Shade's plan." He slumped down further in the chair.

"I didn't want to lose anybody either, but now we know our leak is still out there."

"Kathleen and Duncan were good people."

"They still are good people." The mechanical voice, void of inflection, sounded more sterile than Corinthian remembered. "I'm still reading their vitals; the trackers have not been removed. They're still alive, and from the looks of their signatures, they've been sedated."

"Then, there's a chance we can get them back?"

"As soon as we get the new construct finished, we go in and we make everything right. We get Duncan, Kathleen, and my body. We destroy whatever progress they have made. We find a way to kill Jacob. After that, we go back to Andre's big plans for the world. We go back to being middlemen and finders."

"What about the leak?" Andre leaned against the table.

"We just have to stay vigilant," Shade said. "Only the two of you, Rado, the girl, and myself, will know the real plans now. We have to set it up so we can do it without warning. That way, there is no chance that a leak can give away the wrong information. Our people will just have to understand. We meet in here with the white noise on. No one knows anything until the very last minute."

Section Five: Bleeding the Wounds

"I've located her." A series of pictures flashed on the screen.

"She's currently employed by Jakota as a drug runner. The cameras have spotted her making the same run for the last two nights. Send Gregg. We've got to do it now, while we have a pattern to work with."

"Consider it done." Corinthian inspected the stills. "Are you absolutely certain this is the girl?"

"I've run it a thousand times, Corinthian. She's the only one of those kids I can find. She'll take some work; we have to buy her, detox her, and train her. She's already sold herself; we're just going to give her a new master."

"What time?"

"Nine. Have Gregg in position early. Make sure he has the right dosage of tranquilizer. We don't want her dead."

"Of course not, Shade."

Leaning against a dirty wall, clutching a cigarette between her fingers, Indigo tried to keep herself awake. It had been too long since she'd had any real sleep. Seattle stretched out around her, towering structures of metal, fiberglass, and plastic. Indigo did what she could to survive, and today that made her a runner.

As her eyes grew heavy, she reached into her pocket for a small bottle of octagonal pills. She shook a pill with a small double P embedded in its surface into her palm. PhoenixPhire was the very latest in club drugs. She swallowed it without hesitation. A man started toward her, watching her. Her instincts screamed undercover cop. Deftly pocketing the bottle, she wondered when it would kick in.

Feeling charged, more awake, Indigo smoothed her long jacket with shaking hands. The last of her forgotten cigarette sputtered out in the rain. Moving down the street, away from the cop, she felt the fog coming over her. Her body was revved up, but her brain was going numb, getting slower.

"Watch yourself." An unfamiliar hand came down on her shoulder to steady her. She was almost too high to register the pinprick sting that accompanied the hand. Suddenly Indigo was laughing. She tried to control herself, but all contact with her body had been lost. Her legs buckled and she collapsed into the large man's arms somewhere between hysterics and paralysis.

3

Indigo opened her eyes slowly when she realized she was still alive. The room around her was small and nearly empty; she was lying on an old mat with a foam pillow under her head. Everything was blurred, her eyes refusing to adjust to the harsh lighting.

Heavy footsteps approached in the hallway and stopped at the door. Indigo closed her eyes and slowly reached into her jacket pocket for her knife only to find it wasn't there. She listened as the person entered the room and shut the door. It took everything in her not to jump up and try to make a break for it. She lay still and listened as the person set something down on the dresser, plastic and paper rustling.

"You don't have to worry. I won't hurt you." He waited for a response but got none. "I'm not stupid. I know you're awake."

Indigo opened her eyes and struggled to sit up. The man was tall and solid. His eyes, which were inspecting her, were blue and clear. "What do you want from me?"

He sat down on the floor. "Hungry?" Indigo nodded. "Good. I brought dinner. Hope you like Chinese."

Wordlessly, she took the small paper carton he held out to her. She shoved the noodles in her mouth with her fingers, licking off the greasy residue. It felt like it had been months since she'd eaten. He sat there watching her in silence. "How long have I been here?"

"Not long, maybe eight hours. A relatively short time for what you put in your system."

"How do you know that?"

"A simple blood test."

"Why'd you bother?" She rubbed her hands clean on her dingy jeans. He smiled politely at her. "Are you going to talk to me?" She could feel the adrenaline in her system mingling with the newfound fear.

"I'll tell you what you need to know and no more." He leaned forward, predatory. "The people I work for have plans for you, but we need you clean."

"Clean? What are you talking about; I am clean."

"Shut up. You've been using steadily for at least three months. And not some harmless tester drug, but the stuff that stays in your system until it kills you."

"Who are you?" She pushed herself back, against the wall, trying to get as far from him as she could.

"My name is Gregg. I'll be your caretaker until you're ready."

"Ready for what?"

"We'll go over all of that later."

"What am I supposed to tell Jakota?" Indigo pulled her knees up to her chest.

"Nothing. That's all been taken care of. You're ours now."

"You bought me?" She asked, eyes wide.

"It made sense. We need you; he was willing to part with you. You're no good to him doped up anyway."

"Screw you."

"Look, Indigo, we want to help you. You may not believe it now, but as you sober up and come to your senses, you'll see the chance we're giving you." He stood up, shaking his head slightly. "There will be someone watching you, should you need anything."

"I need a bathroom. Don't I at least get that?" She glared at him, her eyes darting around the room for any small chance at escape.

"Of course." He tapped a control panel beside the door. "The button on the right will open the bathroom door. The other buttons you can ignore. They won't work for you."

He pressed the large button on the bottom of the panel and the door opened, barely allowing him to pass his large frame through before sliding shut. Indigo recognized the click of the autolock as it closed.

"You son of a bitch!" She spun in a circle, looking around for any sign of a camera. "You can't do this to me!" But they could. She was property. Chattel. No better than a slave. And it was her own stupid fault. No one sold her out but herself.

"What now?" Gregg walked into the room next to Indigo's cell.

"Now we wait." Corinthian turned to face him. "That's all we can do until we get her system leached."

"How long will it take?"

"No way to tell. We'll know more when I get her initial scans and tests finished. It's a waiting game now; maybe a month, maybe more."

"I'll be in the Mess." Gregg left the room in quiet disbelief.

"What do you think of her, Shade?" Corinthian bent over a monitor.

"I like her." Shade said. "From what I've seen of her, and from the information in the file, she's got the constitution to handle it. And the attitude."

"I hope you're right." He tossed his body down into a chair in front of the massive computer. "If you aren't, then all of this has been for nothing."

"I know I'm right." Corinthian pictured the smile that would have gone with those words.

5

Indigo was left mostly alone to her hell. Gregg visited her daily with meals when she could keep them down, and brought in IVs when she couldn't. A different voice, a thick, dark voice, calmed her when she was hallucinating.

There were gaps of time when Indigo had no memory at all. Images imprinted on her mind, faces over her, things poking and prodding at her. She chalked it up to her detoxification process and never questioned it.

When it had been almost a week since her last episode, Gregg came with her lunch and asked if she was up for a visit from a doctor. Indigo didn't have a chance to answer before the door slid open to admit a woman with a cart and a tall, thin man who had to be the whitest man Indigo had ever seen. He looked like one of the monsters out of her hallucinations.

"I need you to hold her still, Gregg." The pale man took something off the cart and waved it over her, reading whatever appeared on the tiny screen. "She is officially clean." He smiled, his teeth not quite as white as his skin.

"Does that mean we can start the rest of the process?" Gregg kept his hands clamped on her arms as he spoke.

"I think it does."

"I am in the room, you know. I'm not deaf or stupid; at least treat me like I'm here." Indigo strained against Gregg's grip and glared at them, amazed at the clarity of her thoughts.

"Have you started to explain what's going on?" The tall, skinny, pale man continued to talk over her.

"I will, Corinthian. Let's get her showered and dressed first." Gregg turned her to face him. "Come on." He turned away from her and she almost ran for the door.

"Can I at least have a cigarette before we do anything?"

"Sure." Corinthian reached into a crumpled pack and pulled one out. "Just do yourself a favor, smoke it quick. We've got a lot to do." She took the cigarette and allowed him to light it for her. She breathed in the smoke hungrily.

"Will you please explain what's going on?" She took another long drag and shoved a chunk of ash blonde hair out of her eyes.

"All right. We have some new tech we're trying to market. We need a model."

"Why me?"

"You fit our requirements." He said.

"Exactly what is it you want me to model?"

"A cybernetic armor. For you it means a surgery and an extra ten pounds."

"What could I possibly need surgery for?"

"The armor we've designed works with your body, but it requires the implantation of several sensors. We will also be placing a small implant in your foot, a tracking device and trademark all in one."

"Do I have a choice?"

"Not really." Corinthian smiled at her again, showing his ghoulish teeth. "We have a vested interest in you now, seeing as we did buy you. I will say this, though: you'll have more choices and more power over your own destiny here, with us, than you ever would have had with Jakota."

Section Six: Shade of Indigo

Looking into the mirror, Indigo hardly recognized herself. The thin wiring woven into the fabric of the suit changed position as she shifted. Her head had been shaved for one of the surgeries, and her hair was only just beginning to grow back. Her blonde locks were gone, her natural coffee colored hair growing in.

No one had told her yet what the suit had been designed for, or better yet, why it had to be connected to her through implanted chips. Gregg hadn't told her all of what was involved. No one was answering her questions, and she was in no position to require it.

Indigo paced her small cell. She knew he was next door and that he was watching her. They had her on constant surveillance. She could hear the hum of the cameras and the minuscule reverberation of the microphone in the flimsy panel ceiling.

She had spent days trying to adjust to her heightened senses. Odors were the worst. She could smell her own blood that had been washed out of the room. She could smell little hints of her own fear and desperation.

There was nothing she could do but wait for her new owners to tell her what was to come next. Her gut told her that it all added up to more than just armor. Her gut also told her to trust Gregg, if not Corinthian. Indigo had no choice but to be ready to become whatever her recreators had planned for her.

Gregg knocked once before coming into the room. "Are you sick of this place yet?"

"And then some." She crushed out her cigarette. "What do we do now?"

"We have some diagnostics to run."

"Are you any closer to telling me what's going on?"

"Yes, just be patient, Indigo. We'll allow you to keep your name, but only because it was never your name to begin with."

"You ran my prints?"

"Yes. We have a friend who is a coroner back East. According to all the records now, you are dead and cremated. He ran your prints, attached the file to an unclaimed Jane Doe and officially, you are dead. As long as you don't do anything stupid, no one will ever know. It works out pretty well for all of us."

"I guess I'm ready then."

"Good." He smiled at her and led her out of the room. Indigo paused just outside the door, trying to count the people inside the building. She enjoyed testing her new heightened senses. She focused her attention on getting an accurate number of people in the warehouse. She could see three, hear another two, and smell another six past that. Including Gregg, Corinthian, and herself, that brought the total to thirteen.

A very young woman stepped closer to her, inspecting her.

"Indigo." She extended her hand, but the girl didn't reach for it.

"Let's go." Gregg took her arm and led her deeper into the warehouse. He led through a maze of machinery and crates to a section near the middle where the floor felt different beneath her feet. She stepped carefully on the cement, searching for a door. She hadn't gotten within two feet of it when Gregg palmed a small sensor and a door eased open, its hydraulics hissing. She followed him down into the room followed by a small handful of others, the last of whom pulled the door closed behind him.

The bunker beneath the warehouse was twenty feet square. On two walls, a massive computer made up of several towers and monitors and servers stretched out. The other walls were empty and sterile. Gregg led her to a long table in the center of the room and positioned her across from the computer.

"Indigo," Gregg sat down beside her. "The people in this room are the heart of our team. Andre," an older graying man nodded, his eyes twinkling in the dim light. "The girl you met upstairs, Lonna, is his daughter. Rado." A tall, broad shouldered man with long black hair in a thousand tiny braids crossed his arms across his chest and kicked his feet up onto the table. "And of course, Corinthian and myself."

"What's this team for?"

"Shade. More or less anyway." Gregg motioned Corinthian over to the computer. "What's the verdict?"

Corinthian read some words flashing on one of the monitors. "So far so good. If all our calculations are correct, which they should be, she should be able to handle it."

"We have a lot to explain tonight, Indigo." Gregg smiled re-assuringly. "First things first. This is Shade," he gestured to the computer, "or at least a version of her. Before she was killed, Corinthian was able to download her entire consciousness onto a special carbon-based chip. What's in that mainframe started as just a shadow of the woman, but it's grown, much more than anyone expected it to."

"This suit isn't really armor, is it? Those surgeries I went through, the wires in this suit, none of it makes any sense. What is it really?"

"When you are wearing it, the suit becomes a power source."

"A power source for what?"

Corinthian broke in. "We are going to install a construct, a condensed version of the Shade persona. We don't think there will be any ill effects from the process. The only thing you may have trouble with is adjusting to having a second voice inside your head."

"And just what do I get out of this deal?"

"The chance to be something great." Rado muttered as he tried hard to hide the slight flush of his dark skin.

"Excuse me?" Indigo scowled.

"Simply put, Indigo," the old man shifted uneasily, "you will have access to everything Shade knows through all her cameras and bugs and outstretched arms into the nets. It will allow for silent communications. The mainframe and the construct, which is what we want to put inside you, can share information instantly and silently. Aside from that, I suppose your ultimate benefit is being well taken care of until you die. We have to keep you happy and healthy for Shade so, in a way, our loyalty to her becomes our loyalty to you."

"When?" Indigo leaned back in her chair, running her hand through the dark stubble on her head.

"Not tonight. I need to run some more diagnostics and double check everything one more time." Corinthian smiled at her softly, more sweetly than he had before. He said something that Indigo couldn't quite make out and another monitor jumped to life with an image of a body, the internal organs visible. It took Indigo a moment to realize it was footage of her surgery. She watched almost in awe as the short film showed them inserting a series of chips at intervals throughout her body, wiring it into her spine. Indigo reached around herself, to the base of her spine where they had placed a metal plate. They hadn't told her anything about the wiring.

"What have you people done to me? There's got to be at least thirty chips implanted in me." She stood and moved closer to the monitor. "You've turned me into a living computer and never told me a thing. I should have had a choice in this."

"Would you have done it?" Rado's voice filled her head as his dark eyes bore into her.

"I'll never know, I was never asked." She glared at him. "I'll never know what I would have said if anyone had bothered to fill me in. If any one of you had decided that something like this should have been a choice and not the condition of my survival."

"We couldn't take the chance." Rado looked away.

"It hardly matters now." Corinthian looked up at her. "What's done is done."

Indigo crossed her arms over her chest both annoyed and resigned. "Now that I'm here and I'm on my way to being what you designed I have no choice. I never had a choice. Let's get this done. What comes next?"

"Tomorrow, when everyone is ready, we'll begin the download." A disembodied, almost feminine voice filled the room. "If it works, then we'll discuss what comes next."

Indigo turned back to the head honchos. "If? All this nonsense and you aren't even sure it's possible?"

"Let's get you fed and settled in." Andre tried to smile, but it faltered.

Rado was the first one out of the chamber. Indigo watched him closely; there was something about him that made her uneasy. Perhaps it was his size; he could crush her without so much as a second thought. Maybe it was the way he looked at her, with such deep familiarity, like he really knew her. She couldn't put her finger on it.

Indigo followed the group through the warehouse and up the stairs into a kitchen and took the seat next to Rado. Indigo watched the group closely as she ate the stew they set down in front of her. They were close to each other, like a family, but there was a great deal of tension, too. The tension all seemed to emanate from Lonna, Andre's daughter.

Lonna just didn't fit in. She looked out of place within the gang of men. She was the old man's daughter, explaining her presence, but Indigo couldn't shake the distrust she felt. She didn't get that feeling from anyone else in the group, not even the people she hadn't met that seemed to fill the warehouse. She tried to shake off the notions she had. Everyone she'd met had conspired against her from the start, she shouldn't trust any of them, but the only one who set off alarms was a little girl.

After dinner, Andre led Indigo down a long hallway to a small room. "This is where you'll be sleeping."

"Thanks." Indigo followed him inside and shut the door behind her. "Can I ask you a few questions now, just between us and the cameras?"

"Sure."

"What's really going on here?"

"Really going on? What do you mean?" He leaned heavily against the door.

"I don't understand what you really need me for."

"Shade needs you, and we need her. She needs a body, in this case, yours, to effectively carry out her plans. She can't do what she needs done while she's completely housed in that system in the bunker." Andre eased himself down to the floor.

"Bullshit. Who was this woman that you are all risking your lives for her?"

"Shade was something different to us all. For me, she was the kind of child I'd always wanted, brilliant, talented, a natural leader. I found her when she was fifteen and brought her in. She made this team what it is now." Andre pressed his head against the door.

"I'm trying to figure this out and none of it makes sense. Why does she need me at all? You would listen to orders and do exactly what she wants. What am I really doing here? And don't tell me it's just because it's suddenly possible. I don't buy that."

He smiled and leaned forward. "You cannot repeat what I am about to tell you. Not to anyone." Indigo nodded her head. "You are the first, and possibly only, member of a new kind of army. If things had taken a different path, you would be one of many soldiers. This construct allows for silent communications and movements in unison. We might be headed for a war, if things don't go our way. Your first mission will be to get our leader home where she belongs."

"You make it sound like she's alive."

"She is," Andre nodded.

"You're serious? Shade is alive?"

"Yes, but I think I may be the only one who knows it. You were designed for this, engineered by the fertility clinic your parents went to. We spent a long time trying to find you, only to find out you were killing yourself. There are more like you, and we're trying to find them, but the clinic must have worked really hard to cover their asses when the people they worked with were murdered. So far, you're the only one we've been able to locate. Everything that is about to happen—it's been in the works for decades. And no one saw the signs coming. Shade worked her fingers to the bone to get us to the point where maybe, just maybe, we can prevent the war that certain individuals are trying to start."

"You are all crazy, aren't you?"

"No. I wish we were. It would make everything so much easier. We have to move heaven and earth to keep certain factions from taking over, and the only way we can do it is to have better technology than they do. You and Shade are the keys. You give us the upper hand."

"I don't understand. You're trying to keep a group out of power, so what? Get an army and do it."

"Indigo, these people don't care who they hurt, who they kill, what they have to do to get what they want. We're racing against the inevitable. We do have the upper hand; the fact that you are here and not dead proves that. The fact that we beat them to the technology proves that." He sighed. "The first thing we have to do is get Shade back from them. Period."

"I'm sorry, but if you're really trying to stop a war, isn't that more important than some collateral damage?"

"Not to us."

She shook her head, but smiled as he left her room. Indigo was tired, but adrenaline pumped hard through her blood, chasing sleep away. She paced around the room, trying to wrap her head around the information. In all likelihood, she'd die on the table during download. If she didn't, she would be something new, something the world had never seen before. That should have been enough to silence her objection, but something wasn't fitting quite right. On the small chance that her recreators weren't completely insane, what made them any better than the people they fought against?

Some time later, after she'd been asleep for an hour, Rado slipped into her room. He looked down at the sleeping woman with awe. In just a few hours, they would know if everything they had worked for was worth it. He wondered if Indigo had any idea what she was getting into. Gently, he ran a finger down her jaw.

There was something about her he felt drawn to, and he didn't like it. He didn't know her from Eve, but his gut screamed that it was his job to protect her, to watch out for her. It had begun the moment he saw her, strapped to a bed, thrashing around, fighting the demon that was killing her. He had never felt the need to protect anyone but himself, not even Shade, and he'd loved her.

Indigo's eyes shot open when she heard the door inch open. She could see Corinthian's silhouette in the doorway and sat up. "Is it time?" Her voice was weaker than she wanted it to be. Out of the corner of her eye, she spotted Rado stirring in the corner. He'd slept there, watching over her. Maybe he was afraid she'd try and sneak away in the middle of the night and not go through with it.

"Yeah. Are you ready?" She flung back her blanket and sat up. "I'll take that as a yes." He smiled broadly. "Come on then. Rado? Let's go."

Rado stood up shakily and followed Corinthian and Indigo out of the room. He knew he had to be there, but would have given anything to run as far from it as he could. As they entered the bunker, he eyed the long table with trepidation. It was prepared for her, the white sheet covering its surface, looking very innocuous. He knew better.

At Corinthian's direction, Indigo pulled out of the thin suit and lay down naked on her stomach. Her nerves were jumping and her eyes darting from Corinthian to Rado. Corinthian pressed a hand on the base of her spine, sliding the metal plate to the side and attaching a series of wires.

"Are you okay, Indigo?" Corinthian bent down to look at her.

"Nervous. I'm just nervous. I'll be fine. Let's just get this done."

"I can't do anything until you settle down. Your blood pressure is off the charts." Corinthian stood again. "Rado, will you give it a go?"

"Sure." She heard a chair being dragged closer and turned her head so she could see him. "Indigo, I can understand why you'd be scared."

"Can't we just knock me out or something?" Her voice wavered as she spoke.

"I'm sorry, Indigo, but we need you awake. If you're under when this transfer happens, we won't be able to monitor you properly. As much as the download is important, it means nothing if we lose you." Corinthian tried to keep his voice light despite the weight of his words.

"Oh God." Indigo felt herself trembling beyond her control. "Will you keep talking to me?"

"Of course." Rado put his hand on her back.

"Thank you." She smiled as she finally recognized the dark honey voice. "So, it was your job to watch me all this time, and now it's your job to calm me down, right?"

"I'd be doing this just the same even if it wasn't." He rubbed her back with one hand and held her hand in the other. "Indigo, I'll be right here the whole time. I won't let you go."

"Thank you." She squeezed his hand. "How long is this going to take?"

"About five minutes, Indigo." Corinthian typed something into the computer.

"I'm scared." Indigo looked up at Rado, her eyes brimming with tears.

"I know you are. Now hush." He used his free hand to touch her face. He was watching her closely as the interface began. As she started to scream, Rado caught a glimpse of her eyes. "God, it looks like lightning."

"What does?" Corinthian pulled the thermal blanket up over her twitching, screaming body.

"Her eyes. Look." Rado was practically hypnotized by the flashes of light.

"What in heaven is that?" Corinthian leaned closer, entranced.

Indigo could hear herself screaming and feel her body twitching as the implanted circuitry jumped to life. She felt as if she could lift the whole world off its axis. Images seemed to pour into her mind, flashing faster than anything had a right to. Indigo tried to focus on Rado's face, but she could only catch glimpses of his dark skin just beyond pictures of places she'd never seen, people she'd never met. She tried to feel for his hand, to see if it was still holding hers. She tried to speak but couldn't.

"Corinthian, is this supposed to be happening? Is it supposed to take this long?"

"I don't know, Rado. This is a first for all of us, remember?"

"It's been seven minutes. I don't think she can handle much more."

"Shade says we're nearly through. Another thirty seconds."

"I just hope it doesn't kill her."

Indigo's body began to lurch on the table, seizing. "Hold her down, Rado! We only have a few more seconds." Corinthian readied a shot of antiseizure medication.

"Look at her. We're killing her." Rado touched her face.

"We're done!" Corinthian gave Indigo the shot and waited for it to subside before removing the wires and closing the panel.

"How soon before we know if she'll be all right?"

"I don't know. We'll just have to wait it out." Together, they rolled her onto her back and covered her with a blanket.

◆ ◆ ◆

Indigo. A woman's voice poured through her head. It was like nothing she'd ever heard. *You've got to fight now. You won't make it unless you do.*

"Shade?" *Yes. You have to live, Indigo. Everything depends on you now.* "What good will it do? What happens if I don't fight?" *I'll show you. If you survive and complete your mission, the world will continue much as it is now. If you die on this table, everything is lost.*

Images flashed quickly through the darkness of Indigo's mind like a fast-paced slide show. A boy, surrounded by men in white coats poking and prodding. The boy, a young man, giving orders to kill whole families to get the data they are hiding. The same man, a hard man, standing over a bound woman, screaming for the answers. A great army, thousands of soldiers moving in perfect synchronization, heavily armed. Mountains of broken bodies lying in mass graves dug by giant machines. Blood running through streets like a flood. One man standing above it all, calling the silent command to destroy the world. His face familiar, his smile hideous and vile as his power becomes complete.

Some of this is memory. This man exists. He has the means now to create his army. If you don't want the world to look like that, you have to fight. "How?" *Wake up. Do whatever you have to do and wake up now.*

Section Seven: The Business at Hand

Indigo tried to focus her ears to catch Rado's voice. She had been rendered deaf, blind, and mute. Her body was lost to her, all control assigned to something outside herself. Delving deep into her stores of will and strength, she grasped for any thread to tie her to the world she belonged to. Slowly, she began to feel the blood in her veins, began to feel her lungs filling with air. And then his voice broke through.

"She's coming to!" Relief rang through his voice. "Indigo. You can do this. Come on. Come back. Open your eyes."

His voice pulled at her and she grabbed onto it with every ounce of strength she had left. Indigo tested her control, begging her hand to respond to her command. As her hand clenched the open air, she felt it immediately as he grasped it in his. Suddenly she could feel his hand stroking her head, squeezing her hand. She forced her eyes open to find his face only inches from hers.

"Welcome home, Indigo." He smiled broadly, relief oozing off him, exhaustion evident. "You gave us quite a scare." She opened her mouth to speak, but he shook his head. "You need to take it easy."

Indigo slowly moved her head from side to side. Her voice was a dry, hoarse whisper. "We've got to get to work."

Corinthian breathed a weighted sigh as he checked her vital signs. "It looks like it actually worked." There was awe in his voice. "How do you feel?"

"Indigo?" She felt Rado's hand settle softly on her shoulder. *It feels nice to be touched. I'd forgotten.* Indigo looked up into his face and smiled.

"I think Shade says hello." She let him help her sit up. "I don't know if I'll ever really get used to this. Having a voice in my head that isn't just me being crazy. If I'm not careful, I'll end up one of them though—one of those crazies wandering the streets, talking to themselves."

"We'll try very hard not to let that happen." Rado smiled at her, his gaze traveling over her, but not unpleasantly, as he handed her the cybernetic suit. "Do you need some help putting this on?"

"Let me try standing first. Then I'll tell you." She slid off the table, grimacing at the ache. When she felt confident that her legs would hold her, she pulled herself into the wired fabric. "All of this is so new. Part of me feels like I'm seeing everything for the first time."

"Part of you is." Corinthian put his hand on her arm. "I think we can qualify this as an unmitigated success." The awe in his voice chilled her. "I want you to take it easy for a few days. We don't need any complications right now."

"I appreciate the concern, but I don't know that I can take it easy right now." Indigo shook her head. "There is too much that needs to be done. She wants to go to the armory, she wants to see the schematics again just in case my eyes offer a different perspective, and she wants a cup of coffee. I don't think she's ever going to shut up until she gets what she wants, so I doubt I'm going to have much choice in the matter. It's time to get back to work. This needs to be over."

Corinthian's expression changed, cooled. "Look, if you don't get some rest, if you don't let her rest, you'll self-destruct and this all will have been for nothing."

Fine. "Fine." Indigo repeated the words running through her head. "At least give me a smoke and a coffee."

"That, I think we can manage." Corinthian smiled, more pleasantly. "Rado, will you take them . . . ah . . . her, up to the kitchen and get her what she wants?"

"Come on." Rado was trying hard not to look at her, not to meet her eyes, as he carried her up the stairs.

"Are you going to be all right with this?"

"Who's asking?" He continued to look away from her as he pushed open the mess hall doors. "Forget it. I think I'll be fine, eventually." Rado's voice was quiet, reserved. He sat her gently in a chair and handed her a cigarette.

"You loved her very much, didn't you?"

"I did. It's taken two years just to accept that she's really gone. I know she never felt the same for me; I've always known that."

"Did you ever think that maybe she didn't want to risk being hurt again, losing everything again?" Indigo lit the cigarette and inhaled deeply. *I have truly missed this.*

"That wasn't it. Not really." He poured two cups of coffee. "She didn't want anyone to replace Claude. She never wanted to get past his death. She enjoyed widowhood too much. It made her untouchable."

"Isn't that exactly what you're doing? You aren't any closer to letting her go today than you were two years ago."

"Yes, I am," he insisted.

"You look at me and you see her. Your people bought me to become part of her, or let her become part of me, and it worked."

"We thought we were going to lose you today." Rado's words were as guarded as his eyes.

"But you didn't. And you got some small piece of Shade back in the process, didn't you?"

"What are you saying?"

"I don't know exactly." She drank deeply. "Maybe I'm trying to figure out where I stand."

"What?"

"I saw the way you looked at me, and then refused to look at me. I am just trying to figure out if the look was meant for me or for the fraction of Shade that has taken up residence in my head."

"I don't have any answers for you. I wish I did." He looked deep into his coffee as if he could divine answers from the grounds. "When I know, I promise you'll be the first one I tell."

Andre drove the tractor-trailer across a small section of Seattle, toward the Sound. Though Indigo herself didn't recognize it, the entity in her head did. The dark stench of salt-drenched, rotting wood, seawater, and industrial sludge rose up all around her. Even if Andre hadn't brought her, Indigo knew she could have made the journey.

They turned a corner, onto another side street that led right to the docks and then to the run-down looking warehouse. On the inside, it had to be anything but run-down if half of what Shade wanted to retrieve was stored there. Indigo followed Shade's directions for the numerical code combination while Andre entered his thumbprint. The door slid open silently and the interior lights came on. A thick coat of dust layered the floor, disturbed only by Andre's footprints.

"We'll have to tear down and clean everything up when we get back to Headquarters."

Indigo moved down a long aisle of crates. She moved quickly in the direction Shade told her to go until she reached an oddly shaped mass covered with a black tarp. She flipped back the tarp and gasped in delight. Sitting on a motorized platform was a small, two-person helicopter, its propeller blades tied down and the whole of it painted matte black with a pixel pattern. Quickly, she maneuvered the platform up the ramp and into the back of the trailer. It was a bit of a tight squeeze, but it fit just as Shade promised it would.

Andre was at her heels with an armload of high-powered rifles. Indigo moved quickly, gathering up anything Shade told her to. She wasn't quite sure how to use all the weapons and explosives, but orders were orders.

"Anything else?" Andre called out as he opened the truck's door.

"We'll have to come back for the blasting caps. She wants the electric ones."

"I'll come back for them myself." He nodded and climbed into the cab.

"Great. Go on, I'll be right behind you. Don't worry. I'll get the doors." Indigo grabbed a black helmet up off a shelf, wiped it off, and shoved it down on her head. With two long strides, she was next to and then astride a black motorcycle.

I built her myself. I designed most of it from some old diagrams of a Yamaha YZF 750 Genesis. It hasn't been used in a long time, so be careful. Hopefully, she won't fall apart on you. I know you've never done this, but I'll walk you through the whole thing. It'll be a cakewalk.

Taking a deep breath, Indigo turned it on and released the clutch. She followed Shade's directions explicitly and pulled out of the bay. She got off the bike for a moment to shut and lock the doors, all while keeping an eye on Andre in the truck. She was just starting to enjoy the ride when they reached the warehouse and pulled inside.

"What do you think you are doing on that thing?" Rado stormed up to her and nearly ripped the helmet from her hands.

"Whoa. Slow down, Rado. I was only doing what I was told to do. She wanted the bike, so I brought the bike. I thought that was what I was supposed to do. What I was designed to do."

"You could have gotten yourself killed! No one has ridden it in years." He cursed at her. "You could have destroyed everything we've worked for."

Can it! "Can it! You have no right to tell us what we can and cannot do." Indigo cringed to hear herself speak of herself in the plural. But she was plural. She was an 'us' now. She and Shade were partners in her body. There was no escaping that.

"You know I'm right." Rado threw the helmet at the truck, barely missing Andre.

"Rado!" Corinthian and one of the guards ran toward them. "Knock it off! She made it back, didn't she? She's fine."

A scowl lined his dark face. Indigo didn't like seeing him so upset. She argued vehemently with the voice in her head and decided to do things her own way, despite Shade. "Rado, I didn't know you'd react this way. I won't ride it if it's this big a deal." Indigo stepped toward him, her voice softer. "I don't need it."

Rado turned away from her and fled deeper into the warehouse. "Do whatever you want." He yelled back over his shoulder.

"Well then." Andre picked the helmet up off the ground. "Let's get this baby unloaded."

Several men and women worked quickly to unload the truck, spreading the weaponry out on four long tables in the main bay. It would take them at least a week to get everything cleaned and prepared. There were three rocket launchers, two single use Dragons and a SMAW, half a dozen chain-guns, several AK-47s, and a crate of M-16s. A box of grenades, homemade claymore mines, and several olive-drab metal ammo cans took up one table. Several feet away, on another table, they arranged plastic-wrapped 1 ¼ pound blocks of C-4, tubes of TNT, M60 fuse igniter, time fuse, a spool of detonation cord, and six crimper tools.

Indigo wrote down Shade's very specific instructions for each bomb's construction while Andre went back for the blasting caps. The electric caps might be safer to transport, but there was no sense in taking chances with so much explosive nearby.

By the time Indigo fell into her bed that night, she was too tired to notice Rado sitting in a shadowed corner. He watched her pull out of her clothes and crawl under her blanket nearly naked. He watched her sleep. He was desperate to find something in her face that belonged purely to Shade. Or maybe he was desperate to find something that belonged purely to Indigo. He wasn't sure, and that uncertainty plunged through him like a knife.

When Indigo opened her eyes, she saw Rado sleeping in the corner. There was no point in waking him, so she dressed and started Shade's morning routine. It was easier to comply than to argue, and the construct did have a point. The better shape she was in, the better her chances at survival, and there was no guarantee she'd have much time to prepare.

She was in the middle of a set of sit-ups when Rado opened his eyes. "Good morning." She smiled at him, a gleam of sweat on her brow. "Did you sleep well in my corner?"

"I'm sorry. I'll get out of your way." He started to stand.

"I wish you would stay and talk to me. You've been either avoiding me or yelling at me." Indigo leaned back on her elbows.

"I'm just having a hard time with all of this."

"Of course you are. Let me ask you something. What would you do if Fumetsu Kokoro found a way to bring her back to life?" *Indigo, what do you think you're doing?*

"I don't know." He hung his head, his long black braids brushing his shoulders. "I really never thought about it. Do you think that's even possible?"

"What do I know from possible? Look at me. A few years ago, would you have thought something like this was possible? I want to help you. I am going to need you on this mission. I need for you to be all right."

"I'll be there when you need me."

"Is that all?"

"You'll be fine either way. Shade can walk you through anything. With her under your skin, there is no one who can stop you." Rado sighed as he stood. "I'm sorry I fell asleep here. It won't happen again. I just wanted to see if there was anything of hers in your face. I thought I saw something in your smile, a small glimmer of Shade. I think I was wrong."

"I am sorry."

"Don't be. It's better that way." Indigo watched him leave. There was more he needed to say, she could see it in his dark eyes, but he was too stubborn to let her in.

That was a stupid thing to do! Shade scolded her. *Do you have any idea what he would do if he knew the truth? He'd charge in un-prepared and get killed. Do you want that on your head?*

"No. But he needs to be prepared, at least a little bit. And if you can't see that, then it isn't me who is the fool."

Section Eight: All's Fair . . .

The team was busy going over the plans when Indigo walked down the stairs into the bunker. Gregg had just received confirmation; he'd landed a job on Fumetsu Kokoro's security detail, working the night shift. It was a requirement that all employees live inside the large compound, and they were expecting Gregg and his wife within forty-eight hours. They hadn't expected that particular catch, but it would put Gregg in a better position than they'd hoped for. The only problem was finding him a suitable 'wife.' They hadn't planned on anyone having to meet the woman except on paper.

Gregg looked anxiously at the faces of his friends. "Do you have any clue at all when you'll be ready?"

"No." Indigo surveyed the men in the room. "We won't know until we do it. We need to keep it that way."

"So, who's going in as my wife?"

"I will." Indigo smiled. *Absolutely not!*

"There's too much for you to do here to be on the inside. We won't risk you on this part of the mission." Corinthian was nearly shouting.

"Not Lonna." Andre leaned forward.

"Definitely not." Indigo sat down. "So, who does that leave us?"

"Jenna might work."

"Thanks Rado. Gregg, what do you think?" Indigo looked at him, watching the plan settle in his head, on his shoulders. Watching him sag under the weight of not knowing the details.

"If she's up for it, that's fine."

"Good. Rado, you run it by her. If she thinks she can handle it, then it's a go; if not, ask Shannon. Now, down to other business." She tapped her fingers on the table. "We still have our little problem with our leak. As far as anyone outside of this room is concerned, we will not be ready for at least four to six weeks. We'll get everything ready even if we have to do it ourselves. I want that timeline cut in half."

"I think we can manage that." Andre spoke for the rest of the team.

"When we go in, we'll go in with four teams. I want one team at both the CEO and the head of the research department's homes. I want one team for external demolitions. I'll take the fourth team inside. Rado, you and Andre put the teams together. Make sure you have alternates."

"Is there anything else, Ma'am?" Rado's voice was harsh but his eyes glittered with laughter.

"No. That's my tall order for today. You'll just have to ask me again tomorrow." She laughed. "What now?"

"I think that's everything." Corinthian leaned back in his chair.

"Good. Then we can get cracking." Rado stood. "I've a tall order to fill." He was laughing as he left the bunker. Gregg followed him and Andre was about to when Indigo tapped him on the shoulder. Instead of leaving, he shut the door and the mainframe reengaged the white noise.

"I need both of you to sit down for a minute." Indigo leaned against the wall. "We need to talk." She waited until Andre was situated. "The two of you and myself are the only ones who know the truth." *Indigo, watch your step.* "When I take that team inside, you know Rado will fight to be there. You two have never talked about it, have you?"

"You knew?" Andre turned to Corinthian.

"Yes. When we talked, before she went to that meeting, she told me to keep my mouth shut. When I heard what had happened, I pieced together what she'd had in mind."

"You let her go through with it?" Andre stood, moved toward him like he was going to hit him, and Indigo stepped in the middle with her hands up. Andre wisely sat back down.

"What choice did I have? You know her as well as I."

"Enough! The two of you have had a long time to mull this over. Have either of you taken Rado into consideration?"

"We were told not to. At least I was."

"Rado is one of my men. It has eaten at me all this time." Andre put his head in his hands. "What do you want us to do?"

"We send Rado to get Duncan and Kathleen. I'll go for Shade myself."

"She doesn't know you from Eve." Corinthian scowled.

"There's a code word. It was the last thought in her head before download. She had everything planned out. After I get her, we are going to stay away from here until after Rado gets back and you show him the video."

"Video?" Andre looked to Corinthian.

"The footage was on one of the discs Rado brought back from the Kuo people. No one has seen it but me. It documents some experiments that were run on both children. It's horrible," he turned to Indigo. "I can't let him watch that."

"He's going to be furious no matter what. We don't think we should spring this on him. He'll never believe it's her otherwise."

"What will you be doing while we take care of that?"

"We'll see when the time comes." Indigo shook her head. "And you should know also, Chen knows. He's known since Shade hired him. He was once sent to kill Shade. It caught him by surprise when she got back up. It didn't take much convincing after that for him to leave his previous employer. It must have been much easier for you people when your enemies were so straightforward, when everything was just about business."

"You're sure he's not the leak?" Andre asked.

"I'm certain. When we go in, maybe he should come with me. Just in case there are any complications. This way, I'm not walking through that place alone.

"Makes sense to me." Corinthian nodded. "You talk to him, Indigo; we'll take care of everything else."

The three of them walked out of the bunker and got to work.

They loaded up the equipment Gregg and Jenna would need in suitcases and trunks. The moving van was just barely big enough to accommodate the equipment and the facade of furniture and clothing. Two of their own men would drive the van and help unload it. Gregg and Jenna were busy going over the details of their cover. Indigo stood off to the side and watched.

Most of the team was engrossed in their jobs, but Lonna was sitting off on the sidelines, watching. Indigo couldn't shake the feelings she'd had when she met the girl. *Cut her a little slack. She's just a screwed up kid.* "You're all blind because you love her too much." Indigo sighed. "We know the leak isn't one of the insiders, right?" *Right.* "Who else has had the information? She's had plenty of opportunities to sneak away because no one watched her. She fits, Shade." *I hope you're wrong.* "But what if I'm not?" *We'll have to watch her. When the day comes, we'll have to find a way around her.* "Let me take care of that."

Indigo walked over to Lonna and sat down beside her. "How are you doing?"

"Fine." Curt response with no eye contact.

"What do you have against me, Lonna?"

"Nothing." She shrugged.

"I don't believe that for a second."

"I don't care what you believe. Shouldn't you get back to work?" Lonna's tone was about as hateful as Indigo had ever heard.

"I guess I should." Indigo retreated deeper into the warehouse, looking for Rado. When she found him, she hesitated. She had no guarantee that he would believe her. "Can we talk?"

"Sure."

"Not here. Let's go to the bunker." She turned away and Rado followed at her heels. Once they were safely in the bunker, she spoke. "I think I've found our leak, but I don't think anyone is going to believe me."

"What do you mean?" Rado sat down at the table.

"Who has the best motive?"

"None of us do. None of us has any motive." He shook his head vehemently.

"Really? Think about this then: say you've lost almost everything. You have only your father left in the world, but someone comes into his life and steals him from you. What would you do?"

"You can't be serious. That's not possible."

"How so? How did they find Shade? Where was Lonna when she was drugged out? How do we know who she met or who she talked to?"

"What would she possibly gain?"

"She'd have Shade out of the way." Indigo prodded.

"Shade is already out of the way."

"Is she really? What are we doing then? What has everyone so preoccupied?"

"No. I suppose it's possible. I don't want to believe it." He rubbed his face. Indigo could understand. He wanted Lonna to be that little girl he remembered, the sweet, innocent girl who was just always there. Like their mascot. "What do we do?"

"I need your help. The day we go in, we have to drug her. She can't go with us, and she can't have those four travel hours to warn her contact. Can you do it?"

"Maybe. If I start eating with her. If I do that, then, on the right day, I can slip her something."

"You'd better start tonight. You know we can't tell Andre, right?"

"He'll never believe it without proof."

"I have no proof, but my gut is screaming. She won't let me near her, but you, she adores you."

"I really don't want it to be her. But I can't deny the logic either."

"I'm sorry. I'm glad we talked."

"So am I." The look in his eyes made her jumpy.

"We should go up and see them off." Rado nodded and they left the bunker to say goodbye to Gregg and Jenna. After they were gone, Andre and Corinthian busied themselves setting up the surveillance equipment. Once Gregg and Jenna got their equipment installed, they would have full access to the company's network.

"How's that surrogate coming, Jacob?" Shade's smile was cruel. Her words the only weapon she had left.

"I expect you already know the answer." He stood at the foot of the bed, close enough to breathe in her scent, but not close enough that her tether would allow her to touch him. "Failed again."

"You've said it yourself, time and time again; we are not the same species as them. You can't expect their feeble bodies to accept an alien fetus. You can't have it both ways."

"Shut up, you worthless bitch." his rage rolled off him, contaminating the cell.

"What are you going to do now?"

"We try the natural way again." He leered at her, his eyes raping her.

"Why bother? You know full well I'll just force my body to reject it again. I will not bear your child." She spat at him, earning herself a quick slap.

"You would kill my child even if, in going through with it, you could replace the one you lost?" His dark eyes bore into her.

"What did you say?" She sat up on the bed, straining against her tether.

"Struck a nerve, did I?" He smiled. "Poor Marron. Didn't realize I knew about Claude? About the baby?"

Shade wanted to rip him apart, wanted to feel his life flow out, watch his eyes as he took his last breath. He owed her his pain.

There'd been a job, almost a year after Shade joined forces with Andre. Andre had been hired to find young Marron Buchanan. By this time, she'd already married Claude, one of Andre's enforcers, his protégé, and love of her life. Claude went to meet the employer, to tell him no. Shade bugged him; put a listening device in his boot. She wanted to protect him.

It didn't surprise her much to hear Jacob's voice. To hear him get annoyed with Claude for refusing the job. The meeting went well, for what it was. He was on his way home to her when they gunned him down. She heard him die; sputtering in the gutter for breath and no one helped him. No one even tried.

The shock of it caused her to miscarry Claude's baby. She made it four months without her body rejecting the child. For four months, she'd had everything, and then, in moments, she had nothing. Nothing but bodies to bury.

"Marron? Come back to the real world, Marron." Jacob's voice intruded on her sacred ground. "Don't think I'm going to let you go to your happy place." His hand connected solidly with her cheekbone. "I don't like when people refuse me. If I had known then what I know now, I never would have killed him. Just had him followed until he led me right to you. To think how many years were wasted looking for you."

She refused to let him into that place where she still loved.

"How did you know about the baby then?" Her mind raced, pieces of the truth falling into place. Things she should have seen but missed. All the hope she had of success fell from her like so many unshed tears. There were only so many people who knew. Only one of them vulnerable enough for him to prey on. "Lonna was just a baby!"

"She was old enough to know what she wanted and grab opportunity with both hands. Besides, she was older than you were when you married that overgrown fool."

"You are sick." She turned her back to him, wrapping the tether tightly around her hand, stretching the thick leather, pulling hard at the O ring embedded in the wall, testing.

Seeing his opportunity, Jacob sprung onto the bed and grabbed her, pulling her hard against him. "The minute you abort this next child, I will kill you. I will cut you up and burn you and you will never get back up."

"Try it." Shade flung herself out of his grip, rolling away from him. She planted her feet on either side of the O-ring and, using the tether, pulled it cleanly from the wall. "I would rather die than carry your child." She swung the tether, brought it down hard over Jacob's chest, knocking him back. She hit him as hard as she could. Pulling back for a second blow, the sharp pang of a tranquilizer dart caught her under her arm. Shade managed three more lashes before she collapsed.

Jacob was there when she woke, a snide smile on his face. Shade tried to sit up, but restraints pressed her firmly to the bed. "I will get you pregnant, and you will not abort the child. I won't allow it. I will have you sedated throughout the entire gestation period. But I'll let you be fully present and accounted for during the conception." His smile widened, predatory eyes fixed on hers.

"You must be desperate to go to this length, Jacob. What happened? Lonna cut you off?" The thought of anyone touching Lonna in that way made her stomach turn.

"I should have thousands of soldiers by now. Clones of myself. But no. Normal humans are incapable of carrying them. I learned a lot from the pieces of that imposter's body when your people came here the first time. Even more from the two that came with her. I know she wasn't operational. She was a puppet. Pulled by radio strings. Kathleen admitted as much." Shade's heart sank. "Oh, didn't I tell you about that? Yes. Your dear friends Kathleen and Duncan are both here. Sedated and quite useless now, but they're here."

Shade remained silent, not giving in to his goading.

"There is something that I'm missing, and I believe your people have it. All I need is their location. Now that Lonna can't get in touch, we've gone back to the old-fashioned way of things. I have people out there right now, hunting." He touched her face, a motion that should have been kind and sweet, but Jacob made it dirty. "Would you care to bet me the fate of my child that I'll find them before they come for you?"

"Fuck you." She slammed her teeth together, trying to bite his hand, and earned a solid punch in her belly that knocked the wind out of her.

"Don't mind if I do." He pressed his lips to hers, hard and cruel as his hands tore at the thin white fabric she wore.

Indigo spread out a rough sketch of the compound on the conference table in the bunker. The squad leaders pressed in closer to see. "This is the new Fumetsu Kokoro compound. They've made some improvements since the last attempt. Here, on the north side, is the main entrance and these buildings are all housing. Devon, I want your squad positioned around the perimeter. Use the launchers and take out the bridge to the main gates and then the housing units here and here." She marked the drawing with large red X's, then drew a green circle around another building. "Leave this building alone. That is where Jenna will be. As soon as the first explosion hits, she'll be on her way to the rendezvous point. The east side of the compound is mostly storage from what we can tell. Hit this building here." Another X and another circle. "But don't hit this one, as my squad will be on the inside. Matt and Sean will give us the distraction we need on the ground while Andre does the same from the air. Rado will go after Duncan and Kathleen. I'll be getting the research. This building," another green circle, "do not touch. I'll take care of it on the way out. We'll escape through the water on the south end. Until we start rocking, radio silence must be maintained. We can't let them know we're coming." Indigo laid out two other drawings. "Squads three and four will take two of the armored trucks, one to each of these addresses, and destroy them. As long as you get these two men," she handed photos to the leaders, "the other occupants may live. All of this must occur at exactly 21:00 hours. Clear?"

The men around the table mumbled and nodded their approval. "When does this go down?" Devon leaned back in his chair.

"We won't know until the very last minute. I want us ready to go within a week, but we may not go for six or seven. Get your gear together. Train your people. Be ready and stay ready."

"This is still about the leak, isn't it?" one of the squad leader's asked.

"Yes."

"We thought it was Kathleen or Duncan."

"Outside of this room, that is still what you think." Indigo looked pointedly at each of the squad leaders. "Am I understood?"

"Yes." They spoke in near unison.

"Good." She watched them leave. Rado lagged behind. "Is there something else, Rado?"

"Do you really have to go in?"

"I'm the only one with Shade in my head. I'm the only one who will know what to look for."

"It's too big a risk, Indigo." He stepped toward her hesitantly, like he might approach a skittish fawn.

"I am replaceable. I was brought onto this team and modified for this reason. This is my purpose; to do what I am told without question."

"You aren't wholly replaceable. Not to me." A heady rush passed through her as Rado reached out to touch her arm.

"I . . ."

We don't have time for this, Indigo, Shade snapped.

Indigo stepped back with some reluctance. "Can you hold that thought until after this mission? If you still feel that way when this is all over, we'll talk about it. There is too much to do right now."

"If that's what you really want." He nodded.

"No, but it's what we need to do." She switched gears as fast as she could, putting enough distance between them to allow her to think clearly. "How are things going with Lonna?"

"It won't be a problem. I've been watching her more closely. I can't believe we missed the signs."

"Her contact was smart. He picked the one person in the group who was both vulnerable and exempt from scrutiny. At least, she used to be."

"We would have kept failing if not for you."

"We haven't succeeded yet. We're only closer."

It had been three weeks since the meeting. Indigo was tired of pacing, tired of waiting. Her people were as ready as they were going to get. She'd watched them go over the details a hundred times, making sure everyone knew their part. They were starting to get antsy, and it wouldn't be long before they were so ready as to be reckless. She couldn't wait any longer. She found Rado with barely enough time to put their plan into action. While Lonna was having her dinner, Indigo spoke to each of her squad leaders and got them moving. Everything would be ready to go and they would be on the road within the hour.

Indigo waited outside Lonna's room for Rado to carry her in. After they'd strapped her to her bed, they left the room, locking the door behind them. "How long will she be out?"

"At least twelve hours. That's enough for it to be started. Now, we just need to get Andre out of here before he realizes she's drugged."

"Between the two of us, I think we can manage to keep him running."

"I hope you're right."

"Come on, we've got to go over everything one more time. Let's make sure there are no mistakes."

Indigo glanced over her shoulder into the shadows, assessing the position of Rado and her other squad members. Adrenaline pumped through her system like a drug. *Pull your mask down, Indigo. Turn on the infrareds. Give the signal. Go!* In the green light, the window smeared with glow dust lit up like a lighthouse. *There's your door.*

Indigo crouched down, hooked her finger and gave the signal. Rado, Chen, and the other men crept along the wall behind her as she moved quickly across the courtyard before the spotlight had a chance to circle back on their positions. She leapt easily through the maze of infrared motion sensors, the bands visible in her night-goggles. In moments, she had the unlocked window up and she was in. Rado and the men followed suit and were standing next to her in the basement of the building within seconds.

Silently, they split up. After dropping explosive charges with rigged cell phone detonators along the foundation, Indigo reached the elevator shaft. Shade's voice barked commands in her head and Indigo followed them explicitly, Chen always just a step behind her, silent and sturdy. *Up the ladder to the second level, wait for the hum of the elevator, press tight to the closed doors; let the cage slide past and step onto the roof. Gregg should be inside.*

The elevator lifted up again, moving fast to the top level. The moment the doors opened, the first explosions hit and the power flickered out. Indigo and Chen slid through the maintenance door and into the hall. The hallway was empty but for the three of them. They moved fast, down the hall, chasing after Gregg as he led them to the room where Shade was being kept.

"Move, Gregg." Indigo leapt up and kicked in the door. The woman on the bed was exactly what she'd expected. "Evolution." Indigo could barely get the word out.

"Are you what I think you are?" Shade pulled against the chains that held her to the wall and held them out to Chen, who quickly picked the locks and freed her.

"Yes. The construct phase was a success." Indigo slid out of her jacket and pants and threw them to Shade. "That gown is too light; they'll spot you." She stood in only her cybernetic suit. Unzipping the pack, Indigo tossed the extra gun on the bed. *Sean is out. He killed two guards. He's on the run, but he's out of the building. Get moving.*

"How did you pull this off without Lonna blowing the whistle?" Shade pulled herself into Indigo's clothes.

"Rado and I drugged her. We were lucky we figured it out in time."

"Where is Rado?" Shade turned to Chen and offered a quick salute.

"He's getting Duncan and Kathleen." *He has them. He's on his way out.* "Come on."

"Yeah. Let's go."

Together, the three of them ran across the hallway to an office. Indigo anchored the line to the wall as Chen worked quickly with the glass cutter, opening a large hole in the glass near the sill. Shade motioned Chen out first, then followed, rappelling as fast as she could. Indigo glanced around the desk, grabbing a stack of files and a locked metal box. She had stuffed them in her pack when a security guard burst into the room. With one fluid movement, her right hand pulled her gun free and her left hand took hold of the line. She leapt onto the windowsill and fired a bullet into the guard's left eye.

She looked beneath her where Shade was just reaching the ground. It was a very long way down. Going through the plans on paper hadn't prepared her to actually scale down the side of a building. Not from the top floor. Not when it was several hundred feet back down to Earth. *Get moving!* It was strange to hear the voice inside her head when the woman herself was standing on the ground beneath her. "Here goes nothing." Indigo crouched against the building. She held the line loose in one hand while the other held the breaking lever on her belay device.

Doing her best to both keep control and not look down, Indigo watched the windows of the building slide past. Her stomach lurched at the drop, bile rising into her throat. She should have practiced more, from higher than the roof of the warehouse. Relief swept through her the moment her feet touched the ground and she freed herself from the rope.

Set it off! Indigo pressed the speed dial on her phone and started the explosions. As the ground shook and the building burst into flames, Indigo and Shade ran. Chen followed them, covering their backs as a man started shooting at them through the dark. Chen put down the cover fire long enough for them to get away before the gunman was joined by a few friends and Chen stopped firing. *The only way Chen stops is if Chen is dead.* There was sadness in the internal voice. Indigo cursed quietly, commiserating. He did his job. *He died protecting the two of you. Don't let that be for nothing!*

The whistle of rockets filled the air, hitting home just as they'd planned. The ground shook and the night sky was alive with fire. For one brief moment, Indigo looked back over her shoulder, seeing the fire, the night booming with secondary explosions. Part of her was numb. *There isn't time to catch your breath, move!* Indigo took the lead, heading for the fence. It took only a moment to find the hole that had been cut and slide through it into the water.

Rado's team got Duncan and Kathleen out; they're on their way to the rendezvous point. Sean and Matt are dead. Gregg and Jenna both got out. We achieved our objective with very few casualties on our part. Base knows you are safe and out. The Shade there has told them that you have been delayed. We should have bought enough time for them to explain about Shade.

When Indigo and Shade reached the shore, Indigo pulled the bike out of the bushes.

"She still runs?"

"I did some maintenance when I pulled her out of storage. She runs."

"Good. You have access to the mainframe, right?"

"Yes. What do you need?"

"We're going to take out Jacob. He's never here at night. He has a home not too far from here, fifteen-minute radius, land vehicle. Near a nursery or a greenhouse of some kind with non-native and tropical species. Chlorinated pool in the yard or the house. Um, there's something else, another smell, paint? Cross-reference construction or remodeling permits in the radius. And it'll be gated." The glint in her eyes was maddened.

"And you know this how?" Indigo stared at her a moment.

"I pitched a doozie of a fit one night when I knew he wasn't here and it was too windy for air travel. I pay attention to his smells, his everything. He's very careful, but he'd never think about sterilizing the scents on him."

"Not bad." Indigo smiled and nodded, a little in awe of the woman she'd only known by legend.

"Found two possibles. No. One. The other is in probate. Hang on." *I'll give you directions as you go.* Indigo handed Shade the extra helmet and pushed her own down on her head. As they sped through the darkness on streets she didn't know, Indigo followed the directions and pulled to a stop just in sight of a large, three-story home in a very upscale community.

"Do you have any other weapons on you?"

"I didn't have much room. All I've got are the two handguns and the weapons system on the bike."

"Give me a minute to think. What's your name, anyway?"

"Indigo. How about this: we ride up to that gate and put a hole in it. I'll drive you through the front door. If we're lucky, the first guards down will be better armed."

"Sounds like half a plan. Kill anything that moves except Jacob. Just disable him. I have some things I want to tell him before he dies. Do you know what he looks like?"

"Unless he's had implants like you did, I have a visual."

"Good. They know by now about the compound. They'll be expecting us; at least, he'll be expecting me."

"Let's not disappoint, then. Keep your helmet on. It will give you some protection, if not from their guns then from their cameras." Indigo pulled her helmet back down. "Ready?"

The machine lurched forward, roaring through the night. They were ten yards from the front gate when Indigo fired two rounds from the bike's launcher. The iron gate fell open, the bike flew through the opening, and up the drive to the house. Shade was firing her gun, hitting the six guards that were stationed by the door. They dropped the bike after shooting in the front door.

Guns popping, they entered the house. Shade dropped beside a dying guard and stripped him of his machine gun. "Where is he?" She shook the uniformed, frightened man.

"Not here."

"Bull." She shot him between the eyes. "I'll take the upstairs." She darted up the stairs, leaving Indigo to defend her position with a newly acquired assault rifle from one of the other dead guards.

Shade flew from room to room, her adrenaline on overdrive. In her hunt, she felt more alive than she had in years. Adrenaline pushed away her fatigue as the nanobots did their work on her muscles inside. With every empty room, her frustration grew, her rage overcame her. Jacob wasn't going to get away with it. Not this time. She stepped into another empty room and screamed. Nothing but a tacky game room. A bar.

There was gunfire from downstairs, but Shade didn't have time to worry about the girl. "Jacob!" She yelled. "Get out here and fight like the soldier you were supposed to be!"

"You don't need to shout." A gun poked her in her side. "I really don't want to kill you, you know. All you had to do was give me nine months. I might have let you go then." He pressed his cheek close to hers, his breath hot on her neck, his muscular chest pressed against her back.

"Too bad for me, then." She put her finger on the trigger of her gun, aimed it at him through Indigo's leather jacket, and fired. Jacob roared in shock and pain, firing back at her as he fell backward and as Shade dove for the bar. Luck moved with her as she found shelter behind the bar; Jacob continued to fire, bullets biting into the wood and ricocheting off the stone. She peered around the corner to where Jacob lay writhing. She didn't have long before he'd get up. He was designed the same as she. No wounding would keep him down. Most killing wouldn't keep him dead, either.

Shade took aim and fired, hitting the bony part of the hand that held the gun. His gun, and two fingers, went flying a few feet across the room. He crawled after it, quicker than she expected him to. She shot him again, in the back, in the heart, in the head. He dropped to the ground, as lifeless as he got. There wasn't much time. She had no way of knowing how much he'd doctored his own system, how many nanobots swarmed through every ounce of his blood, how quick his healing process was.

She scanned the room for something she could use. She grabbed two wine bottles off the shelf closest to her and cracked them open on the edge of the bar, leaving herself with two sharp cutters. She hacked into him, separating as much flesh from his body as she could and flinging gore all over the room with the curved glass, as far apart from each other as she could. The glass wouldn't cut through bone, so she shot the spinal cord at the base of his neck to separate his head.

Shade put his eyeless, tongueless head on the bar and grabbed for the liquor bottles. She smashed bottle after bottle on the floor, against the walls, and poured one over Jacob's head. Satisfied with the saturation, she grabbed a last bottle from the bar, a nice old Scotch.

"Such a good cause." She whispered as she cracked open the bottle. She stood in the doorway, took a long drink, and reached into the pocket of Indigo's jacket. She smiled as her fingers touched the lighter she knew would be there. They shared the same consciousness to some degree, after all. Using a linen napkin from the bar as a wick, she tossed the Molotov Cocktail deep into the bar and ran for the stairs.

"Did you find him?" Indigo was waiting for her.

"I did." She nodded.

"And you think he'll stay dead?" Indigo eyed her with a small measure of distrust.

"Wanna see before the pieces catch fire?" Shade grinned. "I think he's in enough pieces that he'll burn too fast for the bots to heal him. We've got to get out of here though." Shade looked harder at the girl. "You've been shot."

"You're going to have to drive. Just get us out of here and to a motel somewhere." Indigo leaned against the wall, clutching her shoulder and taking as much weight off her bleeding leg as she could.

"Don't pass out on me. Let's go." Shade half carried Indigo back to the bike. "You have to hold on tight. Do you think you can?"

Indigo nodded weakly as Shade helped her onto the bike. "Just make it fast." Her voice was barely a whisper now.

Shade climbed on in front of Indigo. With Indigo's help, she attached the carabiners on Indigo's belt to the belt loops of Shade's pants and sped away, paying no attention to the sirens headed for the house or the explosion that rocked the night, setting the horizon behind them on fire. "You set a bomb? Smart." Shade laughed brightly, the sound carrying through the wireless comms in the helmets.

Section Nine: Reunion

Rado stormed into the bunker where Andre and Corinthian were waiting. "Where is Indigo?"

"She's safe." Corinthian looked over at Andre anxiously. "Sit down. We need to talk."

"Is she okay?"

"She's injured, but she's in good hands. Sit down." Andre motioned to a chair between him and Corinthian.

"Injured? What happened?"

"I won't tell you anything more until you sit down and listen." Andre barked.

Rado dropped himself into the chair. "What is going on, Andre?"

"We need you to watch something. We couldn't tell you, you have to understand that. If we'd have told you, you would have charged in and gotten yourself killed." Andre nodded at Corinthian, who touched a key. When the monitor jumped to life, Rado's body stiffened.

The sterile laboratory was familiar, he'd watched countless hours of footage from those discs, but he'd never seen this one. A baby, Shade, was strapped to a cruciform operating table. Her tiny body lined up against the edge of the table, held down by padded restraints, her right arm held out to the side and secured by another restraint around the small wrist.

A masked doctor gave the baby a shot of something, a local anesthetic maybe, and stepped aside, allowing two other masked figures in surgical scrubs to approach the baby. One took a scalpel and sliced open her arm. The other took a hammer and broke the baby's wrist. There was no sound on the video, but they could tell the baby was screaming, her little legs struggling to break free of the restraints, her face red, her open mouth quivering with confused anger and fear.

Rado stood up and started pacing, wanting to look away but unable to stop watching the baby's silent scream. "If her mother wasn't already dead, I think I'd kill her."

"You aren't alone in that. Watch." Corinthian had his back to the monitors, refusing to look at the horrors on the little screen.

The mainframe Shade moved the footage faster, like a time lapse. Rado watched in horror as first the cut healed as if it had never been there and then the bones knitted themselves back together. All the while, Shade kept screaming, kept fighting against the bands that held her firmly to the table.

"Oh my God." Rado was shaking.

"She wasn't just part of her mother's project. She was her mother's project. Her blood carries machines. Tiny nanobots that reproduce, that repair themselves and their host. The footage goes on for hours like this." Corinthian stepped closer to the computer and pressed the button that turned off the video. "I don't want to see the rest of it again."

"What's the rest of it?"

"They cut her throat and let her bleed." The rage in Corinthian's voice was tangible.

"Mother of God." Rado's knees gave out and he dropped to the floor. "If I had brought her body home that day, she would have woken up?"

"Yes."

"She's still alive?" Rado's voice broke.

"Yes."

"And you've known this all along?" The rage filled him, shook him.

"I'm sorry, Rado."

"We left her in that place where they did God knows what to her for two years! They did God knows what to her, and you're sorry?" He got up, powered by his anger.

"Rado," Corinthian put his hand firmly on his shoulder. "That was the plan from the beginning. That's what Shade wanted."

"Don't touch me!" Rado pulled back his fist, but Andre grabbed it.

"It doesn't do any of us any good to fight about this now. She's alive and she's safe. Indigo will bring her home."

Rado pulled away from Andre. "I can't believe you didn't tell me." He shook his head.

"We couldn't! We were sworn to secrecy. We didn't even know we both knew until Indigo sat us down." Corinthian shifted his chair to better see him. "It was the only way she could get inside and find out what he knew, how far he'd come with his own soldiers. Her capture had to be as real as possible, and if you had known, it wouldn't have been. She knew that they knew what she was, what she could do, but they didn't know that she knew, too."

"Oh my God. This can't be real. None of this is happening."

"Rado, it's all true. Indigo is with her now." Andre sighed.

"She tried to tell me this before." Rado's mouth curved. "Indigo tried to prepare me, to keep my mind open. This is why she wouldn't talk about us."

"Indigo is a smart woman." Corinthian turned back to the mainframe.

"Indigo. Is she okay?"

"She was shot. Once in the shoulder and once in the leg. Shade is with her."

"Is she conscious?"

"She was. About ten minutes ago, she passed out. We lost the connection."

"Where is she?"

"She's with Shade. She's safe."

"Not good enough, Andre. Tell me where they are. I'm going to get them and bring her home. Indigo risked her life for something she didn't understand. You may not think her health and safety are a priority, but I do. Now, tell me where she is." His fists clenched, the vein at his temple throbbed. His fury filled the air around him, tainting it.

Corinthian looked at the mainframe for a second. "They're at a motel about an hour and a half from here. It should be easy to find."

"Get me directions. You tell these other people what you need to tell them, and I'll bring Indigo and Shade home." Rado stood and started for the door.

"Do you need me to go with you?" Andre asked.

"As a matter of fact, yeah." He grabbed the directions Corinthian had printed out. "You drive."

The drive was spent in silence. The radio was airing news about the attack on the Fumetsu Kokoro compound and its leadership. There was nothing about the news that they didn't already know. Rado's thoughts were racing. Shade was alive. It was too much for him to comprehend. When they pulled in to the motel's parking lot, Rado pulled into the slot beside the bike.

"What room?"

"214." Rado and Andre rushed up the stairs and to the red door with the right brass numbers. Andre knocked softly. "It's me. I've got Rado with me." They heard the soft click of the lock, the shifting of the chain, and the door opened.

"Shade." Rado's voice barely escaped his throat.

"Hello, Rado. Hey, old man." She opened the door wider so they could enter. "I'm glad to see you both." She hugged each man in turn but when she looked into Rado's eyes, she discovered that he wasn't the only one in shock. "You aren't here for me, are you?" She smiled broadly when his eyes flickered past her to where Indigo lay, motionless. "Go on. She's unconscious."

Rado stepped past Shade and rushed to Indigo's side. She looked so small and fragile. He sat lightly on the edge of the bed and took her hand in his. "You did it, Indigo. You're going to be all right. I'm going to take you home."

"Old man, we need to talk." Shade turned her back on Rado. "We're going to go load the bike in the van. Give us ten minutes and bring her down." Rado nodded. "Come on."

Shade and Andre had reached the parking lot before he spoke. "Is there something wrong?"

"Yes. We know who our leak is. When I realized it, I thought everything was lost. Indigo figured it out, and between her and Rado they were able to get around it."

"What do you mean? Why didn't they tell me?"

"You wouldn't have believed them. I don't think you'll really believe me now. Lonna has hated me for a very long time. She's known from the beginning that I was alive."

"I'm not hearing this." He stumbled and sat on the curb.

"I am sorry, Andre. Rado and Indigo drugged her so she couldn't send a warning to Jacob. That's why we're all still breathing."

"You're wrong. You have to be. My baby wouldn't do that."

"Think what you want. I've told you the truth. Just remember that."

"She's my baby, Shade. I can't believe she would do something like that. She'd never betray me." He clenched his jaw, the veins in his neck throbbing.

"I know it's going to be hard for you to come to terms with because she is your daughter. And I don't believe she did it to hurt you. She wanted to hurt me."

"Hurt you? Why would she want to hurt you?" He shook his head. "No. You're wrong. You have to be wrong."

"For now, until we get back to the new base, we'll pretend you're right. We'll let her explain it to you herself."

"I won't believe it."

"I understand." Shade opened the doors to the back of the van. "We'll never fit all of us and the bike in the van. I'll pull off somewhere on the way home, somewhere nice and secluded, preferably wooded, and destroy it."

"Why?"

"It'll be getting a lot of air time when they get the surveillance footage from Jacob's house—what they can salvage after Indigo blew up the place, anyway. It won't be safe to have it."

"Did you at least get him?"

"I did, and it was the best thing I've done in years." She sat down next to him.

"And you're sure he'll stay dead?" He looked at her, uncertain still of their success.

"I think that's fairly safe to say. Little pieces burn a lot faster. And a lot more thoroughly. But, when it is done, we'll check for ourselves. Right now, we need to let the cops get their investigating done." She took a deep breath of night air. "It feels so good to be out of there, let me tell you."

"I'm sorry it took so long. There were a lot of factors we weren't expecting."

"I think you and Corinthian chose well."

"We didn't choose at all—there was another piece to the puzzle, a fertility clinic. The construct, the chips, everything will be rejected by normal people, but your mother paid off this clinic to change a few pieces of the DNA to suit their needs. She helped them create the designer children for her own requirements instead of the parents' requirements."

"Such a great mother I had, don't you think?" Bitter sarcasm clung to her words like dew.

When Indigo opened her eyes, she was lying on a bed in a room she recognized. They'd brought her home. Home. She'd come to think of Shade's group of people as family in less time than it should have taken. Probably in part because of the construct. They were her home.

They knew now, all of them, about Shade. Rado knew, too. What that changed was up to him. *He brought you home, Indigo. He stayed with you during surgery. He hasn't left your side much.* Indigo looked around. There was an IV in her arm and monitors stationed next to her. Rado was slumped in a chair, sleeping. How much blood had she lost? "Rado?"

His eyes sprung open at the sound of his name. Leaping out of the chair, he was beside her almost immediately. "You're awake!" He took her hand. "You had me, us, worried."

"Sorry about that." She smiled at him.

"It doesn't matter now. You're safe." Rado lifted a cup with a straw for her to sip.

"Shade?"

"She's fine, thanks to you." Rado smiled at her, a ghost in his eyes that was far less solid than it had been when she met him.

"How long have I been out?"

"We've kept you under sedation for nearly a week. We couldn't take the risk that you would push yourself too much."

"Why are you here?"

"I was worried." He squeezed her hand lightly.

"These monitors would have kept vigil. You could have stayed with Shade."

"Indigo, you said we would talk about all this when the mission was over. I think we should."

"Is there anything to talk about?"

"Let me explain something." His lips brushed against hers, his breath hot on her skin.

Corinthian entered the room quietly. "Sorry to interrupt, but you're not well enough for that kind of visit. You're barely stable yet. I need to check you over." He sounded apologetic. "You need your rest."

"I guess I can manage rest for a little while, until I get bored anyway." She smiled up at Rado for a moment. Until she thought about Andre, and her smile dropped away. "What happened with Lonna?"

"After we brought you and Shade home, Andre had a talk with her. She never admitted to anything, but she stormed out that day and hasn't been back."

"Andre must be a wreck."

"He is." Corinthian nodded.

"Did anyone tell her that Jacob's dead?"

"Yes. She didn't believe us at first, until the news stories started." Corinthian checked her pulse, shined lights in her eyes. "When the firemen got it under control, they found Jacob's head. His skin was pretty well melted, but his brain, it was still pulsing. One of the firefighters gave an interview, talking about the terrible brain he saw through the hole in the skull. It must have been played a hundred times now."

"Where is it now?" Her eyes narrowed.

"Shade stole it from the coroner's office. It's currently in the labs here. We'll study it until we have no use for it and then chop it up into tiny pieces and feed it to some dog or fish somewhere." Corinthian smiled.

"What happens now? What do I do now that it's over?" The reality hit her then. She'd fulfilled her purpose. "My job is done. You don't need me anymore."

"Are you kidding me?" Corinthian laughed. "You are the most advanced soldier that exists in the entire world. And maybe the only one that will ever be created. In our line of work, your talents are priceless."

"You are more than welcome to stay. I imagine work is going to be as steady as it ever was." Rado took her hand in his. "I'd like it very much if you would stay."

Shade walked in, her presence filling the room with an odd tension that Indigo recognized. "I'm glad to see you're awake."

"Are you?" Indigo shifted uneasily beneath her gaze.

"Of course I am!" Shade strode to the edge of the bed and took Indigo's other hand in hers. "I can't even begin to explain it. I've worked all my life for this." Shade's smile seemed genuine.

That's as genuine a smile as you'll ever get from her. Trust me. Hearing the voice in her head soothed Indigo, just a little. She'd become so accustomed to having that constant companion that she would have felt deeply, irreparably alone without it.

"When you're on your feet again," Shade released Indigo's hand. "Now that I'm back and we're back in business, I'm sure some of our former clientele will be back. Besides, I have a few things I'm looking into that I'd like you to help with."

"Really? Like what?" Indigo wiggled in the bed until Corinthian pressed the button that raised the back up higher, until Indigo wasn't staring up at all of them like some lost little Dorothy.

"That box you snagged from the office, it held a couple of jump drives. There's a pretty detailed accounting ledger of just who took bribes from Jacob and his company to let certain things slide. There are some pretty heavy hitters on that list. A few national leaders, judges, senators, congressmen, leaders of other countries. It could be prime material to call in some favors with."

"Or just expose them." Indigo offered with a smile. "Leak the information; get the dirty hands out of the till as it were, maybe even get some decent leadership for once."

"You're just like Andre." Shade shook her head. "No wonder

he likes you. So, are you going to stick around? See if we can't do more than save the world?”

"If you're really serious . . ." Indigo started to say something more, only to have both Shades interrupt her.

"I am," said Shade. *She is.*

"Then I'll stay."

Rado squeezed her hand and smiled.

Author's Note

This story is one of the best of my oldest work, the seeds of it were laid many years ago in the early days of the internet during something of a writing exercise. For many years, I don't think I consciously understood some of the choices I made in writing it but as I've grown up, the story has matured and aged pretty well, I just didn't completely get it until I had a few decades of growing up under my belt. Shade was a turning point for me, from the childish books I was writing in middle school and high school to something with a bit more depth.

There is a little of me in all my characters but especially in Shade and Indigo – I've used both those names as internet handles since the first time I met the internet and those lovely usenets. Fortunately, I've grown up to be a bit softer and warmer in my old age than my characters got to be.

Shade isn't perfect by a mile, but she does have a few good points – her intelligence, her resilience, her persistence. I may have plans for her in the future but never as the focal point. This is her story. She may touch on other stories, weaving in and out of stories in her universe, but she is far more content to be a shadowy figure on a rooftop, plucking strings and setting events in motion. There are other stories in this universe, perhaps coming sooner than later.

ABOUT THE AUTHOR

Born in Denver, Colorado, Sarah Wagner got her first taste of people watching from inside the 75-gallon tank that served as her playpen in her parents' tropical fish store. She liked it so much, she continued to people watch whenever she could and it has led to some very interesting characters.

She comes by her love of science fiction naturally, thanks to her devoted Trekkie of a mom. Science fiction was her gateway genre, leading to fantasy, horror, and superheroes. She hopes to be able to pass this deep love along to her children.

Sarah spends her time torn between the worlds in her head and this one. Her husband and two sons do a wonderful job keeping her relatively grounded in this one. She writes in a little corner where clutter breeds and dust bunnies find refuge.

In what free time she can eke out, she loves to read and drink coffee. You can find Sarah's short stories in a wide variety of publications including the Sha'Daa anthologies, Ruins Metropolis, and a wide variety of other publications. You can find Sarah online at www.sarahewagner.com, queenofmygeekdom.wordpress.com or follow her on Twitter @Shade53 or on Instagram @shadeinink.

OTHER BOOKS BY SARAH WAGNER:

Guardian Of The Gods

Thosha-Tol isn't supposed to exist. For the first years of his life, the only person who can even see him is the guardian chosen by the Goddesses who created him. Thosha-Tol is Jaffine, the last race on a steadily advancing planet who still follow the laws of the Goddesses, rejecting all technology in favor of a simple life. But Thosha was created to break all of their laws. In order to save his Goddesses, Thosha-Tol will need to travel where no Jaffine has dared, away from his homeland, his planet, out to the stars where the god killers have gathered. Using the simple magic he was born with, Thosha-Tol must battle creatures that died out before history began and find those who pulled them out of the deadlands. When it matters most, Thosha-Tol finds himself betrayed and abandoned by his Goddesses, forced to choose who he wants to be. The guardian of the gods as he was born to be or the killer of gods he has the power to be.

Christmas In Bear Ridge

SOMETIMES...

Bear Ridge is the cutest little town that no one can remember. It gathers magic like faerie dust to a wand, especially at Christmas. Toni Bell hasn't believed in magic since her parents died. She's been on her own for more than a decade, driving from town to town, job to job, gig to gig, living out of her truck turned ɪny home, making a point to never get attached. She's on her way to the West Coast for New Year's Eve, and plans to be on the road for Christmas, hoping to avoid the heartache being reminded of how alone she is brings. But a wrong turn, a loose dog, and a bollard pole change her world.

IT TAKES A LITTLE MAGIC

Stuck in Bear Ridge until her truck can be fixed, Toni decides to make the best of it only to discover everything she's ever wanted, and never dared to wish for, were all within her grasp. Nicodemus Panait makes her want to believe in magic, miracles, and Christmas, but she's afraid that all he offers will prove too good to be true. Nico knows what his forever looks like, but he has only until Christmas to make Toni see it too. Fortunately, he has fate and love on his side.

Hunter's Crossing

To save the world from a demon apocalypse, hunter Leilani Scott and sorcerer Blake Pratt will have to risk everything: their lives, their souls, and their newfound love.

THREE WORLDS, ONE SAVIOR

Hunter Leilani Scott hasn't been on the job long, but she knows an uptick in monster attacks can't mean anything good for humanity. The powers responsible for protecting the borders can't —or won't—put a stop to it. In fact, the only person willing to believe her is sorcerer Blake Pratt. Distrustful of anyone or anything not entirely human, and certain the handsome magic-user knows more than he's telling her, Lei senses they'll have to act as one as she crosses into realms where human life is forbidden. She and Blake will risk everything—their lives, their souls, and their newfound love—to fight an army of demons to stop an apocalypse.

Eldercynne Rising

Reina Cahill is about to learn the truth about herself by returning to a world of shapeshifters and sorcerers, of ancient secrets and older magic, a world where she will win the friendship of monsters and the love of a vigilante sorcerer and save the world.

DESTINED TO RULE

Reina Cahill is used to taking on the problems of others. As the owner of a store purveying all things witchy—and also as someone hiding inexplicable powers of magic and empathy—she's learned people offer not only their business but long and lingering psychic emanations of their ailments and emotions and even their humanity. Every customer is like an open book, and yet each reminds her that she is unique, alone, a refugee from a traumatic past impossible to fathom. But the man outside her shop tonight is different. He feels like...home.

That home is not familiar, though it holds answers to many questions. There are those who seek Reina's death. To survive, she must return to a place of shapeshifters and sorcerers, of ancient secrets and older magic, of dragons and witches and a crown yet to be seized. But Reina's responsibilities will only grow. She must win the friendship of monsters and the love of a vigilante sorcerer, and finally she must claim her Eldercynne destiny and save the world.

Gilded Scars: Finding Beauty In The Broken

Poetry and short prose exploring the scars life leaves behind and the beauty and victory in being alive. The scars that make us who were are, that serve as shining badges of strength and resilience. Especially those scars that are not on the surface. Poems dealing with life, love, grief, loss, anxiety, depression, and parenthood.